Francis Dana

Leonora of the Yawmish

A Novel

Francis Dana

Leonora of the Yawmish
A Novel

ISBN/EAN: 9783743367166

Manufactured in Europe, USA, Canada, Australia, Japa

Cover: Foto ©Andreas Hilbeck / pixelio.de

Manufactured and distributed by brebook publishing software (www.brebook.com)

Francis Dana

Leonora of the Yawmish

LEONORA OF THE YAWMISH

A Novel

BY

FRANCIS DANA

NEW YORK

HARPER & BROTHERS PUBLISHERS

1897

TO

A. F. S.

THE ONE CRITIC OF WHOM THE AUTHOR STANDS
DREADFULLY IN AWE, AND FOR WHOSE PLEASURE
THIS CHAIN OF FANCIES IS WOVEN, THE STORY IS

Lovingly Dedicated

INTRODUCTION

FAR in the Northwest stands a forest whose heavy shade broods over many thousand square miles of plain and hill, whose rough arches and massive roofs are pillared on trunks that are towers and monuments of dead ages. Only a few years ago its recesses were unknown to men—sacred places where Nature slept in her strength and beauty, unharassed by civilization, unpolluted by the touch of traffic, alone in solemn peace and grandeur.

Now here and there among the broken, desecrated solitudes may be heard the sound of axe and saw, the harsh blasphemy of striving men, the plunging of goaded oxen in the brush; while every day some hundreds of the moss-bearded giants bow their grand heads, groan, and yield up the life of centuries with a roar and a thunderous sound of crashing limbs.

Except in the mountain fastnesses (where the hunter finds enough to do to avoid the misfortune of tumbling downhill), the deer may no longer lie secure; and the jolly black friar of the woods, the comfortable bear, no longer takes his simple, inexpensive meal of berries in peace and quiet, but must keep ear and eye and restless muzzle alert for the coming of unbidden guests, who may invite themselves and bring their knives and forks with them.

The older trout of the mountain-streams and forest-girt lakes have reason to complain of the times, and to wonder why insects, of late years, have such tough hides, sharp stings, and long tails that reach upward into space, and what becomes of the good fellows who disappear so suddenly at breakfast.

The sanctuary is broken, and the voice of the forest is sweet and sad, as fir and cedar lean one to another, sighing with fragrant breath, and whisper softly of their coming fall.

The fairest spots of the wilderness are parcelled out into "sections" and "quarter-sections" with geometrical precision, and claimed with legal formality in the land-offices; the "timber-cruisers" (scouts of the devastating army of "loggers") have calculated to a nicety how much lumber the pillars of Nature's temple, wherever they are accessible, will yield to the saw.

Where the streams widen and deepen as they near the salt-water, floating logs jostle and push each other between the banks, as a drove of cattle in a narrow lane, on their way to the towns and cities that have sprung up within a few years past along the rainy shores of the sound. But there are places where, for all that man can do, the woods may stand forever and add to their time future ages when humanity may be as dead as it was perhaps unborn when the sun shone full upon their mother-soil and the first tiny shoots peeped out to see the light.

For in the middle of the forest, between the ocean, the sound, and the strait, Nature has her fortress and refuge—a circle of frowning mountain walls, moated by cañons that roar from the depth to the height, and topped with battlements of sheer rock or gleaming ice and snow, where she may laugh with the voice of the upland stream at the march of artificial life, and where man, if he come at all, shall come as a guest, not as a master.

The passes are few and difficult, and, at the time of which I write, no one knew what lay within the forbidding circle. Although among the white settlers, who were fast becoming more and more numerous in the forest, there were plenty eager enough to explore, both from the restless curiosity and love of adventure that belong to our race and from the invariable assumption that gold may be found in any given wilderness until the contrary is proven, yet, as the passes were then unknown, and as the mountain-sides between the rocky perils of base and summit presented mile on mile of precipitous ascent, shaggy with stiff, thick-set brush and tangling vine-maple, and strewn here and there with loose rock or the locked branches and piled-up trunks of fallen trees that storm and avalanche had hurled down upon the slope, and were so rendered quite impassable even to the most sure-footed beasts of burden, every adventurer who had

yet attempted the expedition had failed; finding that
he could travel but slowly, that the mountains were
higher than they looked, that three miles was a fair
day's march, and that it was impossible to carry provisions enough to last the journey through.

For such climbing, with a heavy pack on one's
back, greatly stimulates the appetite, and the temptation to lighten the burden and assuage the cravings
of the inner explorer by the one simple and agreeable
process of eating is hardly to be resisted. Game is
scarce upon the outer slopes and among the foot-hills,
so that one cannot depend on his rifle, and must husband his supplies.

Those who had tried, however, solaced themselves
for their defeat and endeavored to mend their repu-
tations as woodsmen and mountaineers by telling
the most wonderful tales of what they had seen and
encountered; of the marvellous country doubtless
hidden by the mountains; of the things they might
have accomplished there (but for the stupidity of their
comrades, if they had had any, or, if none, the lack of
them); of rich, open plains where the deer grazed in
vast herds; of bison, too; and of obliging game that
sat and smiled, and might have been shot but for the
pity of it; of great lakes with remarkable fish; of
masses of precious metal just out of reach: and some
went so far as to hint darkly at discoveries that cor-
roborated certain Siwash legends, telling of wild
voices heard laughing and singing in the night in the
woods and on the heights; of smoke-wreaths seen

rising from the valleys, or tall forms gliding among the trees.

While the people of the region gave no great credit to these stories, particularly as none of those who told them seemed in any hurry to revisit the delightful scenes they so heartily recommended to others, still they did not hesitate to repeat them freely, with such improvements as might suggest themselves, so that the mountains began to acquire an immense reputation, and the unsophisticated son of the East who visited those parts might well wonder as he listened to the tales of the "mossbacks,"* and grow curious to find out more for himself.

The aborigines did not know what was there, for they were content to stay by the coast with their canoes and nets, or farm the fertile reservation-lands after their own shiftless and primitive fashion, or work for the whites in the season when the old war-canoes are brought out and tribe after tribe goes up the Dwamish and along the coast to the hop-picking.

It has always been enough for them that there are clams to be dug on the tide-flats and salmon to be caught in bay and stream, and that the elk come down in winter to huddle together in herds on the chilly lowlands and be slain and salted at pleasure.

Superstition, moreover, kept them out of the mountain region, for they had a legend, invented perhaps by some chief of former days as an excuse for being lazy when he ought to have been adventurous—

* A "mossback" is an old settler.

a story of a mysterious and dreadful race, of great stature, fair to look upon but terrible to meet or speak with, abounding in wiles and mystic lore and wizard's tricks—cruel, dangerous, unprincipled, and altogether the worst company imaginable, who dwelt in the unknown country behind the heights, and would let no man trespass on their domains.

If the modest disinclination to intrude where they were not wanted had not been enough to keep the coast Indians from meddling with the unknown country, it is likely their own sluggish, indolent nature would have held them back; for the Siwash is entirely without the spirit of attack that is so strong in the Indian of the plains, and his peculiar kind of heroism consists in passive endurance of rain, mud, pestilence, and a diet of clams.

DRAMATIS PERSONÆ

"We are no other than a moving row
Of magic shadow-shapes, that come and go
Round in this sun-illumined lantern, held
In midnight by the master of the show."
—OMAR KHAYYÁM.

THOMAS N. MOORHEAD was living in enforced idleness, on hope and a strong constitution, in a little out-of-the-way office in a busy city.

C. NORMAN MOORHEAD was hard at work trying to amuse himself here and there, and found the task irksome.

OLD MR. WILLOUGHBY went a-fishing most of the time, and passed the other available hours in reading all kinds of books.

MOLOCH went cheerfully about his work day by day, and sang and whistled a great deal, after the manner of his race.

MRS. NELLY MERIVALE was making ducks and drakes of the late lamented Abner Merivale's hard-earned dollars, pounds, francs, and marks abroad, and wondering a little, now and then, what should be done when these were gone; but the matter did not trouble her much, because she had plans, and there was just enough uncertainty to please her.

MRS. BRADLEE was very comfortable at home, minding her own business, which was that of finding out about other people's affairs and arranging them for their good and to her own satisfaction. Sometimes the other people were grateful—sometimes not. In either case she felt that she had done her duty by them, and was glad.

And Leonora—Leonora reigned in her own realm supreme. When it was invaded, the invader became her captive. When she in turn was led into captivity, it was only to extend her empire.

These seven played a play together upon the Great Stage, and none knew whether it was Comedy or Tragedy till the end.

There were others also, but theirs were minor parts, and only incidental,

LEONORA OF THE YAWMISH

I

In the heart of the Northwestern forest, where a river runs between the foot-hills of the Olympics and a bold outstanding spur of the outer range, on an evening in early June, when the eternal twilight of the woodland was deepening into night and the shade that lurks all day in the sombre foliage seemed to be stealing down, fold on fold, to the earth below and veiling every object in blackness, a cougar, much at a loss for guiding precedent, lay crouching on the trunk of a fallen tree, watching two figures that moved to and fro in the dusk, some fifty yards away, and trying to decide whether they, or either of them, would be of any use to him personally, and whether, in any case, he had better experiment upon them or let them alone.

He had begun to incline to the former opinion, and his lithe body was already swaying to and fro as he felt his strength and shortened his muscles for a spring, when suddenly there was a slight crackling sound, and he waited.

The noise grew, and a red glare arose from the

earth and blazed upward in a way that made the shadows of the night draw back and sway and waver round it and the waters of the stream beyond it gleam darkly and flash as they sped by.

The wary beast, who had never in his life seen anything of the kind before, felt that the matter was by no means in his way—that the two creatures were strange food — unwholesome — inadmissible. He withdrew very softly and sought a more conventional supper of the mountain-beaver* that dwell in their villages on the slopes.

The two men busied themselves in making camp, cutting the tops from young hemlocks with their hunting-knives, strewing the tender, fragrant twigs thick on the ground for bedding, and gathering firewood to last out the night, which in that deep river-bottom between the hills was cool and fresh with the breeze that came sighing down from a range whose late snows still defied the summer sun.

They unrolled their blankets and spread them over the twigs, and from the stores that had been rolled up in them made supper—one gigantic biscuit, big enough to do justice to the wants of two hungry men, a delicious fry of bacon, some sauce of dried apples, and a can of strong coffee—and, reclining on their blankets, fell to and ate each from a tin plate : the one with his fingers, the other with a knife and fork which he took from a Russia-leather case; the one in zealous gulps, the other with disdainful nose but hearty appetite.

---

*Not a beaver at all, but a kind of marmot, larger than a woodchuck, and not unlike the prairie-dog in habits. One of their villages sometimes riddles a whole mountain-side with holes.

The man who ate with his fingers was a short, bandy-legged fellow, with a heavy, impassive face of rare ugliness.

When he had eaten he squatted immovable by the fire, so silent, so stolid, and so still that he looked for all the world like some quaint idol carved in dull brown wood and clad by some irreverent hand in a queer array of ill-fitting old clothes.

He was a "Siwash"* of ordinary type.

The other man gathered up the dishes and went to the stream. He did not care to intrust the responsibility of washing to the Indian, to whom that science seemed an utter mystery.

When he had returned and laid the dishes in a row along a mossy log, he flung himself on his blanket, and, taking a brier-wood pipe from his pocket, began to smoke, lying with his head pillowed on one arm and his legs stretched out towards the blaze.

He was a tall fellow, of graceful proportions, clad in a rough gray suit of fashionable cut, and encased at one extremity in a gray cap with a visor, at the other in tall boots of russet leather, laced at the ankle and the side of the knee.

His name was Moorhead. He was a man of leisure. He had come into the forest for his own amusement, which had been a great mistake on his part, and had employed the Siwash as a guide, which soon proved to be another.

For a long time the two were silent. The firelight seemed to have hollowed out a room in the mass of darkness.

* "Siwash" is the Indian attempt at "savage," and is applied to all the Pacific coast Indians.

One tree made a central pillar—those nearest about it and the black shade around them were the walls, beautiful with tracery of fern, graceful sprays of evergreen, festoons of creeping plants, tapestry of hanging moss.

Neither of the two men noticed the loveliness of the place. The Siwash gazed blankly at the fire; the other lay smoking and contemplating his russet boots, lifting his eyes now and then with an uneasy glance at his guide, who seemed to occupy his thoughts not altogether agreeably.

He had reason to be troubled, for the guide, as such, was a failure. The fitness of things had seemed, to Moorhead, to demand an Indian guide. He liked the idea, and the Siwash are harmless and have a reputation for docility.

He had been so far governed by prudence as to select one that could understand a reasonable amount of English, and for the first few days had found him intelligent and willing. But from the time when they had left the Sound and entered the great forest the linguistic powers of the guide had been gradually on the wane, and now, at the foot-hills of the Olympics, he positively refused to understand any English at all.

" To-morrow," Moorhead had said, " we ought to come to the mountains."

" Halo kumtux Boston wawa," * had been the calm reply.

This was the more irritating as Moorhead knew that the sudden ignorance of tongues proceeded from unwillingness to carry out his own plans. He had

---

* " No know American talk."

told the Siwash, at starting, what he meant to do, and that worthy had assented cheerfully. Now he obstinately refused, and Moorhead did not know why. Any inhabitant of the Puget Sound region could have told him, if he had asked, and then he would have hired some one who was not an Indian. But he was one of those gifted persons who take it for granted that they know what to do better than any one can tell them and who do not talk freely with comparative strangers, so he had not asked advice.

His object was to go over into the unexplored country behind the outer range of the Olympics, a thing which, be it from laziness or from superstition, or both, no Indian will do.

Now, by mischance, Moorhead could have found few Indians lazier and none more superstitious than this guide of his, and this was why, when the foot-hills were before them, the unhappy creature refused to go farther.

Moorhead's heart was set upon the expedition. When he found English of no avail, he drew from his pocket a little blue book and began to study it intently.

The Siwash smiled.

Presently Moorhead looked up and spoke in a strange tongue in which bad English, bad French, and bad Indian are blended in awful discord.*

The words, though spoken haltingly, were in the young man's most persuasive tone; but the Siwash only shook his head and lapsed into his usual stolidity.

* Chinook, the common language by which the many Coast tribes, whose proper tongues are Babel, converse with each other and with the whites.

The argument went on. Before each fervent appeal Moorhead was obliged to have recourse to his blue book, a glossary of the Chinook jargon compiled by a missionary, and largely used by the whites in their dealings with the Siwash. The guide answered only by negative gesture and grunts of disapproval.

Having exhausted in vain all the persuasive phrases he could find in his glossary, Moorhead took from his pocket a flask, and poured some of its contents into a tin cup.

The dark eyes of his companion glittered with a wistful light. Moorhead, smiling, passed him the cup, in the hope that the mellowing influence of the mixture might bring him to a more compliant state of mind.

The Siwash are poor bottle-men,* and cannot sit decorously over their wine or spirits, but are prone to give way suddenly, under the spell, to extravagant behavior. This one swallowed the liquor in one great gulp, and held out the cup for more, after which he soon became talkative and garrulous, gabbling so fast that all effort to stem the torrent of his words was unavailing; nor was it possible by the most energetic use of the little blue book to find out what he meant.

Moorhead turned away in disgust, and took no more heed of the poor fellow's ravings till a sudden silence called his attention. The fire, neglected during the

---

* The Coast Indian is singularly susceptible to alcoholic influence. The effect is sudden. From a stolid, placid creature of amiable temper he becomes a jabbering idiot or howling maniac, as the case may be. Even then, however, he seldom attacks a white man, but employs his newly acquired energy in quarrelling with his brethren or in mere vocal atrocities.

altercation, was burning low, and darkness hung close about the embers.

Moorhead could just make out the form of the Indian, dim against the black background, and see the glint of his eyes. He saw that he was trembling all over and pointing across the fire towards the water. As he leaned closer to the embers, his face showed like a vision in a nightmare; the dark-brown skin had a dingy pallor, and the staring eyes showed white above and below. He muttered to himself in his native tongue, and held out his shaking palms with the half-imploring, half-forbidding gesture with which actors greet ghosts upon the stage. " What's the matter?" said Moorhead, in a hurried whisper, and trembling in turn, for he was not a particularly brave man himself, and had caught some of the horror from his companion's face.

The Siwash had forgotten not to understand. "Hiyu kanim—hiyu skookum tamahnawis!"* said he, whispering too.

Moorhead knew these words, and was instantly relieved. He had thought it might be a bear at the very least, and it was nothing but ghosts.

He looked towards the river, and, seeing only the occasional gleam of the water as it caught the reflection of the dying fire, laughed angrily. The stream was too small for canoes. "You infernal fool," said he, "shut up and stop your nonsense. There's nothing there."

The Indian gabbled.

"I shall let him know my opinion of him," said

* " Plenty canoe—plenty mighty spirit!"

Moorhead. He threw a log on the fire, stirred up the embers, and, as the blaze sprang up, took his glossary and proceeded to copy out a not inconsiderable part of its contents.

The Hudson's Bay Company, who first compiled the Chinook jargon for the purpose of holding such communication with the Indians as was needful for the uses of trade, doubtless perceived that occasion might arise when it would be convenient to bestow terms of reproach and obloquy upon their dusky acquaintances. At all events, Chinook is not lacking in choice invectives culled from its several sources.

Moorhead collected as many of these as he could find, and, when the Siwash had regained his composure, read fluently from his note-book a sound philippic. The Indian made no reply, and showed no sign of interest, but presently rolled himself in his blanket. Moorhead followed his example, and, wearied with a long day on the trail and the unwonted exercise of carrying a pack, was soon asleep.

Late in the night as the fire flickered and died away, the Indian rose and sat brooding in the dim light, watching the young man's slumbers with hateful eyes like some ugly demon come out of the night to do him harm in the hour of helplessness.

But the Coast Indian is not sanguinary—he fears strife and white men, even asleep, so that Moorhead was safe enough from all peril of life and limb.

Only that when he awoke, next morning, he found himself bereft of his rifle, provisions, every portable thing that he had had, except what was on his person —alone, without food or arms, utterly deserted in a pathless wilderness unknown to him.

II

MOORHEAD awoke and was afraid. There was nothing frightful in the scene about him, where the gracious loveliness of the woodland summer greeted every sense with pleasure.

The night-breeze had flown away on its chilly wings, and now the air was warm and still, rich with the drowsy fragrance of cedar and balsam.

The soft forest twilight was broken here and there by gleams of sunshine that found their way in between the leaves and shone on the flashing water, on the thick warm masses of the moss that clothed the trees and on the ferns that grew in it and hung in feathery grace from the branches a hundred feet overhead.

The stream by which they had camped came down the mountain with a tinkling sound, and its rapids far below gave back a pleasant murmur. The morning-song of a wood-robin or two fell faintly from the tops.

But the ugly scene of the night before—the horrid face of the frightened, crazed Indian, with his gruesome fancies, the desolation, and the darkness—still lingered in his mind, and he had a feeling that something was wrong.

He sat up and found that he was alone. "That miserable imp has been playing me a trick, perhaps,"

he said, and called out, "John!" "John!" came the
echo, short and sharp, from the near distance, and
"John!" from the mountain-side not far away.   All
along the range of foot-hills the word "John!" was
passed along from top to top; and when for a moment
silence had come a belated echo fell back from the
upper rocks far overhead, like a voice from the sky.

But "John," if he heard, did not answer, and
Moorhead, seeing that the camping outfit had vanished with him, did not trouble the echoes again.
For more than two hours he hunted in every direction for some trace of the deserter, but there was
none that his unpractised eye could see. As well
track a fish in the ocean as a Siwash in those dim
leagues of verdure.

He looked carefully about the ground to see what
the Indian had left behind in the way of personal
property. Only the blankets on which he himself
had lain, the clothes in which he had slept, and the
contents of their pockets.

The discovery that there was nothing to eat made
him hungry at once.

Happily he had in his pocket a fishing-line with
a single hook attached to it, and in searching about
the banks of the stream had seen fish darting in the
water.

He cut a vine-maple shoot for a rod and went
a-fishing. When he reached the pool where he had
seen the fish it occurred to him that he had no bait.
He sharpened a stick and dug in the ground—there
were no worms. He scraped the moss from dead
wood—there were no grubs.

Apparently fishing was out of the question. He

threw himself down on the ground, after a long search, tired and hopeless. Presently a yellow-jacket came buzzing about him. He drove it away, and then remembered with sorrow that it might have done for bait. Perhaps it would return. At last, after many attempts, he struck it with his cap, was stung in the thumb while putting it on his hook, and cast it into the stream.

He was no fisherman, but, luckily for him, the trout of those parts, being rustic, unsophisticated trout, did not perceive his mistakes in the gentle craft and came to his lure. A great patriarch of the stream came with a swirl, took the hook bravely, felt the prick, and with an angry rush darted close to the opposite bank, swung round a projecting root, and, having twisted the line tight about it, wrenched himself away and sped into the darkness under a shelving rock.

The smaller fish scattered in the struggle, the pool was calm again, and in the clear green water Moorhead could see the hook, his only "lawful and visible means of support," hanging to the snag. He could not afford to lose it; so in he went, and, after no little splashing and disturbance, recovered it, and came shivering out of the icy water.

No more trout would bite in that pool, and after another hunt for bait and a great deal of fishing in unfavorable places he sat down, lighted a fire—for, happily, he had a few matches left—and cooked two of the three fish he had caught, thinking meanwhile what course to adopt.

It certainly was not wise to spend any more time in so unprofitable a place, and he determined to set out at once. The only question was, whither?

He had no idea from what direction he had come, nor how to find his way. When he had finished his meal he strapped his blanket on his back, put his one trout in his pocket, crossed the stream, and started right up the mountain-side, in hopes of seeing from the top some familiar landmark in the distance from which he might take his bearings. This done, he meant to come down to the same place, fish in the pool with better success, and take the nearest way out of the forest.

This plan, though wholly impracticable because he had no compass, seemed feasible enough to him, and served to cheer him and keep his mind from the dangers popularly supposed to surround a lonely man in a wilderness, particularly that of being starved and that of going to keep some other creature from starving.

The very act of climbing gave him enough to think about for the time being. He had the right to consider himself a tried mountaineer, having been up the proper mountains abroad in the regular way, and had the names of his victims branded on an alpenstock which held a conspicuous place in his comfortable rooms at home. For a while he wished he had brought his alpenstock, for at first he travelled easily enough except for the thick growth of salal, with slippery leaves and tough twigs, that stood knee-high on the slope. But soon he was glad that he had left that useful implement behind, for it would have been only too much of an encumbrance.

The ascent became gradually and almost imperceptibly steeper, till, stopping for breath, he began to notice that he was holding on hard by the bushes with both hands and digging his heels into the ground at every step, with the sides of his feet turned towards the earth.

He took a realizing sense of his position and for the first time looked behind him.   He was no longer walking up a steep slope, but climbing a nearly vertical wall.

Below, as far as the timber would allow him to see, was an almost sheer descent falling between the stately, solemn rows of trees, whose mighty roots, grasping the earth, held them upright even there—falling away into dim obscurity of still foliage.   Above, for several hundred yards, a still more upright mass covered with the same growth ; beyond, a cessation of objects and a glimpse of sky through the gap left by a fallen tree that now hung head downward, with its roots entangled among the tops of its brethren.

"There," said Moorhead, beholding the sky-line and falling a victim to the usual delusion of those who climb in the woods, "must be the top !"

He scrambled up and arrived, panting, at the gap, only to see that the ascent took a little turn inward there, and then rose in another towering mass of rocks and timber to another sky-line, "where," he said to himself, "there may be still another confounded mountain piled on this one, and so on *ad infinitum.*"

By this time the heights were black against the western sky, and the sun had long been out of sight on the other side of the mountain.

"If that next shelf above me should be the top," said he, "I may reach it to-night : I've an hour yet before dark."

But though he made the best of his hour that

young limbs and desperate energy could, the end of
it found him still below the timber-line, in the
shadowy forest on the mountain-side, weary, hungry,
and more sadly lost and bewildered than ever.

Not wishing to be caught in the utter darkness
that was fast coming on, he gathered enough dry
wood for his fire, spread his blanket on the ground—
for he could not afford to waste energy in getting
soft foliage for a couch—cooked his trout, which was
by this time a little the worse for wear, and devoured
it ravenously, unsalted as it was.

He had meant to keep a little of it to help uphold
his strength in the toil and faintness which, he knew,
must be his portion on the morrow; but the piece he
saved was so very small that he thought better to use
it as a complement to a moderate repast than as an
appetizer for none at all, so it followed the rest of
the fish at once.

He had picked a few salal-berries on the way up.
They were juicy and mellow, but they had an unpleasant sticky sweetness that made him very thirsty.

He could hear the sound of water, and tried to
find it by the light of a resinous stick, but his torch
seemed only to burn a little hollow in the blackness
and to make all the rest more impenetrably thick
than ever by contrast. The waters mocked him in
the echoing woodland, sounding now on this side,
now on that; now near, now far away.

Bruised by rocks and scratched by brambles, he
went back to the fire and blanket that were his home
for the time.

Until then, hard exertion and the concentration of
will on an end to be achieved had kept him from

realizing his helplessness to the full. Now fancy had free play, and he not only saw and felt his real danger, but began to multiply the sense of it by needless imaginary fears.

The evening pipe had not its usual soothing effect on his weary, unfed system. He grew nervous and restless, hating the awful stillness, yet not daring to break it; starting at the rustle of a leaf or the drop of a cone from overhead.

The horror of solitude came upon him as he lay among the grim trees and rocks under the black distorted branches, with their rustling, waving drapery, in the red glow of the fire.

The immensity of the objects about him oppressed and overawed him — the feeling of distance from mankind, the idea of height and depth above and below.

His former experiences had been bounded by the club, the drawing-room, the hotel, and the conventional routes of travel. Accustomed to no more fearful solitude than that of some pleasant grove in the country, he felt an unreasoning fear, like that of a little child whose mother has gone away it knows not whither and left it in a strange place, in the mystery of darkness to wait and shiver and call for her and listen, winning no answer from the silence.

At such a time one begins to think of places in his life when he might have done better by others.

Moorhead, generally self-congratulatory, now found himself thinking very sadly over certain events that presented themselves to him in a guise more vivid than complimentary.

" Poor old Tom !" said he. " Well, he'll get it all

now, and I hope not too late to do him any good—I
hope not too late!"

Then it suddenly occurred to him that this hope,
which he felt truly and deeply at the moment, was a
hope for the consequences of his own death, which
he had begun, in his fright, to deem very probable,
since it was evident that he could neither live in the
woods nor find his way out of them; and he added,
"If I die, that is."

Now a question formed itself in his mind—not, as
it seemed, his own question, but one asked with
authority, which he must answer.

"Do you not mean to do him justice if you live?"
And Moorhead answered, very solemnly, "I do, and I
will."

The promise comforted him awhile, and gave him
the fresh hope that comes with the consciousness of
something worth living for, if it be only the righting
of a wrong. He felt a claim on life. But gradually
his nervous fears came back. He began to grow
sleepy. The firs whispered, and sighed, and murmured over him; the mocking water among the rocks
—the water that had played such a game of hide-and-
seek with his thirst—laughed with an unearthly me-
tallic voice, with a strange harmony of its own that
rose and fell in rhythmic cadence, suggesting a choral
band of woodland beings that danced with mirth and
wild music in the darkness on the mountain-side.

Sleep only brought him strange dreams. He could
reason down his nervous fancies, but whenever he
withdrew his will from the effort they took new
strength and came back in innumerable shapes to
trouble him afresh.

Unused to so hard a couch, chilly and hungry, he shifted his tired form from one uneasy position to another, or crouched, half-suffocated with smoke, close over the fire, till it seemed that he had been there the greater part of his life; and still there was no sign of day.

III

As soon as dawn enabled him to see about him, fantastic troubles began to disappear and real ones to take their places.

His faintness made him dread bestirring himself and cooking breakfast, yet (so prone is the human mind to discontent) he was even less pleased when he realized that he need not trouble himself with that function, which entire lack of material would have rendered an empty formality.

The morning air was delightfully refreshing. The whisper of the boughs seemed less mysterious and more soothing; the water laughed no longer as in mockery, but cheerily. Now he might drink, and delight at the prospect made him forget his despair a moment and brought him to his feet.

He found the stream, revenged himself upon it for its trickery of the past night, and, greatly refreshed for the time being, strapped up his blanket, ate the rest of his salal-berries, comforted his soul with the thought of the promise he had made concerning Tom (whoever Tom may have been) and of his own enhanced value in the eye of Fate as the promoter of a good object, and took counsel with himself as to what was next to be done.

This, he decided, was to follow the nearest watercourse. So he might avoid the thirst that had tormented him, become in due time the glad possessor of fish, and finally reach Puget Sound, where he might easily find a settlement or hail some passing boat.

The brook that had been his enemy became his guide and source of supply. He followed it with some trouble where it plunged down the southerly slope he had climbed the day before, and was much relieved when it stayed its abrupt descent, and, bending along a nearly level "shelf" to the eastward, kept on in that direction over a place where an immense landslide had piled up earth upon the mountain-side in ages past, and had built a gentle, rolling slope with mounds and hollows—a pleasant kind of country, full of woodland grace and loveliness, and very different from the steep he had just traversed.

A deer started from cover and stood a few seconds with ears erect, wide eyes, and moving nostrils, then dashed away. Moorhead hated the man who had stolen his rifle, on the groundless assumption that he would have been able to hit the animal.

The water led him more and more to his left, till it nearly reached the base of the mountain, having made about one-third of its circuit. As he went on he could hear, faintly at first, then louder and louder, the mellow thunder of a river. Encouraged by the sound, which promised food and suggested the possibility that so large a stream would have tempted men to settle far in the woods, he pressed on faster, and in doing so used up too much of his small reserve of strength.

Whether through the absence of that famous alpenstock of his, or for lack of guides, ropes, and the other conveniences to which, as a practised mountaineer, he was accustomed, or because of his anxiety about his precious welfare and valuable health, or because of the unfair advantage of gigantic size with which the things of the mineral and vegetable world about him seemed endued, or for whatever reason, he was exhausted — head and arms and legs and lungs were growing faint.

The stream, with its deep channel, capricious course, and experience in dodging obstacles, was no easy guide to follow. As nervous force sustained him, he kept on, without knowing how heavily the effort to increase his speed told upon his failing powers, till the roar of the river sounded very near.

Having brought him to this pass (which proved to be no thoroughfare), the stream played him a farewell trick, and, like a laughing girl who suddenly springs away from her bewildered escort with a flashing backward glance and a glimpse of bewitching white drapery as she runs, leaped, tossing its foam and rainbow spray upon the air with mirthful ripple down a rough ledge of granite and over a sheer precipice, leaving the poor waif sadly at a loss how to follow farther.

He, standing at the edge of the forest on the ledge, saw a towering range of mountains opposite, and at their base, not far before him, a fair valley, with green meadows, tree-crowned knolls, bright pools of still water gleaming in the light, or lying dark and cool in shadow, and here and there a glimpse of the river through the soft fringe of cottonwood, alder, and willow that marked its course.

At the head of the valley the two ranges nearly met, and the river roared through the deep cañon that parted them, while looking upward through the chasm he could see the eternal snows of a higher range. No traveller could look upon a fairer land in which to rest; but long as he would, and look as he might, he could see no way of reaching it alive.

The ledge on which he stood projected a little from the forest and was bare of vegetation, so that he could see far along on either side. He saw that he had crossed a range by a gap between two heights. Close on his left rose that on whose southerly slope he had spent the night, and down and round which he had been journeying since dawn. To the right and eastward stood another peak, and between and along the northern bases of both extended the precipice on which he stood.

Just before him, where the stream fell over, the ledge jutted down and out at a perilous slant. Wishing to scan the face of the steep and see if it afforded any hope of a descent, he cautiously crept down on the slope of the projection and lay prone, with his feet almost at the verge, one of them resting against a slight angle in the rough surface; his arms outstretched and his hands clinging to the rock as best they might.

Having seen all he could of the front of the cliff and found that, although most of it was quite impassable, a jutting out of green foliage near the foot, at some distance, seemed to betoken a gorge or water-bed to the eastward, he determined to explore in that direction. But his obliging destiny, beholding his need of a means of reaching the valley, supplied one then and there.

His strength, already taxed to its limit, would not

bear him up the rock ; he slipped a little, caught a cramp in his thigh, lost his nerve, struggled wildly in a long moment of agony, put too much faith in a little tuft of grass that grew in a crevice, lost his hold as it gave way, and fell.

IV

THE waters of the river Yawmish are born of sun and snow on one of the inner and loftier heights of the Olympics. In brightness and cold purity they flash into being and come springing down their native crags into a green glen that nestles on the huge shoulder of the mountain—a safe and pleasant pasture for the deer — unapproached by feet that are shod. They race over the green in the freshness of new life, tumble tinkling into a rocky basin, and thence with a merry noise come coursing down the steep, gathering strength as they go—down across the timber-line, through the echoing woodlands to the cañon and in and out along the pediments of the mountains, where, grown to a torrent multitude, they fling a peal of thunder to the heights. They pass the outer circle by a chasm in the wall and roll away through a lovely valley, where they spread abroad and linger here and there in little lakes beneath the shade, then gather their forces into a strong, swift river, and, rounding in foam and tumult the end of an outstanding range, go roaring through the forest to join the waters that have gone before them in the Sound. They are of a bright clear green, and with the foam upon their tossing heads look like masses of fair beryl flecked with snowy quartz.

It was that same outstanding range from which

Moorhead had fallen, and he lay in the valley, unconscious of the loveliness around him.

He had fallen far, but a tall cedar had caught him on its spreading arms, and the boughs had tossed him upward and let him fall, still from a dreadful height. The young trees below caught him again, and would have held him but his clothing tore, and he fell from bough to bough, down to the springy undergrowth, and thence rolled over upon a clear space covered with deep rich moss that grew on the wood-mould like a fleece, without stick or stone to mar its luxury.

So he lay, senseless more through exhaustion than hurt, and breathed, and lived. When he awoke he had lain there a long time, so that the moss was warm beneath him. With faint, uncertain senses, as in a dream, he heard the drowsy music of the river, and knew the sweet aroma of the cedar blended with the honey-odor of balsam.

A sunbeam slanting down through the foliage rested warm on his face.

He lay still with closed eyes, half unconscious in the luxury of rest and warmth, sweet sounds and fragrant air, not stirring, hardly thinking.

Then he seemed to hear words gently murmured in a tone of awe and pity.

"Oh—he is dead!"

He was hardly awake yet, and the words were to him such as one hears in a dream without wondering at their strangeness, whatever they may say. "He is dead!" He understood that he himself was meant; but he felt no surprise, for he was in a state of passive submission of mind and body, making no effort to know, but faintly receiving such impressions as reached his half-awakened senses. So he was dead? Yes; well, he was willing. It was pleasant and restful—gentle warmth was about him, sweet odors and delightful sounds.

"Death is good," he murmured, drowsily. Something cool and light touched his hand: his eyes opened a little; he saw dimly, still as in a dream, a face looking down upon his. A pale, fair face, with glorious brown eyes, dark with pity and alarm, gazing kindly and anxiously into his own. A sweet, wholesome, womanly face—he saw it more distinctly now as the mist of faintness began to clear away from before his eyes—full, tender, sensitive lips, cheeks sweetly rounded, and those lovely eyes full of good will, under strong dark brows, a fair broad forehead shaded by waves of gleaming gold-brown hair.

A gentle lady's face, bright with sense and understanding, formed by delicate thoughts, rich in the finer feelings.

He lay and looked, with no wish to move or think, without care, without wonder; languidly, passively, dreamily happy.

The soft voice spoke again in a low, soothing tone: "Speak to me—tell me—are you in pain?"

"I don't know," said he, sleepily, "or care."

"Ah! but you look sadly," said she. "Will you try and sit up? Shall I help you?"

"I don't think I care to—much," he answered.

"But you *must*. Yes, you must try."

He felt a firm, light touch on his shoulder and on his arm. "Come now!"

He tried to move, and groaned, for the effort was

agony; his muscles were stiff, and he was bruised and helplessly weak.

"Oh! I have hurt you," said she, "I am *so* sorry! There—lie and rest a little longer and I will bring you help—never fear."

So saying, she rose from his side, a graceful figure, smiling down at him; turned and passed swiftly away among the surrounding bushes. He tried to rise and follow her, but fell back racked with pains, which brought him quite to himself and left him fully conscious, but not certain in his mind as to whether his visitant had been a living human being who had really promised him help, or only one of those visions that come to a failing mind in its weakness, seen when the eyes are closed and invisible when they are open.

He tried to think how she looked and what she had said, but could only remember vaguely a lovely face close to his; a sweet, low voice that gave comfort and hope; a slender form that vanished in the bushes ere it was fairly seen, leaving an impression of grace and beauty and strange but rich attire.

Yes, it must be real; doubtless she would come again. And yet his mind had been so wrought upon during the night past; he remembered that as he lay fevered with thirst, listening to the water, he had imagined nymphs dancing on the mountain, and old legends had come back vividly to his mind.

So he lay, arguing with himself, now inclining to this opinion, now to that; now feeling hope of present aid, now despairing in utter helplessness and loneliness.

He was yielding more and more to the latter state

of mind when he heard the voice again, clear and cheery :

" We're coming. Can you hear us ?"

The bushes rustled, and there stood his nymph with her attendant satyr—a negro of powerful frame and surpassing blackness. He was rather of the gorilla type of beauty, with long arms and huge hands, immense chest and shoulders ; his hair was grizzled, and the crown of his head bald, and glorious when the sunbeams touched it.

" A long tumble, sah," said he, with deferential manner and very little of the accent of his race. " Am you broke at all, sah ?"

" Everywhere, I think," said Moorhead.

" May I take the liberty of feeling for shattered bones, sah ?" asked the black man, kneeling beside him, and passing a great hand deftly over his person.

Having ascertained that the bones were all in place, the sable personage turned and drew from the bushes a large arm-chair, covered with soft furs, and set it down beside his patient, lifted his body while the girl took his feet from the ground, and seated him in it ; then, kneeling behind it, thrust his own arms through two broad thongs that were fastened on either side of the back, and, slipping them over his big shoulders, rose and strode steadily away with the chair on his back, and Moorhead sitting in it as comfortably as his condition would allow, while the girl held aside the undergrowth to let them pass the more easily.

Moorhead saw that they were going along a beaten path beside the river, but nothing more ; for when he had begun to recover from the intense pain caused by his being lifted, and to become used to the slight swaying and jogging motion of the chair, he fell into a dead faint.

When he came to he was in a room with log walls, on a comfortable bed, and the negro was bending over him.

"You'll be better now, sah. It was an awful fall—a stupendious fall—sah!"

"An awful fall," said Moorhead. "Yes, I suppose so."

"'Low me to help you to bed, sah," said the negro; and having raised him, sat beside him on the bed, supporting him in one big arm while he gently undressed him, turned down the bedclothes, and placed him safe between a snowy pair of sheets.

"There, sah, am you quite comfable?" he asked.

"Thank you," said Moorhead. "I'm very hungry, could you bring me some food? I'm well able to pay—"

"No question of payment, sah," said the negro, hastily.

"But I'd rather pay," said Moorhead.

"Sorry, sah; but it's beyond the bounds of possibility," said the other, with suave dignity and a great deal of manner.

"Is this—your house?"

"This is Mr. Willoughby's house, sah. I am Mr. Willoughby's butlah, sir. Now, sah, if you please, I will bring you some broff."

He bowed himself out, and soon returned with a bowl from which a delicious savor of venison arose.

Moorhead ate ravenously, wondering the while who Mr. Willoughby could be that had a butler in such a place.

" May I see Mr. Willoughby ?" he asked, when he had finished ; "I should like to thank him."

" I think not. Mr. Willoughby seldom receives guests, sah. If you please, sah, sleep am the most important agent for the renovation of your faculties, sah." He placed on a chair by the bed a large tin-pan and a hatchet.

" What are those ?" Moorhead asked, rather apprehensively, with sudden recollections of those stories told to gladden our childhood's dreams, wherein travellers are slain and salted during their sleep in out-of-the-way places in the woods.

" Those are an improvidential gong, sah. If you should want anything, and will be pleased to beat on the pan with the hatchet, I will come. 'Low me to 'stinguish the light, sah. Good-night, sah ;" and the lamp and the butler went out and left Moorhead to the enjoyment of undisturbed rest.

He, though used to the greatest luxury, had never known any such as he felt now.

After weary days of wandering and nights spent on the ground, the first cool touch of linen, the first soft pressure of a comfortable bed, are more delightful than anything that can be bought for money.

The balmy air came gently from the open window ; the woods and waters made soft music in the valley. He enjoyed it a few moments and slept.

V

THE wanderer was too much shaken by his fall, too much excited by unusual adventure, to sleep a natural, wholesome sleep — too much exhausted to awake when his bruises gave him pain.

So he dreamed, and in his dreams the events of the last few days were blended in a tangled chain of frightful fancies.

He seemed to be still toiling alone in dark, trackless, precipitous places; groping by night in the brush, and pursued among the rocks by creatures of the woods with Siwash faces — beings who peeped from behind trees and leered and made wry mouths at him, or sang and danced as they circled round him or eluded his wrath; and if ever he came out of the darkness, or escaped, or was about to lay hands on a foe, suddenly he seemed to fall into infinite depths, while mocking laughter sounded round him and hands seemed to clutch at him from the empty air as he fell.

But now and then throughout his dreams a lovely form drew near, a lovely face looked into his with kindly deep-brown eyes, a gentle cool hand touched his own, and a soft voice spoke soothing words.

When he awoke a light was burning in the corner of the room, and beside it sat an old man reading and smoking a big pipe.

His head was large, with a noble, rugged forehead,

deep-set eyes and shaggy eyebrows, drawn into the habitual frown of one who reads much by night.

His hair hung to his shoulders in fine gray locks, and a huge silvery beard lay on his chest; altogether, in spite of his careless pose—for he lounged in a chair tipped back against the wall, while his stockinged feet reposed in another—he was a venerable figure.

Moorhead lay and watched him, trying meanwhile to remember where he was and how he had come there, and to sort out the real memories from the dreams. Soon the sight of the pan and the hatchet reminded him of his last conversation, and it occurred to him that this must be the owner of the house and of the butler.

"I think, sir," said he, and stopped, for his voice was strange to him, so hollow and faint that he would never have recognized it as his own—"I think, sir, you are my host?"

The old man took the pipe out of his mouth, laid his book on the table, and looked annoyed; then rose, took up the lamp, and came over to the bedside. He was a man of great stature and proportionate breadth, lean, sinewy, and deep-chested, but stooping a little as one who spends much time in study; and wore an old dark-blue smoking-jacket, a gray flannel shirt with white necktie, very loose blue trousers, and black stockings. He leaned over Moorhead, looked into his eyes, and felt his hand and forehead. "How do you feel?" said he.

"Rather weak, thanks," said Moorhead, after a short self-investigation, "and very thirsty."

The old man went out, and brought back a tin cup of water from one of the cold eddies of the mountain-stream. Moorhead drank eagerly and fell back, much refreshed, on the pillow. "Now," said the old man, "try and sleep," and sat down again to read.

Moorhead watched him and wondered why he was there. He was anxious to talk and hear all about himself first, and then the people of the place, but hardly knew how to begin. The old gentleman had an air of not wishing to be disturbed.

Presently he asked, "Have you the time, sir?"

"Yes," said the old gentleman, petulantly, taking his pipe out of his mouth with an impatient manner and consulting his watch—a large gold timepiece of old fashion—"Half-past nine, more or less."

"No later than that? Why, it must have been about eight when I went to sleep; and surely—*surely* I've slept longer than *that*. Why, it seems ages since I came to bed!"

"It isn't," said the other. "It's only four days and a fraction."

"Four! Oh! I've been ill then!" said Moorhead.

"Damnably," said the old gentleman, "and if you talk any more you'll be worse."

The patient was still awhile, but, having considered his condition and inwardly expressed his concern for himself, began to be annoyed at the silent presence with the book and pipe. He had nothing with which to amuse himself except unsatisfactory conjectures, and that picture of quiet enjoyment irritated him. He began to wish the old gentleman away.

"I must not trouble you to sit up with me," he said. "I'm causing you great inconvenience, I fear. It is very kind of you to take care of a stranger, and—"

"Not in the least," said the old gentleman. "I
didn't care to have you die about the place. I don't
keep a public cemetery for wayfarers. The alternative was to nurse you and have you able to travel as
soon as possible. Do you mind the light?"

"Not at all," said Moorhead, "but allow me to—"

"Then try and keep still."

Moorhead said no more, but began to think over
the memories of the few days past. They were rather
vague, and blent with dreams that had come to him
in his feverish illness. He remembered the night on
the mountain, but the dream-pictures were woven in
upon its darkness. He remembered his fall, and the
awakening—the journey on the butler's back.

What kind of place was this—this house in the backwoods, with log-walls and a butler?

This man who sat and read looked quite capable of
such a possession. His features showed refinement;
his voice was that of a gentleman; his words, curt and
eccentric as they were, had not been rudely spoken.

Then that face—that lovely face and form that had
come in his dreams and driven away the ugly fancies—
was that a memory, or a fancy also? He could not
tell.

Pondering on this, he slept a cool, delicious, wholesome sleep, from which voices on the porch by his
door awakened him.

"No," said that of the old man, "I shall go and try
the trout. Moloch has supplied me well with wrig-
glers, and I hope—"

"But," said another voice, very gentle, clear, and
sweet, "you have been up all night, and surely you
need rest."

3

"I often am, and I do *not* need rest; besides, it is a perfect day for fishing."

"Was our invalid—"

"Whose invalid?"

"Our invalid."

"Why ours?"

"'Who is our neighbor? A certain man went down from Jerusalem to Jericho—'"

"Yes, yes—I know," said the old man, in a low voice. "So your mother would have said, Leonora."

There was silence, broken by the sweet young voice.

"Well, how is he? Was he in his right mind when he woke?"

"Y-es—yes; quite, I should say. He seems to be doing very well."

"Poor fellow!" said the other; "he has lost all his good looks."

"Such as they were," said the old man. "Good looks, like everything else, are a matter of comparison. The human race is not beautiful, and he does not excel the average. You see you have no standard of comparison."

"Oh! *I* think good looks are real—positive—"

"Not his," said the old gentleman, with an ugly chuckle. "Less still now. Where's my rod? Oh, thank you. Good-bye; I must be off to catch my speckled friends at their sunrise breakfast."

Moorhead thought him as disagreeable an old man as he ever had met.

The voices had stopped, and footsteps had succeeded them, going away in two directions. The door stood wide, and the curtains were drawn from the

open window.   From his pillow he could see, framed
by the vines that hung about the window, a glowing
object cleaving the sky like a tongue of rosy flame—
a sharp snow-peak that, looking far over the horizon
line, saw the approach of the morning, while the lesser
heights still slept in the gray dawn, and flushed at
the sight with glory.

The door framed a different picture — a garden-
path leading to a dim grove, and a glimpse of water
through dusky foliage.

The peak began to brighten, and turned from rose
to gold, and then to clear white as the full light
settled on it ; the flowers by the path began to show
their colors and the waters to sparkle.

All this did not appeal to Moorhead, who was thinking of what he had overheard.   He lay uneasily—impatient till he heard the voice of the old butler singing at his morning work.   Then he seized the hatchet
and beat upon the tin pan.

" You're awake, sah, an' bettah—much bettah,"
said the butler.   " You rang, sah ?"

" Yes," said Moorhead.   " Is there such a thing as
a mirror—a looking-glass—to be had ?   Then bring
me one."

The mirror showed him a highly indignant face,
quite thin and pale and by no means attractive, but
unmistakably his own.   His " good looks " were not
permanently injured—he could see that—and on reflection he forgave the unknown speaker for saying
they were gone, because it implied her consciousness
of their having existed ; and he took some pleasure
in the inference that, when they should return, she
would recognize them again.   Not that he cared es-

pecially for her, but he wished his good looks to meet with general recognition from her sex.

He knew her voice as that which had spoken to him after his fall and in his dreams, and was glad to feel that she was real.

The good butler helped him to a chair, made his bed, patted out the pillows, and, having propped him up and settled him comfortably, went out to get his breakfast.

Afterwards, while his convalescent appetite was doing justice to a bowl of strong venison broth, several new-laid eggs, and delicious toast crisp without hardness, a new picture stood in the frame of the door.

A tall, slender girl of queenly bearing, lovely in feature and expression.

She wore a dark-green skirt of some strong, pliant material that draped her person gracefully to the ankles, and a loose hunting-shirt of soft doe-skin made after the Indian fashion, with heavy fringes on arm and breast and shoulder and richly embroidered in green and gold.

Her belt was of the same material, stiff with embroidery, and held, in loops, a row of Winchester cartridges on the left side, and on the right a hunting-knife with a hilt of ivory and gold, in a sheath of black fur, and a light holster with a revolver of no small calibre, beautifully mounted to match the knife.

A heavy gold chain hung round her neck and was knotted on her breast, whence it fell beneath the belt.

Her feet were clad in dainty moccasins, likewise embroidered; a little golden snake with emerald eyes twined her left wrist in spiral coils.

Moorhead sat and looked and wondered. "Who and what is she ?"

Surely she could be no ordinary woodland maiden—no settler's daughter. Her look and bearing were not those of a rustic, gentle or simple; her attire, peculiar and almost barbaric as it was, had a certain *chic*, a dash of *style*, that can generally be attained only by a diligent study of the fashions. She was nobly formed; her neck, beautifully round and white, rose straight and comely from a splendid pair of shoulders, well knit and athletic, yet neither too broad nor too square for womanly grace. She was slender, yet beautifully and not weakly moulded, and health shone in her deep-brown eyes and glowing sun-browned cheeks. She held a bunch of yellow violets in her hand.

Moorhead thought—as every young man thinks when suddenly confronted with new feminine loveliness—that she was the most beautiful woman he had ever seen, and perhaps on this occasion he was right.

"I am glad to see you getting well again," she said (and her voice was the one Moorhead knew). "For a while we were afraid for you."

"So I have heard," said Moorhead. "In fact, Mr.—Mr.—"

"Mr. Willoughby ?"

"Yes, thank you; Mr. Willoughby told me he did not keep a public cemetery, and was nursing me to avoid burying me."

"You mustn't mind my father's jokes," she said. "He says strange things sometimes."

"You are Miss Willoughby, then ?"

"Yes, so I am; though no one ever called me so

before. *You* would, of course," she said, thoughtfully. "Yes, I am Miss Willoughby."

"Queer—seems to be in some doubt about it," Moorhead thought. "But this is all queer."

"My name is Moorhead—Norman Moorhead," said he, "and I owe you an apology for descending so abruptly on your premises."

"It was a little precipitate," she answered. "But since you had to fall, I hope you will find that you have fallen among friends."

"Indeed, you have been friends to me," he answered, "and now I beg that I may have the privilege of being one of yours."

"A most exclusive privilege," said she, "for you will be the *only* one, except my father and Moloch; but you are not to talk, I forgot. I have read that the temptation to talk is irresistible—to a woman. I must prove the contrary. You must be very quiet and get well soon, for I have many questions to ask you, all about the world outside. When I begin you will have no peace, so make the most of the present. Have you everything you need?"

"Yes, but Miss Willoughby, one more question, who is Moloch?"

"Moloch is the butler."

Moorhead let his curiosity get the better of him. "And may I ask why you live here?"

"Because it's my home."

"But—" he began.

She put her finger on her smiling lips, shook her head, then made him a grand, stately courtesy, and was gone.

"Am I dreaming again?" said he. But the yellow

violets on the threshold, where she had dropped them, answered him that he was awake.

He took up the hatchet and pan, hesitated a minute, laid them down, crept feebly to the door, and took the flowers.

VI

THE mountains and woods breathed strength into the atmosphere; the Pacific sent inland a wholesome flavor of salt spray, tempered with the warmth of the Japan current; the air was rich in health.

Moorhead sat on the veranda by the door of his room; as yet he had been unable to go farther. He had had a dangerous illness, but was not likely now to die of anything but curiosity. That noisome malady had taken full possession of his mind, and he spent his time in forming theories about the old gentleman and his daughter, Leonora, in whom he was beginning to take a lively interest.

His room opened only outward, and he had not yet seen the inside of the house. He had not been allowed to talk much, and any attempt on his part at continued conversation was sure to result in his being left alone, with an admonition that he needed rest.

What puzzled him was the question how such people as the Willoughbys could possibly be at home in such a place. He had one of those peculiarly conventional minds that resent anything unusual in the ways of others—he was strongly attracted towards the Willoughbys. They were evidently people of high breeding and thorough refinement; there was even a certain stateliness about them and a charm of manner that tempered the eccentricities of the old gentleman and made his daughter's loveliness irresistible ; yet it seemed to Moorhead that there must be something wrong about them, because, from his point of view, they were out of place.

They must, of course, have a reason for living in a wilderness where there were no neighbors apparently—some cause for avoiding their fellow-men. As for their unwillingness to talk to him, it might be owing to his weak condition and need of rest—and it might not. Mr. Willoughby evidently wished him away. He had visited Moorhead once or twice, for a few minutes at a time ; and while he had been, as far as manner goes, the pink of courtesy, since the night when the patient had waked and found him sitting in the room, he had hinted very plainly that he wished him to get well in order that he might continue his travels. Behind all this there must be something very wrong. Moorhead could not doubt it, and it made him uneasy. What was it ?

He was sitting and pondering, for lack of better employment, on this question, and his reverie was profusely illustrated with mental portraits of Leonora. (He had begun to take the liberty of thinking of her as Leonora, a practice he would have condemned, if he had caught himself at it, as not the thing, for he was, superficially, a devout worshipper of the Thing.)

A rustle in the bushes startled him, and he saw her coming out of the woods, erect and alert, stepping lightly, with a rifle in her hand. She waved her hand to him with a gracious gesture, smiling, and called the butler, who came from some covert where he had been sawing wood.

" You'll find a mule-deer on the upper trail, Moloch.

Better take a cayuse with you to bring him home. He lies right by the big laurel, under the ledge."

"Yes, Miss Leonora," said Moloch, touching his grizzled tuft of wool.

Moorhead was wounded again in his sense of the fitness of things. A goddess of the chase is all very well in fable or marble, but a girl with a Winchester is different, and he thought such lips would be better employed .in discussing light opera, dress, and the character of a neighbor than in announcing a successful "kill" and disposing of the quarry, and that a fan would become the little hand better than that splendid instrument of death, with its curiously carved stock and heavy gleaming barrel of dark-blue steel. (The girls of Moorhead's set had not yet gone in for outdoor sports as they did a few years later, or he might not have cared.) However, poor thing, she was not in the way of seeing opera, and had no neighbors to discuss, and dress, as a subject of conversation, would be thrown away in such a wilderness. As for the rifle, it was her means of marketing, the purse that furnished her change when she went shopping. Poor girl!

Having dismissed Moloch upon his errand, she came to the porch, leaned upon the objectionable rifle, and looked critically at her patient. "You are much better," she said, approvingly. "You feel so, I hope?"

"Thanks to your care and hospitality, Miss Willoughby."

"Your voice is strong," she said, gleefully. "I really believe you are well enough to talk."

"I am sure of it," he said. "May I?"

"Yes, you may. Please do."

They were both silent awhile. To wish to be allowed to talk is one thing, to be asked to talk is another.

"Then," said he, "I shall ask questions."

"Oh! But it is I that must ask questions," she said, "and you will be able to answer them for me. I have so much to ask! Tell me—tell me all about the world beyond the woods."

"That is a great deal to tell all at once," said Moorhead, somewhat startled by this wholesale demand upon his stock of information. "And the world is not very interesting. To me your life here in the forest seems infinitely more worth talking about."

"You are good enough to say so," she said, "but if you had lived here always, as I have, it might not seem so. Besides, you can see what there is here, and I have seen nothing of the world outside."

"Do you mean you have really lived here all your life, Miss Willoughby?"

"All my life—and I so long to hear about people and places, and my father will never speak of them, and Moloch is almost as bad. If I ask him questions, he says, 'I dunno. Ask Mr. Willoughby, Miss Leonora.' Now I have you to tell me everything."

Moorhead looked vexed. It was more clear than ever that something was wrong with these people. However, there was something attractive in instructing the quite unenlightened mind of so fair a listener. What is more delightful than a good audience?

"'Everything' is a good deal," said he — "more than you will care to hear; but I'll do my best. Where shall I begin? At the creation?"

She looked gravely at him, and her eyes darkened a

little. "The creation is a solemn thing," said she, "and not to be spoken of lightly."

"I beg your pardon," said Moorhead.

"You have done me no wrong," said she.

"I mean," said he, "for speaking, in your presence, in a way that you do not approve."

"My presence and approval have nothing to do with it," she said. "Well, begin with—the cities—tell me about cities." Her face had lost its grave look, and wore the expression of an eager child waiting for a promised story.

"The cities," he said, after a long pause, finding that his supply of information on the subject did not flow as freely as might have been expected. "Really, I—I don't know that there's much to tell about the cities. They are — why, cities are much alike, you know !"

Leonora looked disappointed. "You don't seem to understand," said she. "*I* have never seen a city. In the first place, what do they look like ?"

He tried his best to describe a city, but, not knowing very well where to begin, where to end, or what to say between, failed dismally. Try to describe a city yourself to some one who has never seen any, and see how you like it.

"That sounds dreary," said she. "But then the houses are very beautiful, many of them ? There are the churches, the theatres, the courts of justice, the palaces—are they not very grand ?"

"Why, yes, some of them ; I hardly know how to describe them. Of course, houses are of every kind, from little shanties that are just enough to keep the wind and rain off a man's head as he sleeps, to great buildings with hundreds of rooms; and some are bare and ugly, and some are adorned with all that art can do to make them beautiful — pictures and statues and splendid architecure."

Leonora was now more and more disappointed. "You don't tell me so very much," she said. "I think I can imagine a city for myself, as far as the buildings go. But about the people—where there is so much to do—"

"Really," said Moorhead, in despair, "I believe you were right. I am weak still, and find that conversation is more of a strain than I had expected. By to-morrow I shall be better able to go on with the subject; and meanwhile I will think things over and be prepared to tell you what will interest you."

"Oh, thank you," she said. "That will give me great pleasure. I am sorry for having tired you so with my questions. Here comes Moloch, and I must go and help him with the deer."

Moloch was just coming from the woods leading a little dappled pony, across whose back lay an antlered buck of nearly twice its size, and came at her bidding to show the quarry to Moorhead.

"You killed that great creature all yourself?" said he.

"Yes."

After he had duly admired the antlers and paid her a compliment or two on her aim, she went with Moloch to the back of the house, where he heard the two busily engaged in cutting up the deer.

"I never expected," said he, "to have to begin at the beginning and tell her everything. How pitifully ignorant she is! And how am I to do it?"

However, he felt that the opportunity of addressing such an audience was too good to be wasted, and for the rest of the afternoon he amused himself preparing the morrow's lecture, so that when the time came, and Leonora presented herself, with the same child-like eagerness she had shown on the day before, she should find him ready.

He knew his Baedeker pretty well, and if where the facts seem too insipid he did not hesitate to flavor them with an occasional touch of romance, it was only to please his listener—an object which it did not fail to accomplish, for he had the satisfaction of seeing her smile every now and then with evident pleasure as she sat drinking in his words. After the first shock was over he rather enjoyed her ignorance, as it gave him a chance to be patronizing, and he dearly loved to patronize. It seemed to him that the wonders of modern invention would be a fertile topic, and susceptible of artistic coloring.

"The magic we read about and don't believe in—all superstition, you know—of course—" he began.

"What is superstition?" the simple maiden inquired.

"Why—er—superstition is—well, believing in what isn't true, you know."

"Oh, then, if you happened to be telling me what was not exactly true, I should be superstitious in believing it?"

"N—no—not exactly superstitious. It's hard to explain precisely what superstition means."

"You were saying," said she, after a pause, "something about magic. I have heard of magic. Moloch tells me stories in the winter evenings—stories of enchantments—of witches and strange things that happen—"

"Yet there are stranger things than enchantments," said he. "There is the locomotive—the iron horse that draws a train of houses on wheels—a sort of rolling village—for thousands of miles at such a pace that if a man jumps off while it is going he is likely to be killed—the creature whose life is fire and whose breath is steam—who may be inspired to life and gigantic strength at the will of a man or put to sleep indefinitely merely by kindling or putting out the fire—"

"I had heard of railways," said she. "Have you seen them, and are such things really possible?"

"There are engines more wonderful still," said he. "They carve and weave and work in metal, doing the labor of thousands without weariness, and with such swiftness and accuracy that no quantity of human hands could equal the results. Yet they obey the touch of a man's hand. And what should you say of an enchanter who could chain the lightning and make it do his bidding? Light the cities at night, so that one can read in the streets? Send the thoughts of one person to another hundreds of miles away in a few minutes? Drive great cars full of people about the streets, on regular lines, open to all, so that even the poorest may ride to their work faster than horses could carry them?"

Here he stopped, delighted with his flight of fancy in describing the prosaic electric cars, to watch the effect.

"Oh!" said Leonora, "tell me more!"

"Have you ever seen a photograph?" said he.

"What is a photograph?"

"A sort of picture. There is a kind of little box called a camera, with a sort of eye in one end. The man who knows how to use it turns its eye upon some person or object, touches a spring, and there is a perfect picture of the person or object, line for line, which by chemical process may be printed on paper, and reproduced again and again."

Leonora looked up with eyes that sparkled with delight. "Are you telling me the very truth?" she asked. "Do they *really* have such wonders in the great cities?"

"The very truth."

"You are *not* taking advantage of my ignorance?" she said, with evident anxiety.

"Indeed, I am not," said he.

"Then I must believe you. How sad it is," she said, thoughtfully, and regarding Moorhead with deep, pensive eyes, "that sometimes the boiler bursts, or the safety-valve refuses to work, or the wire breaks, or the fuse burns out, or the trolley comes off, or the slide of the camera gets out of order! Isn't it, Mr. Moorhead?"

It is one thing to instruct a fresh, ingenuous mind in the wonders of the world; another to be led into holding forth for hours in minute detail on trite and familiar subjects.

The change from the pleasure of the former position to the awkwardness of the latter was too much for Moorhead, who felt as if he had been invited to sit in a chair of state, and had had it pulled away and sat on the floor instead. If Leonora had suddenly drawn a revolver on him he could have forgiven it, as in keeping with her environment; but that she should make fun of him was more than he could bear.

Leonora was smiling, and presently spoke:

> "'These things to hear
> Would Desdemona seriously incline:
> But still the house affairs would draw her thence;
> Which ever as she could with haste despatch,
> She'd come again, and with a greedy ear
> Devour up my discourse.

.   .   .   .

> My story being done,
> She gave me for my pains a world of sighs:
> She swore—In faith,' twas strange, 'twas passing strange;
> 'Twas pitiful, 'twas wondrous pitiful;
> She wish'd she had not heard it—'"

Moorhead drew himself up in wrath. Had he been a lady it might be said that he "bridled."

"I owe you a humble apology," he said, stiffly and testily. "Of course, I was not aware of the extent of your information. I tried, at your request, to interest you; but I fear I have bored you extremely. You might have spared me the quotation, however, and I see no reason why I should have been allowed to go on all this time under the impression that what I was saying was new to you."

"Oh, I assure you it has all been very interesting and amusing," said she.

"Very likely," said he.

"Why, I believe," said she, wide-eyed and surprised—"I believe you are really—angry!"

He made no answer.

"It was a pity to tease you," she said. "I am

4

sorry; I had no idea you would mind. You didn't quite understand me when I asked you about the world outside; I didn't mean the kind of things you have been telling me. Of course, I know all that; but how shall I make you see what I mean? Things that one would not learn without seeing them and living there. So, when you began to tell me just the things that I can get out of books I was disappointed; and when you took it for granted that I was so utterly ignorant I thought I'd just listen and let you keep on thinking so awhile and hear what you'd say. I am sorry, very sorry, if you are vexed."

"Oh, don't mention it!" said he, snapping out his words so crossly that after one steady look of surprise, with parted lips and lifted brows, she turned away and left him alone with his broken temper.

Moorhead was full of small conceit, and could not bear being made ridiculous in his own eyes, to which her explanation, gracious and humble as it was, did not make him look any better. He passed a wretched afternoon.

The saddest worm that crawls upon the earth is the man that cannot take a joke.

VII

THE next morning Moorhead woke up with a feeling that he ought to be ashamed of himself. He rose and dressed, and Moloch brought him his breakfast as usual. While he was eating it Mr. Willoughby made him a short visit, pipe in hand.

"You must find it very dull here, Mr. Moorhead," said he.

"On the contrary, sir, I think it the most delightful place I have ever seen."

"So do I," said Mr. Willoughby. "Its charm for me lies in its seclusion. The absence of the human race is enough to make the most desolate desert attractive. Here we have solitude in its perfection— unutterable grandeur and beauty about us—the gifts of nature bestowed with a lavish hand. But the solitude is the sweetest gift of all."

"Yet you must find it dreary sometimes without neighbors."

"Neighbors," said the old gentleman, "are of three kinds: friends, enemies, and strangers. Which do you prefer?"

"Friends, by all means," said Moorhead.

"I cannot agree with you. Strangers, while they remain so, go about their business and do not meddle. They expect nothing of you, and you nothing of them in return. They are independent of you, and allow you to be independent of them. The only question is, how long will a stranger remain so ? For every stranger may become a friend or enemy at any time. Meanwhile, it is hard to find their *raison d'être*, and to see them about is rather a nuisance than otherwise."

"I agree with you in regard to strangers, Mr. Willoughby," said Moorhead. "They are not useful, and are, as a rule, unpleasant — people one doesn't know. But why prefer them to friends ?"

"Friends ? People who force upon you attentions, of which they have no means of knowing whether they will be acceptable or not, even if they took the pains to try to find out, and who expect, in return, that you shall know and do and say exactly what will be agreeable to them ; who advise you about your affairs ; who amuse themselves by talking about and interfering with your private concerns and call it 'sympathy'; who watch your actions and pass judgment upon them and call it 'friendly interest'; who say behind your back what they dare not say to your face and call it 'politeness,' or who take upon themselves to find fault with you and call it 'kindness'; who exact a return for all they force upon you, and if it be not forthcoming, or if it be unsatisfactory, revile you to others as ungrateful, unfriendly, or stupid ; who profess a liking for you, and as its price assume a familiarity with you and a right to your services ? These are friends ! They have one negative sort of virtue."

"What is that ?" Moorhead asked.

"That is, that as soon as you are unable through any cause, such as poverty or other misfortune, to return in kind the obligations they have forced upon

you, they consider themselves at liberty to drop your
acquaintance and become either strangers or enemies.
I speak of the majority; I do not deny that there are
exceptions. But they are too few and far between to
make it worth a man's while to spend his life in seeking them; and if he does so, he will meet with disap-
pointments enough to outweigh a hundredfold the
few cases of true faith between man and man that he
may find. If that is not so, the world has changed
since I knew it. How many men do you suppose have
been betrayed by enemies in comparison with those
who have been betrayed by their friends?"

"Then, on the whole, you prefer enemies?"

"Ah! But a real *enemy* is a rare thing. So few
dare be enemies outright! Yes! an enemy is one's
acknowledged opponent in the game of life; he has
the merit of being interesting at least. And, let him
do his worst, he cannot injure a man as his friend
can. Pardon me, I have said enough to tire you.
You are gaining strength?"

"Very fast, thanks to your kindness," said Moorhead.

"Good. You will be able to travel soon. Good-
morning."

He went away, leaving his guest to wonder what
was his grudge against the human race, and whether
he himself was regarded as a stranger, an enemy, or,
that objectionable thing, a friend. From the father
his thoughts soon turned to the daughter. He hoped
Leonora would come, but soon he saw her walking
fully armed into the woods, and he found himself in
penitence, condemned to expiate yesterday's ill-temper
by a lonely morning.

He sat some hours smoking, and reading a book he had found in his room. It was not a very interesting book, and his thoughts kept wandering away after Leonora.

Mr. Willoughby had gone fishing; Moloch's axe could be heard in the woods beyond the river.

Moorhead became restless, and the spell of languor that had held him since his illness—the sleepy influence of the forest—was broken.

He walked out into the sunlight. The house stood on a small plateau, carefully cleared of all undergrowth, and shaded by several immense cedars and a cottonwood, whose boughs, nearly meeting across it, made a changing network of light and shade on the ground.

There was a broad level space of well-kept grass, and garden-beds in which grew native flowers and others not indigenous to the valley. The harebells, primroses, and blossoming shrubs of the mountains, the lilies, and blue and yellow violets from wood and marsh, sweetbrier, and wild geranium mingled their sweetness with that of red and white garden-roses, carnation, tulip, poppy, cardinal, and columbine.

The house, built of cedar logs split smooth and square, overlapping at the corners, the interstices filled in with moss and clay, consisted of three long, low cabins, the two smaller ones projecting backward from the larger and higher, so as to form a quadrangle. All about it was a broad covered veranda, roofed, like the house, with cedar shakes and curtained with woodbine and ivy, which parted in the form of a Norman arch at the front.

Moorhead walked about it. At the back were various small out-buildings—a hay-shed, a tiny stable (with five stalls for the winter use of the pack-ponies, which were allowed in summer to roam the valley at will), a hen-house, and a cow-shed.

A kitchen-garden grew in a corner of the clearing with a rank luxuriance of vegetables.

Moorhead walked round to the front and looked up through the arch of vines. The door stood open. He hesitated a moment, then, overcome by his desire to know more of these people and their life, went up the steps, knocked (as a matter of form, for he knew there was no one there), and went in.

Coming from the very edge of the wild woods, he found himself in a long, low hall, among pictures, beautifully embroidered fabrics, rich furs, stately antlers, furniture whose woodwork was a series of grotesque carvings that showed the mark of rare genius, pretty things of every shape and kind here and there, and—books.

The wall, for the height of seven feet from the floor, was lined with books, on cedar shelves whose edges were carved in a delicate pattern of running ivy, broken here and there by queer little faces that looked out between the leaves.

Moorhead was no judge of books, but even he could tell that many of the volumes were rare and costly, that the editions were such as the heart of the book-man yearns over, that the library was that of a reader who loved books for themselves and for what was in them. Many lay on the tables and chairs—not as if carelessly left there, but in a way that denoted recent and scholarly use, and nearly all had book-marks between the leaves in several places.

Above the shelves the wall was devoted to orna-

ment. It was covered with buckskin, embroidered
on the upper border with a broad stripe, of a pattern
similar to that of the carving on the edges of the
shelves—ivy, with odd faces peering out. Below
this border it was thickly adorned with pictures—
water-colors and crayons made with more than skill—
and all of scenes chosen from the most perfect spots
of that wonderful region; little nooks where the
water lay among the trees and reflected the delicate
ferns about its margin and the boughs above; towering rocks; a startled deer just rising from his mossy
covert; an eagle sitting on the blasted top of a dead
fir. And there were portraits, in which Moorhead
saw the face of Mr. Willoughby in the strength and
beauty of early manhood, the budding promise of
Leonora's grace and loveliness, the shiny-black countenance of Moloch grinning with pleasure. The other
portrait, by a somewhat less skilful hand, was the
face of a lady he had never seen—a delicate, sweet,
piquant face of singular beauty, and bearing a strong
though hardly definable resemblance to Leonora.
Between these pictures the furs of small animals and
the wings of birds were spread flat on the yellow
surface of the buckskin—mink and young beaver,
wildcat, marten, black squirrel, jay, blue grouse and
ruffed grouse, white ptarmigan from the peaks, and
water-fowl of many kinds and colors. A noble pair
of elk-antlers graced either end of the hall, and one
grander still lifted its graceful strength above the
immense fireplace opposite the front door.

There were two other doorways, one at each end of
the back of the room, leading respectively into the
two wings, and curtained with heavy dark - green

portières embroidered in dull gold and crimson. Along the upper shelf of the bookcases were innumerable pretty knickknacks, evidence of wealth, travel, and exquisite taste; and rifles of various workmanship, revolvers, knives, and a great array of large-bowled, long-stemmed pipes hung from the prongs of the antlers.

The ceiling was of polished cedar, supported on mighty beams of the same. From the central rafter hung three lamps—a large one in the middle of the room, a lesser one at either end.

The floor also was of polished cedar, but of a lighter tint and harder grain than that of the ceiling, and was almost covered with the skins of beasts. One immense black bear-skin with head and claws lay in the centre with two smaller ones at each side, forming a line from end to end. Before each door lay a skin of the gray timber-wolf, silvery in its winter prime.

The chairs and tables were made of the gnarled and twisted limbs of trees, deftly joined; and the feet and every knob and projection were carven into the semblance of claws or faces or leaves, each without regard to the rest, but according to the fancy its original shape had suggested to the workman's quaint imagination.

There were lounges and great arm-chairs, covered with padded skins, and several long, yellow cougar-skins finely cured, lying loose on the backs. There were lighter chairs whose backs and seats were made of the broad white, thick feathered breasts of loon and wild-goose, and whose upper knobs were carved with birds' heads, whose feet ended in birds' claws.

Under the central lamp was an oblong table, of yellow cedar smooth as a mirror, littered with many things.

The small and portable articles in the room were of many lands and varied workmanship—of bronze and wood and silver. The larger were all of such material as the forest and its wild things supplied, and evidently home-made, though with skill and taste little short of genius.

A rough stone six feet square—evidently a rock that had stood there with its foundations in the earth, and about which the house had been built, for no power these people could have had at command would have stirred it—formed the hearth, and the fireplace upon it was a very cavern for size and depth, of big, rough stones cemented with clay that had baked into brick.

There was no need of fires there through the long summer, so the rock within was covered with living moss and clumps of fern such as love the shade, and purple violets were planted there, transforming the rugged hollow into a grotto fit for a fairy hermit.

Moorhead stood awhile gazing about him, lost at first in admiration of the effect of the whole, and then began to examine singly with a curious eye the various things that went to make it up, quite forgetting that he was a trespasser, and staring like a child in a museum.

He wondered more than ever who and what these people were.

" Surely," he thought, " no ordinary circumstances compel them to stay here beyond the reach of civilization. It cannot be poverty, for these books—those ornaments—are a fortune in themselves and have been brought from all lands. It is not ignorance, certainly. And yet they have lived here long—everything shows long occupancy; that carving of native wood is the work of years. This is no mere summer camp, but a home—such a home as only long living can make, but not the home of people who belong to such a place. I don't understand it."

He had thought it all over and had concluded that the old man must have committed some crime and hidden himself here to avoid its consequences, when he was suddenly aware of a presence near at hand.

There stood Mr. Willoughby, his great frame nearly filling the doorway, saying nothing and watching him with a very unpleasant expression.

"Oh! Mr. Willoughby!" said Moorhead.

The old gentleman stood silent, waiting for him to finish whatever he might have to say, and, when he could think of nothing apt and had grown as uncomfortable as a man may be, remarked, dryly, "Do you find what you look for?"

"I—I wasn't looking for anything, Mr. Willoughby," said Moorhead. "I—knocked, and there was nobody at home; so I—er—"

"So you accepted my daughter's invitation and made yourself at home?"

"I—er—Miss Willoughby didn't invite me," said Moorhead, wondering why he said it, for he was not of a frank nature and would usually have thought a confession quite needless. But he was afraid of the old gentleman in a way and told the truth without thinking.

"Pardon," said Mr. Willoughby. "You forget, of

course, my daughter asked you in, or you would not have come. Will you sit down?"

Moorhead sat down, and Mr. Willoughby remained standing in the doorway.

"You have a great many books," said Moorhead.

"I have not counted them," said Mr. Willoughby.

"And some very valuable ones," said Moorhead.

"Indeed?" said Mr. Willoughby. "I hadn't appraised them."

The old gentleman's manner and tone were painfully polite and by no means cordial. Moorhead tried again.

"What a beautiful home you have, and what a pity so few people can see it!"

"Why?"

"Because, when one is surrounded with delightful possessions there is a pleasure in showing them to one's neighbors, I think; that is, sympathy in enjoyment is as necessary as sympathy in pain."

"As to neighbors, I fear I cannot agree with you," said Mr. Willoughby. "As to sympathy, I don't know that it is necessary in any case. At all events, I should have no pleasure in playing the showman—in my own home, of all places. If your chair is uncomfortable, pray take another." Moorhead, by dint of repeated snubs, was beginning to show signs of uneasiness.

"Thank you. I believe I will go to the room you have kindly put at my disposal," said he, and was glad to be out of his unpleasant position.

That evening Leonora came to him and asked him to join them at dinner. He would have excused himself, fearing the old gentleman's inhospitable demeanor, but remembered that he had no choice and could not very well refuse.   His fears, to his great relief, were ill-founded.   Mr. Willoughby said nothing unpleasant, and Leonora was a charming hostess.

Dinner was served on the veranda.   Moloch had abandoned his usual blue overalls and flannel shirt for a suit of decent black and white collar and tie, and waited on the table with the air of a promoter of state banquets.

The dinner was delicious, and after it Leonora asked him to stay; and, finding he could sing, accompanied him sweetly with voice and guitar under the summer moon.

When they parted for the night Mr. Willoughby said, "Now that you are well enough, pray be the guest of our house and table, Mr. Moorhead, while you stay."   And so it was until he went away from the valley.

When he had gone Leonora said, "Thank you, father mine; that was right.   I know how you hate any invasion of our home; but since a guest has been thrown helpless at our door it would be a shame not to treat him like a guest."

"That shall be as you will, my girl; you are mistress of my house.   But I wish you could have seen him when I found him prying about our hearth.   It was very amusing—to me."

"I'm sorry you treated him coldly," said she.   "He has been made dependent on us for the present by his misfortune—"

"*Our* misfortune," said the old man.

"And to make him feel that we do not want him here, and that he is a nuisance, seems to be unworthy of you."

"Really, I don't think I treated him ill," said Mr.
Willoughby. "I found him in the house, and he had
not been asked to come there. That was an awkward
predicament, for which he had only himself to blame.
I not only abstained from any embarrassing questions—
such as asking what he meant by it—but I invented
an excuse for him. I told him you had invited him,
and when he said you had not, I insisted that you
must have done so, and that he must have forgotten
since he had passed the door."

"*Father!*" said Leonora, reproachfully, "*why* did
you say such a thing as that?"

"To put him at his ease, dear," said Mr. Willoughby. "That's what they call it in the civilized
world you admire so much from a distance."

"*Please*, after this be pleasant to him," said she,
rather crossly. "Remember he's our guest."

"Very well, dear," said Mr. Willoughby, meekly.
"I'll try," and betook himself to his books.

VIII

The days passed sweetly in the valley.

Moorhead began to grow strong and enjoy himself, not the less perhaps that he saw but little of Mr. Willoughby, before whom he was never quite at ease.

The old gentleman had a quiet way of looking down from a superior height, both of mind and body, that greatly irritated a young fellow who liked to be important and was used to being made much of in his own world.

Moorhead knew that he was tall, as men go—the old gentleman towered above him ; he was considered well informed—his host was a man of deep learning ; he liked to hold himself a wit—but his sayings always seemed to him flat and trivial in Mr. Willoughby's presence ; he was proud of his manner — but Mr. Willoughby, with all his bluntness and eccentricity, had a certain "grand air" in all he said and did that made mere manner seem cheap and poor.

Moorhead, who could not bear feeling small, dreaded him extremely, and was thankful that his habit of seclusion and study kept him away by the riverside or held him to his books.

One day, nearly meeting him on the river-trail, Moorhead took to cover to avoid him, and was uneasy at the approach of meal-times, because he must meet him at the table.

With Leonora he got on well. They were much together, and the better he knew her the more he felt the charm of her sweetness. He soon discovered that he spent most of his time in thinking of Leonora. Nor could his mind have had a more delightful guest. Soon he found that he was constantly seeking her presence—that he was more unhappy in her absence than mere ennui would have made him.

One day he was reading. His book did not interest him. He kept losing his place. He realized that he was very uncomfortable, and, being given to self-analysis, less with a view to improvement than to pleasure, he put down the book and set to work to find what ailed him. Such diagnosis usually resulted in the discovery that he was bored, and by way of cure he would prescribe himself change of scene.

This time his favorite remedy was loathsome to his taste; he hated the very thought of going away. He soon found that he had only one wish, and its name was Leonora.

When a young man discovers that he is in love he generally hails the fact with rapture, but Moorhead was peculiar; so, instead of offering himself hearty congratulations, he admonished himself, as a father might a froward son who had become enamoured of some undesirable person.

"The deuce!" said he. "This is very awkward. Who is she? What is she? What is that mysterious old father of hers, and why does he hide himself out here?" "And yet," he said, in reply, "I cannot be happy without her." "Then wait, and find out her antecedents." He would not make an unconventional marriage. At last he went so far as to allow himself to hope that Leonora might prove a suitable match, and then set himself to find out.

"Why," said he to Moloch one day, overcoming his scruples so far as to ask questions of an avowed butler—"why does Mr. Willoughby live out here, Moloch, away from humanity and civilization?"

"I ain't sure, sah, that I ought to answer personal questions 'bout my 'steemed employah, sah; an' he ain't took me into his confidence. But I will say, sah, that I have my own ideas on the subjec'."

"And what are they, Moloch? Has he any special reason?"

"Well, sah," said the butler, with the air of one who weighs his words, "the result of my observations on the mattah am that Mr. Willoughby *have* a reason, but I don't know that I am at liberty to divulge it, sah."

"I am a friend—*the* friend—of the family, Moloch. You surely do not think I ask out of mere curiosity or that I should betray your confidence?"

"Well, sah, I'm inclined to think Mr. Willoughby stays here—because he wants to."

"But what makes him want to?"

"'That,' said the Ethiop, blandly, "am a thing that am prob'ly unknown to Mr. Willoughby himself."

So Moorhead gave up Moloch, and, summoning up all his courage, put the question directly to the old gentleman, in person.

"May I ask," said he, "why a man of your attainments shuts himself up from the world, to the mutual disadvantage of the world and himself, and spends his life in this secluded place?"

Mr. Willoughby looked benevolently at the young

5

man for a moment. "You may ask," said he, and resumed his book.

Although leave to ask was so freely and kindly given, Moorhead felt shy of taking advantage of it.

He looked at the old gentleman, who, reading hard, did not wear a responsive expression.

Then he plucked up courage. "Then, sir, with your permission, I will," said he.

"Will what?" said Mr. Willoughby.

"Will ask."

The old gentleman looked up inquiringly.

"Why you live here," said Moorhead, by way of reply.

"I like the fishing," said the old gentleman in a matter-of-fact way; and as he seemed to think this a sufficient reason, and as the affair was quite his own, Moorhead did not feel at liberty to press the matter further; so, with the remark that the day was fine, he wandered out in the valley and met Leonora, who came singing down a trail that led from the mountains. He walked back by her side.

"Miss Willoughby," said he, "how is it that you, who have no home but these woods, and have seen nothing of your equals, are so—er—"

"So what?"

"So very—er—"

"Well?" she said, encouragingly.

"So entirely—*au fait*—so well versed in all things one likes to know—so—ah—unlike what one would naturally expect of a—ah—um—child of the forest, you know."

"I cannot tell," said she. "What *would* one naturally expect of a child of the forest?"

"Not much," said he. "And you, Miss Willoughby, seem blessed with every grace that women covet and men adore !"

"That," said the maiden, thoughtfully, "is a compliment. I have always wondered what it would be like to have a compliment paid me like a girl in a book ; now it has happened, and it hardly seems worth while."

Nevertheless, she was not displeased, and added, gravely, after a pause, "You would like to know something about my life here ?"

"I should be very grateful," said Moorhead, "not out of curiosity; but how can I help feeling an interest in you and yours and whatever concerns you, when you have been so kind to me ?"

"Well," said she, after looking away at the mountain-tops awhile, "I *am* a 'child of the forest' if ever there was one ; but I suppose I don't fill your ideal of one because of my bringing up."

"But who has taught you ?" he asked.

The girl's face grew very grave and tender as she rose and said, "Come with me."

He followed her to the edge of the woods. She drew aside a spray of moss-grown maple that hung like a curtain over a path he had never seen before—a narrow gallery walled closely and low-arched with the interlaced undergrowth, and winding some hundred yards into the wood.

There was a quiet chamber among the trees where no glare of the sun ever shone, and all sounds were hushed by the dense mass of foliage ; where the roar of the river was a drowsy murmur, and the whisper of the cedars was faint and soft—a solitude and a place of sacred stillness and shadow. No bushes grew within it, only tender ferns and moss and creeping vines.

In the middle of the space stood a green pile of stones such as hands of no ordinary strength must have lifted, surmounted by a cross covered with clinging, drooping woodbine.

She stood there a moment, then, with a slight gesture, bade him go before and followed him out into the light.

She answered the question in his eyes. "My mother."

After the visit to the grave under the cedars they began to know each other better and better.

During their pleasant comradeship by hill and stream he learned her story, by chance words and by little confidences graciously imparted.

It was a simple tale enough, no mystery, no skeletons whose uncomfortable bones must be covered up, just this:

Mr. Willoughby, when a young man, had quarrelled with his neighbors. He had been the offender—poverty the offence.

The friends of his family were well-to-do, and so were the Willoughbys themselves for many generations.

At the age of twenty-one, by a series of misfortunes he found himself alone in the world and very poor.

This did not trouble him much. To live in an inexpensive style and do something for his living was a novelty that interested him, and he saw no difference between himself as the heir of a large estate and himself as a clerk with no definite prospects except a raise of salary to look forward to.

He was the same man—tall, strong, and stately in person, gentle and modest of speech, honorable in mind, kindly in spirit, plain in dress.

If there was any change in him personally it was only that while he had had luxury at his command he had been disposed to indulge in it a little too freely, and when he lost his means he put a strong curb on every tendency to folly and extravagance.

Nevertheless, he was changed for the worse in the eyes of his neighbors.

In the beginning of his distress they made all proper conventional protestations of friendship, and then set about getting rid of the intimacy with him of which not a few of them had been proud.

Friends became acquaintances. Some were coldly courteous, some patronizing, but within a year from the time of his final misfortune none were cordial.

His people had been given a little to pride of place, and the reward was his. It might have been otherwise but for his splendid person and attractive manner; but there were many pretty girls in town, and their mammas bristled and ruffled and glared at the dangerous young man like hens in defence of their chickens.

Now, there was one maiden richly favored of nature and fortune both, above all others, and Willoughby had been fond of her since they were boy and girl.

She had a will of her own too, and maternal chiding did not prevail against her. She had been shy of Willoughby while he and his had prospered; but when his troubles came she made no secret of her liking for him—invited him, without consulting her mother, to

her parties; said publicly that she was sorry that he
had not come; was heard to declare that he was the
manliest man she knew; refused two highly ad-
vantageous offers, on his account, it was said; and
altogether behaved in the most forward and reprehensible manner.

This turned popular indifference to indignation.
Parents of marriageable daughters would not have
such an example set before their own darlings.
Parents of marriageable sons could not bear to see
the prize kept from their own dear ones for the sake
of an ineligible.

The young men were jealous; the young women—
though I dare not say that any such sentiment moved
their gentle hearts, particularly as Willoughby had
never annoyed them with any attention—the young
women, dear girls, shared very properly the feeling of
their mammas.

As for his fellow-workers, they never liked him, because his ways were not their ways. In short, it was
a small, nasty, gossiping, jealous community where
the Golden Calf held full sway over the hearts of the
people.

No one could afford to cut Bessy Patterson, but
every one cut Willoughby.

As for Bessy, she was in deep disgrace with her
mother, on whom her present welfare and her prospects
as an heiress depended, and who told her that if she
married that objectionable young man she should only
add to his difficulties the burden of a penniless wife;
that she, Mrs. Patterson, would neither give, lend, nor
leave her a cent to fall into his wasteful hands.

This lasted about a year. Then strange things began to happen. A certain man had an enemy whom he wished to injure. He had waited an opportunity for years and his chance had come, for the enemy— a good, easy-going gentleman with no idea of business and a cheerful doctrine that all would go well in time —had fallen deep in debt, and his notes of hand were abroad in many directions.

The other bought them all in, and was heard to boast that he would "squeeze him"; but when he was on the point of carrying out his threat a stranger appeared and redeemed them to the last cent.

That night the debtor, awake at last to a sense of his position and trying to screw up courage to explain it to his family, received a package. It contained every note, indorsed as paid and torn across the middle. He told a friend or two, and the friends spread the news.

Another man, who prided himself upon having the best of everything in town, was in treaty for a certain piece of land where he proposed to build a great house. It was part of the Willoughby estate—a low round hill with a rich lawn under noble elms—the fairest site in the neighborhood.

Here he would have his stable, he said; there his tennis-courts, here his garden. So he would build his house and show people how to live.

His bargain was not quite concluded; there had been some little disagreement about the exact quantity of land. But he had consulted an architect and a landscape-gardener.

He was walking over the ground with them when he was politely requested by a stranger to take himself off the premises. Why? Those were the owner's orders. Who was the owner? The gentleman who had just bought the whole Willoughby estate.

A splendid pair of horses was brought out by a dealer and exhibited on the drives. Yes, they were for sale. There were many offers, but the dealer knew how to make the most out of his customers and put the horses up at auction. None of the prominent citizens could bear to be outbid; but one by one they dropped out. At last they were nearly going, at the highest figure any one could afford to pay, when a stranger stepped in and bought them at a heart-breaking price.

A poor old man, who had worked hard and suffered much, was anonymously presented with a sum that made him comfortable for the short remnant of his life.

There was money afloat in the town, and no one knew whence it came.

Then people stopped talking about it to talk about something else; for it was noised abroad that Willoughby, in a shabby suit of black, much polished at the elbows, a dreadful pair of boots, and a shocking bad hat, had deliberately walked up to the Pattersons, sent in his card, insisted on seeing Miss Patterson, offered her the privilege of sharing his poverty, and that she had made no bones of the matter, but coolly walked off with him, taken a train for the city, married him, and returned to his humble lodging as his wife.

It was too true. Mrs. Patterson was prostrated and would see no one for a day. Then she told her most intimate friend, who spread the news.

Bessy and her husband lived for a week in perfect content.

Then the gray span came swinging down their humble street, stopped at the door of the lodging, and took them through the town to the Willoughby place, whose gates closed behind them.

"I had this little surprise for you, Bess," said Willoughby.

"What does it mean, dear?" said Bess, a bit frightened.

"Why, I came in for a lot of dross two months ago —distant cousin—no near relatives— Why, Bess! Did you really think I'd ask you to marry me hard-up as I seemed to be?"

"Why, yes, Joe. And—you let me think we had nothing to live on, and preached economy to me all this time, and let me take all the pains I've done to train myself to be a poor man's wife—for nothing?"

"Just for fun, Bessy."

"I'm glad," said she, "Joe dear. I'm glad you gave me a chance to show that I didn't care. I was glad to make your life happier when it seemed a sad one, and I thought I could manage to be more of a comfort than a burden to you even then, Joe. And now I'm glad that I sha'n't be such a burden, after all—only it *would* have been fun fitting up that tiny little house we meant to have sometime when we had saved enough out of your salary—the little house with low eaves, and ivy about the porch, and the little garden, and the cow that I meant to milk myself, and the four hens, and the cheap furniture; and I was to do all the pictures for the walls and cook all your dinners, and I *would* have had it pleasant for you, Joe; and now it isn't to be, and my poor little plans are lost. But I'm afraid I shouldn't have carried them out very well, Joe."

"Now, let's invite all these dear old friends that have cut us, and see if they don't all come."

Again the news got abroad. The people were invited, and came.

They showed a most forgiving spirit and were prepared to forget Willoughby's temporary lapse from place and Bessy's undutiful marriage.

Girls got new gowns for the occasion. Men looked their best.

They were received at the door and shown to the dressing-room; they were announced at the drawing-room door, but no hostess was there to receive them, no host to bid them welcome.

All preparations had been made for a grand reception. The rooms were brightly lighted, and there were flowers in profusion and music behind the palms.

The guests were uncertain what they should do. Some one asked a lackey that stood in the hall where were Mr. and Mrs. Willoughby.

The man had learned his lesson, and repeated it word for word without a fault, solemnly, with a wooden face:

"Please, madam, Mr. and Mrs. Willoughby said that none of the gentlemen and ladies to-night would come to see *them* but only for the use of the good things they could give them; and so Mr. and Mrs. Willoughby beg to be excused and to leave everything at the gentlemen and ladies' disposal. Supper will be served at eleven o'clock."

So the guests went away with a sense of having been kicked and slapped in tender places, for every one of them had dropped the acquaintance of Mr.

Willoughby while he was unfortunate, and every one was obliged to acknowledge to himself the justice of the inference.

The feeling that prompted this extraordinary behavior on Mr. Willoughby's part was so real and permanent that it resulted in his shutting up the house and going away, no one knew whither.

The young bride went gladly with her husband, half pitying, half sharing his state of mind.

Her mother had never forgiven her marriage, even when it had turned out a prosperous one.

He heartily disliked and mistrusted people ; she could get on without them ; they held the fellow-creature a bore and fled him.

A certain good black servant of the bride's family, devotedly attached to his young mistress, came to them and begged to be employed.

"But," said Mrs. Willoughby, "we are going away and shall take no one with us. • I should *like* to take you—but—"

"Then," said her husband, interrupting, "let him come."

"No, no," said the lady, "he has a far better home with my mother, and is happier in his old place in her household than he would be following our wanderings. We must not take him from all the little comforts he has, to share our adventures. I'm sure he doesn't care for adventures. No : your present place is too good to throw away," she said. "But for that I would gladly take you."

The darky bowed (he was the pink of courtesy) and departed. On the next day he came back. "Lost my place," said he. "Nothin' to do for a livin'."

"Lost your place! Why, what do you mean?"

"Yas—yas, 'm. Ah's discharged, without a character too."

"Why, how? Why?"

"Dismissed foh impudence and 'toxication, Miss Bessy."

"*Im*pudence and in-tox-i-*cation*! You?" said the Willoughbys.

"Yas, Miss Bessy; yas, Mr. Willoughby, sah."

The Ethiop's morals and manners were well known to be unimpeachable.

"How cruelly unjust!" said the lady.

"What nonsense!" said her husband.

"No, Miss Bessy; no, Mr. Willoughby, sah. Own fault," said the culprit.

It appeared that after being told that he was not to be dragged from certain comfort into uncomfortable uncertainty—from his snug service and old home to the shifting scenes and eccentric fortunes of the Willoughbys—he had made up his mind to remove the obstacle to the engagement he wished for.

He had therefore appeared before the astonished mother-in-law, his mistress, holding in one hand a tumbler, in the other a bottle of port, and declared respectfully but with decision that he meant to swallow its contents.

This, in Mrs. Patterson's indignant presence, with many a wry face and inward qualm, he had done; nor need we follow him through the few hours next ensuing.

When he came before the Willoughbys he was, as usual, the picture of neat black respectability, and his bearing after the manner of Sir Charles Grandison.

The Willoughbys looked at him and at each other, then burst out laughing, while he stood solemnly rolling his eyes from one to the other.

"Poor fellow!" said Mr. Willoughby. "It is sad to see a hitherto blameless and happy being so cast upon the world without a home, without a character. What do you think, Bess?"

"He shall come with us," said Mrs. Willoughby, "and be, wherever we are, be it in court or camp, by land or by sea, in seed-time or harvest, in summer or winter, in cot or in palace, on foot or in saddle, now and forever, our butler."

So the Willoughbys went away and travelled in many lands, and Moloch went with them, and saw strange sights and learned many things.

They formed no ties, and revelled in their freedom.

Willoughby never lost his disgust of mankind, but grew more and more weary of men and cities, and went into the wild waste places of the earth.

At last he travelled in the Northwest, and, wandering north along the Sound, encamped with his young bride by glade and stream, till one day, following a wounded bear far up the Yawmish, he found the valley and loved it for a home.

There they lived, a happy life enough; he developing a grand manliness and strength in the struggle with surrounding hardships, from which he kept his wife as well guarded as if she had been still in her first luxurious home; and their good butler lived with them and served them well. None came near them from the outer world.

Willoughby still nursed his grudge against people at large, and it grew stronger in his solitude.

She, if she ever missed the life she had left, never let her husband know it.

But Moloch, when he went on his occasional pilgrimages to the Sound for supplies, brought her all the current literature of the time, a vast parcel of newspapers and magazines, and she was well informed of all the doings of the outer world.

Never was woman more free from petty vanities, more self-forgetful, more absolutely wrapped up in home and husband; yet she read the fashions, and the gowns she made with her own pretty hands were never very far behind the times.

She read the latest books too, as soon as they could be got, and could follow her husband through the deeper studies in which he had begun to delight since his retirement.

And all the harvest of her studies, all her knowledge of what is good and pleasant and without blame in the world, she showered on her little daughter Leonora, who had inherited her father's sturdy independence of mind and health of body, and her mother's beauty and grace, taste, and instinct of high refinement.

It may be that Mrs. Willoughby longed sometimes for a different life, but she never said so. Only when her last illness came she said to her husband, "Leonora must not always be here. She must have her chance in the world, and not be wasted in solitude."

And her husband, with what little voice sorrow had left him, spoke and gave his word.

But as the years went on, there seemed no immediate occasion for keeping his promise. There was time enough yet.

Meanwhile he studied and fished and dreamed, and his daughter studied too, and wandered and hunted on the hills, and learned to use an axe and saw and rifle. But she did other things that her mother had taught her, and, like her mother, she too read the fashions.

As for the butler, he served them with all his heart and grew old in their service.

So Moorhead found them in the valley, and this was the story he learned of Leonora.

WHEN a young man is leading a lazy, comfortable life, rambling at will in wild and beautiful solitudes, with no cares and few amusements, with no object in the world but his own pleasure, and when the companion of his happy easy hours is an exceedingly lovely girl, what is he to do but fall in love with her?

Moorhead fell in love—not headlong, but deliberately and wilfully, having first made sure that the object honored with his regard was eligible.

Nor was she sorry to have a lover at her feet; and once there, assured that her dainty moccasins were worn from choice and not from ignorance nor enforced lack of French heels, he was very much at her feet indeed.

Love took the conceit out of him for the time. The little woodland girl became the teacher of the young man of the world, and he looked humbly into her eyes and there learned many things that had not occurred to him before—of the glory of innocence and downright nature, of the false values of his former life and the dreary worthlessness of much that he had held in high esteem, and of the dulness of the pursuit of pleasure in the beaten paths where men toil and sweat and scheme to "have a good time."

Now, when he had made up his mind to ask her to marry him, he found himself suddenly bashful as a boy, and afraid to come to the point.

This was a new experience for him. He had never had any difficulty in offering himself before, and had generally been accepted, though his engagements had died young—let us hope because they were beloved of the gods.

There was something about Leonora, or about his feelings towards her, that made it very hard for the poor young man.

He had intended himself as a compliment—he was surprised to find that he seemed to himself an unworthy offering.

This was all the worse in that he could have recourse to none of the small devices that so greatly assist love-making in civilized places.

Society provides chaperons to manage these affairs, and all its laws and ways combine to make opportunity for commonplace young men who are not up to the slaughter of dragons, either real or metaphorical, or to any of the stage or heroic methods of bride-winning, to make themselves acceptable by such small acts of personal service as lie within the scope of the most limited ability. For instance, the fervent touch, in dancing, which permits a thousand small liberties and familiarities which no man dare take without its sanction—the prompt calling of the lady's carriage—the manner of assistance in putting on her wrap—the expenditure of large sums (or the accumulation of debt) in finding out gifts for one's fair—the standing about in corners and looking fierce when she talks to one's rival—the improvisation of skating or boating expeditions at which she may shine and so be gratified —the aid and instruction in the more manlike graces of bowling or target-practice, or whatever she may

6

affect—the helping her in and out of boats, cars, or carriages—the alliance against her enemies—the open jealousy, often rebuked and always pleasing, of her friends—the taking to evil courses when thrown into despair by her frown, and an infinity of other such matters, show one's devotion and excite admiration or pity or high approval, and these society provides. But Moorhead had no means of showing off either himself or his passion to advantage.

His practical attentions failed. He would have laid the spoils of the forest at her feet, but he hunted in vain and never killed anything; and, as she never returned empty-handed from the chase, a present of game would have been in the nature of an invoice of coals to Newcastle.

He would have plucked the sweetest wild flowers of the vale and offered them on bended knee, but she knew where they grew and he did not; besides, she had them always on the table at breakfast, and more had been a superfluity.

He was quite useless as an escort, for she was more qualified to assist him in the *petits soins* of the trail and the cabin than he her. He grew sentimental, heaved sighs, and made eyes, but she took no heed. Being unable to lead gradually and gracefully to the wished-for climax, he grew desperate and determined to come boldly to the point.

His proposal was not a success. He tried to ask her as she sat beside him, but he could not. Then he made the attempt standing before her, but the words would not come, and he only asked her if she had ever tasted ice-cream.

Next he came into her presence with the set purpose of kneeling before her; but he felt that he would only seem absurd to her and nothing would be gained, so he gave it up.

At last he thought he could speak more easily when walking beside her. The act of walking would relieve him of much nervous embarrassment, he thought, and give him a refuge from the steady gaze of those deep-brown eyes.

One day, as they came side by side down the mountain, where the trail was broad enough for two slender people abreast, he made a great effort and an appropriate speech. It was perhaps unfortunate that he had prefaced his proposal by setting forth the advantage to a woman of having some one to walk by her side through life, and comfort and support her in all its ups and downs; for just as he offered his hand he fell headlong over a root.

She smiled, and, as he was somewhat entangled in the brush and in an awkward position, offered her assistance; but she held out a branch towards him instead of her hand. He refused it; and, vexed at his own clumsiness, went on silently before her, and did not resume the subject at the time.

Always thinking of himself, he was tormented with the thought that he had made himself ridiculous before Leonora.

It might be supposed that the mind of a maiden receiving an offer would turn directly to the man who offered, to the exclusion of all other considerations; but, as it happened, Leonora's had not been taken up with Moorhead or his mishap, but with herself, the fact that she had had her first offer of marriage and all that it meant to her.

Unable to make his own personality very impressive, he had tried his best to interest her in the life beyond the woods, had kept telling her of all she missed in her forest home, till by degrees she had come to wonder and muse about the world without, to wish for the pleasures that society affords and the delight of going in flocks and herds as is man's nature to do, to travel and see and hear for herself the things she had read of in books.

So for the first time in her life she had begun to feel—a little—a very little—the chill and fever of discontent.

Now when Moorhead asked her to marry him it was as if he had opened a door and said, "Come and be free and feast your eyes on wonders here among your kind, and enjoy like other women all the world has to offer."

So, as she cared far more for this than for Moorhead, whom she liked well, but whom she had not yet come to regard as her heart's all, she naturally thought of him last.

While they walked home to the cabin it occurred to her that this marriage meant above all things the sharing her life with him. Well, why not? She looked at him thoughtfully. She could only see his back—it was a well-looking back, with a good pair of shoulders and a firm neck. She knew he had a handsome face. Altogether she liked him very much, and was touched by his being fond of her; she had seen that weeks ago, and was grateful for it. Then, he was the only marriageable man there; the only one she knew, in fact. That did not occur to her, and so had all the greater weight in the poise of her judgment. So she said to herself, "I *do* love him!"

She had a keen enjoyment of new experience, and was on the whole delighted with her first offer.

While he went on in silence, hating himself for having appeared so very ill when he wished to be at his best, she was regarding him with higher and higher approval.

She was very kind to him after that, spoke more softly to him, and treated him with a sweet shyness that he found irresistible. The ice was broken.

He did better with his next offer, speaking to the point and very humbly.

"Yes," was her answer.

It remained to tell Mr. Willoughby, and Moorhead shrank from the ordeal as from the confession of a crime.

He was relieved when Leonora strictly forbade him to say a word to Mr. Willoughby about it.

"He will not consent," she said, "and why trouble him to refuse? It would only make us all very unhappy. You don't understand him as I do."

"Then you will marry me *without* his consent?" said he, with a glad sense of having the better of Mr. Willoughby in a way, and a mad vision of a runaway through the forest.

"No indeed," said she, coldly.

"Then how—?"

"I cannot leave him here alone. My mother left us each to the other's care. She bade me never leave him here—and I promised. She begged him to take me away from this place, that I might not always lack the companionship of others of my age, or the life that women love among their friends.

"He also promised, and he will keep his word—

sometime, when he is ready, and for my sake will get over his hatred of the ways of men and learn to live among people again.

"But if I leave him he will never go. He would end his days here, lonely and sad, without me, and that must not be.

"When he has a new home and will not be left so alone, I will marry you, but not before. If you care for me you can wait for me. I have patience and will not fail you."

He promised to be patient and wondered how he should keep his word, for it seemed to him that the world had never seen so fair a woman, and he longed to show her to his own people at home, to see her great eyes light with wonder and pleasure at the things that were in store for her in the great cities she had never seen, to have her sitting at his table and ruling his house, to give her all that wealth could buy, to anticipate her wishes, to feel that she was absolutely his own and to be with her always.

X

MOORHEAD, happy man though he was, found himself in a very awkward and uncomfortable position.

In the first place, Leonora had no sooner accepted him than her manner towards him became strangely cool and reserved.

Their pleasant comradeship was spoiled, and nothing warmer and nearer came to take its place.

He would have liked to kiss his betrothed, and was about to take that liberty as a matter of course; nor would the evident distress in her eyes have prevented him, but it was followed by such a cold, angry light as made him draw back fairly afraid. Next time he asked permission, and was told to wait.

It soon became clear to him that his position as an accepted lover, far from giving him any privileges, was to be a bar to the slightest familiarity even of speech or manner. Leonora would have no love-making, and treated him with a distant and respectful courtesy which she expected him to observe towards her.

His discontent under these trying circumstances became apparent even to Moloch, who had observed the stages of the courtship, and was both anxious and amused.

Moloch was a classical scholar in a small way, having devoted himself assiduously during the winter evenings to the perusal of a mythology that took his fancy.

"Tantalus," he murmured learnedly to himself, "am not in it with Miss 'Nora's young gentleman."

Secondly, Moorhead's welcome with Mr. Willoughby was wearing out. Whether the old gentleman had any suspicion of the true state of things or not, he began to grow very impatient of his guest's presence, and showed it by a freezing, bitter politeness.

At last, one morning he said, "I should deeply regret seeming to hasten your departure, my dear sir; but I fear you can hardly find your way alone out of the woods, and my man Moloch goes to the Sound to-morrow."

"To-morrow?" said Moorhead.

"Exactly," said Mr. Willoughby; "and after that he will not go again for a long time; so it seems your only chance to leave a place of which you must have tired long ago. So I fear we must be deprived of your society, unless you will be persuaded to grant us a reprieve and allow us the pleasure of your presence for at least a month more; and that would be, really, too much to ask."

It was made so clear to Moorhead by dint of manner that the "too much" was for *him* to ask and not for Mr. Willoughby, that he had no alternative but to express his thanks, his regrets at leaving, and be ready to go on the morrow.

Leonora took it very coolly—nor even at parting might he kiss her.

His stay in the valley had done him good. The life had been simple and wholesome, free from the petty cares and irksome trifles that attend the pursuit of pleasure even more than the path of labor. Leonora had not been indulgent, Mr. Willoughby had taken the conceit out of him, and the discipline had been good for him. The grandeur, peace, and solemnity of the place had given him deeper and greater thoughts and higher wishes than he had ever known before.

The companionship of the girl he loved, the truth and faith and womanly strength of her nature, made him own his faults to himself and wish to be more worthy of her.

Had he been able to stay longer in the valley it might have been the making of him. As it was, he left it in a way to be a far better man than when he came to it, and, in spite of his disappointment and vexation at parting from Leonora, he set out in the fair morning of what seemed a new and different life, full of high resolve and honest purpose.

Old Moloch went before him with three ponies jogging easily under empty pack-saddles, and disappeared among the trees.

Moorhead lingered at the verge of the open and looked back.

Under the woods it was still night. In the open, the stream, singing its eternal song of the woods and hills, shone like liquid fire in the early light and tossed a rosy spray upon the rocks.

Far above and beyond the black woods the mountains held their blushing snows skyward, like great white altars kindling into flame.

The cabin stood warm and still among its vines; its smoke hung on the air in little clouds.

Leonora stood in the arch, all the stately beauty of her form showing clear in white drapery against the darkness of the porch—an image to be remembered of Moorhead long with pride and joy, and perhaps in time with bitter sorrow. She waved her hand, threw him the kiss her lips had refused him, and, when he would have come back to take it, turned away under the arching vines and out of sight.

He followed his guide out into the shadows of the forest.

XI

MOLOCH trudged along in silence with long, swinging steps, brushing the dew from the feathery brake that overhung the narrow trail.

The Cayuse ponies, who were fond of Moloch and knew what he wanted of them, jogged on behind in an orderly manner, looking up at him now and then as if for permission to nibble the rare tufts of grass by the way, making no trouble.

Moorhead came last, dreaming as he walked, going over again the pleasant scenes he was leaving—imagining new ones to take their places.

Then his mind became full of those anxieties that torture a lover at parting. "What may happen in my absence?" he thought, as if his presence had been likely to afford any great hinderance to fate.

"How long will it be?

"Shall I come back soon for my bride?

"Or may we be parted until our youth—my strength and her loveliness—are only memories?

"Or what may not come between us to separate us forever?

"Where is she at this moment, and what is she doing? Is she unhappy at my going? Is she not?

"Is her father really kind to her?

"Can she be happy under the control of such a man?

"Does he care for her?

"Does he not neglect her?

"Suppose anything should happen to him and this black fellow, what would become of her, alone in the forest?"

Just then he was startled by a face staring fixedly up into his from the moss beside the trail — a face whose brown dried skin was drawn tight over the bones, whose eyes were black hollows, and whose irregular fangs grinned, sardonically grim, under dry, twisted lips.

"Look here!" cried Moorhead.

Moloch came back past the ponies, who stopped with sniffs and snorts and tossing of shapely heads, and took advantage of the halt to find pasture.

"Siwash, sah," said he. "Repository, sah."

"What's a *repository?*" said Moorhead.

"Place where the dead *repose*," the butler answered. "Lots of 'em here." And, stepping into the brush, he produced two thigh-bones, a shoulder-blade, and a jaw. "Siwash aren't very partick'ler 'bout 'cedin' the last comforts to the dead, sah. Haven't took the trouble to bury 'em as deep as one might have wished, sah. No, sah."

"They needn't have left 'em in the trail to stare at passers-by," said Moorhead, in deep disgust.

"The repository antedates the trail, sah," said Moloch, apologetically. "Prob'ly the trail wasn't contemplated when these folks come."

Towards the end of the afternoon they heard voices, and a rough bass struck up a song.

The air was hardly to be recognized, but was perhaps what passed in those regions for "Rosin the Beau."

As they came on they heard the following words:

> "So, free from all care and ambition,
> I laugh at the world and its shams,
> And rejoice in my happy condition,
> Surrounded by acres of clams!"

Then a thundering chorus took it up:

> "Surrounded by acres of cla-a-ams,
> Surrounded by acres of clams!
> Rejoice in my happy condition,
> Surrounded by acres of clams!" *

They came to a clearing. There was a long log-house of very rude and temporary fashion, and before it, lying on the ground among the chips, or sitting on logs and stumps, were a score or so of men, sturdy and hardy, and some of great stature, clad in blue-jeans, coarse flannel shirts, and high boots.

Some dozen double-bitted axes sticking in a huge stump eight feet high and six feet across; some cant-hooks and peeveys standing along the wall; some cross-cut saws here and there; a few lean, weary, sad-looking cattle with the goad-marks raw on their haunches; a multitude of chips that lay everywhere, and the aspect of the men themselves, showed the place to be a logging-camp.

The loggers stopped singing and stared at the travellers with curious eyes.

"Good-afternoon," said Moloch, politely.

"Hulloa, nig! Whar be *you* from?" This ques-

---

* From *The Old Settler's Song*, much in vogue on Puget Sound.

tion, being unanswered, was followed by an invidious personality.

"Say, you ole black Siwash nig! You born chicken thief! Whar in —— 'd you git that thar dude?"

This remark was followed by a volley of expressions equally irreverent and irrelevant.

Moorhead would have resented this uncalled-for insult to himself and his attendant, but, seeing that the man was of mighty stature, bull-necked and deep-chested, and of a very healthy complexion, he reflected that his dignity might be even further compromised by taking as an effront the rudeness of an untaught creature of the woods who, doubtless, knew no better.

Moloch seemed of the same mind, for he approached the stranger with his best bow and blandest smile, saying, "'Dress yourself to me, sah?"

"Yes, you old huckleberry coon! —— ! ——! ——! ——!"

The loggers laughed; the speaker was the life and soul of their company, and his wit on this occasion outshone itself. "*He's* the boy!" "That's what!" said one to another.

Moloch, smiling more sweetly still, stood before him and listened to his abuse with all the deference of a well-trained servant. Then he put his arms about him and kissed him.

The others rose and crowded close about. The logger writhed, struggled, yelled, and swore. It was of no use. Moloch's long arms were round him and held his own close to his sides in a tremendous grip.

Then it might be seen that the negro's back was the broader of the two and his chest the deeper;

the great cords in his black neck swelled and stood out like iron ridges.

The big arms held the logger's middle in a crushing grip that tightened whenever the breath came out and did not yield to let in more, till it seemed as if the ribs would be crushed in upon the lungs.

Tenderly, and again and again, Moloch pressed his ample lips upon those of his new acquaintance, till their profanity was hushed and the very breath seemed drawn out of them in one last, long, unutterable kiss. Then he laid him gently, carefully on the ground, and spoke to the lookers-on.

"When the wicked revile you, treat 'em with 'stinguished kindness. This am brotherly love."

There was a roar of applause, and instantly a dozen flat bottles were drawn, uncorked, and thrust cordially towards the emissary of peace.

"Spare me, gen'lemen; spare me! My delicate constitution will not allow me to participate in the enjoyment of stimulating beverages," said Moloch. "My young days am over."

So, with a cheer from the loggers, the procession went its way, and encamped that night in a pleasant place, between three knolls, whose trees locked their branches across the hollow. There was fresh grass for the ponies and a pleasant shelter for the men.

As they sat in the firelight, Moloch kept glancing sideways at Moorhead, and seemed on the point of saying something, but shy of speech.

"Well," said Moorhead, "what is it, Moloch?"

"Miss Willoughby am a lovely lady, Mr. Moorhead, sah. Miss Willoughby deserves the best of everything."

Moorhead did not fancy discussing his lady-love with her butler, however worthy, and was about to say as much, but something in the old negro's face made him hold his tongue.

"Miss Willoughby," said Moloch again, "am very, very much alone in the world, sah. Nobody but an old butler who am devoted to her but don't hardly count, and an old pappah who am devoted to hisself, and the time comin' on for 'em to die off, and then, sah, Miss Willoughby would be all sole alone."

"Not *quite* alone," said Moorhead, in spite of himself, and added, on reflection, "I hope."

"So do I, sah, most earnestly hope and pray," said Moloch. "And if ever a man has her happiness in his keeping, may God bless him as he does well by her!"

Though the old servant's manner and words were respectful and pleading, the strong earnestness in his clear gray eyes was a command, and his comic old face became for a moment full of the majesty of strong will and deep feeling.

"Amen," said Moorhead, quite unintentionally.

Before he went to sleep he said to himself:

"I have had strange adventures, and this is the most startling of all. To have been left alone in the woods, to have survived that fall, is something; to have got engaged in such a place is something more; but to be lectured by my lady's butler and general factotum — confound him! — and that with such delicacy and tact that I find myself saying 'Amen' to his remarks before I know it, is too much."

They passed a quiet night, and from that time on the journey was uneventful, except for the exchange of greeting with occasional settlers, whose cabins became more frequent as they neared the Sound ; quiet souls, who lived much at ease waiting for their claims to become town-sites, and very happy meanwhile in anticipation of the cities they meant to found and the wealth they would acquire thereby.

At evening they looked out upon the green waters of the Sound, and the forest, the valley, and all that had befallen Moorhead therein lay behind him like a dream.

XII

THERE is a city, old, as American cities go; respectable, as cities go in general; enterprising, in a very conservative way; beautiful, in rare spots; and as to other characteristics, *sui generis*.

It has a golden dome that stands above one of its hills—a glad sight far at sea to vessels homeward bound; a stone much worshipped of those truly imbued with the spirit of the place, who visit it where it lies embedded in the foundation of a shop, and painted a bright and glorious red; a few dreadful monuments, and many other like things which are pointed out with pride and reverence to strangers. It had once a tea-party, and is a favorite haunt of persons, dead and alive, intimately connected with the war of the Revolution.

The people are not just like other people, and are very glad.

Here was Moorhead's home; hither he came out of the Northwest, and here, being a Bostonian of Boston, he was received with open arms.

The story of his having been deserted by an Indian guide and lost in the woods got abroad.

He was invited and drawn out on the subject. Societies for the amelioration of the aboriginal lot asked him to come and tell about the shocking plight of the red man, and to offer suggestions as to the best means of developing his latent virtues.

He was plied with questions as to what he had seen and done, and was spoken of as Mr. Moorhead, the new explorer.

Boston dearly loves a little lion; be it but a lion, she overlooks the occasional fact of its being a cub.

So it became the thing to be asked to meet Mr. Moorhead, the explorer (one of *the* Moorheads, but *so* adventurous, and who had been through so much), and to hear him tell of his experiences.

This he did with complaisance, and wrote two magazine articles and a little book. But he said nothing of Leonora.

The engagement was not announced. He told himself that he kept it a secret in justice to Leonora.

He liked to be in good form. It was not the Thing to announce it yet, before her own father knew of it; besides, it would not be giving Leonora a fair chance.

People would judge her by her surroundings, and the judgment would not be flattering.

He did not tell himself the real reason, which was that he was afraid of being laughed at and talked of as the victim of a sentimental attachment to a backwoods girl.

As he spoke of her to no one, he thought of her less and less, till her image, without his knowing it, almost faded from his mind.

At first he had written often to Leonora ardent letters enough, full of himself, his plans for the future, his interests for her to share, and had sent gifts.

But as her answers came seldom — for she only wrote when Moloch was to go to the Sound, and that was but once a month or so, and in winter hardly at

all—he began to write less often and to say less when
he wrote.

Her letters to him seemed constrained and shy, and
did not amuse or interest him much ; indeed, there
was little to write about in the valley.

So two years passed, and the farther he got from
Leonora the worse he drifted into his old faithless,
objectless mode of life.

It is a matter of conjecture how long he might have
kept his secret—"*her* secret," as he called it—had
Mrs. Bradlee not taken him in hand and made up
her mind that he would do well to marry.

Not to marry *her*—she was an elderly widow of single tastes, a cousin of his through the Jacksons. So
she was motherly to Moorhead, and told him what he
ought to do.

" Now that I have twenty good minutes to bestow
upon you," she said one day, when the five-o'clock
guests were gone and the dinner-guests had not come ;
" I have something to say for your good."

 Moorhead looked pleased.   He liked her little lect-
ures, because he usually got a good deal of compliment
from them at the cost of very little advice.   Then,
the advice itself was a compliment, for Mrs. Bradlee
was a personage.

She took him from the parlor—stately and somewhat
dismal, after the manner of the Back Bay ; with a bay-
window looking out on a brick sidewalk, a narrow
road, and a row of uncompromising brick three-story
houses of marked family likeness which stared coldly
from the other side ; with old, dark, deeply cushioned
furniture that absorbed the light, and a sacrilegious
travesty of an open fire built of iron logs that burned

with stiff jets of gas artistically grouped, to represent
a blaze—into a bright, cozy little den where she wrote
her letters, and which she called her "study."

"Now," said she, "we have all been delighted with
your adventures and experiences, which are all very
well for a young man to have, no doubt, and do credit
to his manly qualities; and now, I suppose, you are
pining for more? You have a bold, adventurous
disposition and, of course, enjoy such things."

Moorhead thought, as he sat in comfort, of the
dark woods, the dreadful steepness, the cold winds
on the mountain, the privation, the treachery of his
Siwash, the language of the logger, his own deadly
terror for fear Moloch should get the worst of the
ensuing struggle and the logger turn upon *him;* and
shuddered, but did not deny, even to himself, that he
was pining as alleged.

He loved to be called bold and adventurous, and
had posed in that character so long that he had begun to believe it of himself.

"But," said the old lady, "you must stop now and
be content and settle yourself. Oh yes, you must,
you know. You are not doing your duty to your set,
which misses you. Your place is at home.

"All that was well enough while you were a boy;
but now you have your place to take. "You must
open your house; you must be in the swim; you must
take part in what's going on with the rest of us; you
must entertain as becomes the head of the family; in
short, you must 'do unto others,' etc. One expects
it of you.

"And to do this you must marry. It's *time* you
married. Don't allow yourself to fall into the old

bachelor stage. Old bachelors are utterly useless, except that they are sometimes amusing at dinner, if one feeds them well, and not *too* well.

"You must marry, and you must marry *well* and *suitably!*"

"Oh, I don't think there's any need yet," said Moorhead, uncomfortably.

"You'll forgive my not agreeing with you," said the lady. "There *is* need. It is your duty to *us*. In your position it is not the thing to be a bachelor.

"The family has always held a certain place in society—a place that you are leaving empty. People notice it, and are surprised at you.

"It's a long time since your father's house—and yours—has opened its doors to society.

"*We* have duties to perform, just as others do. They are not in the way of trade; they are not necessary to our livelihood; we don't earn our bread and butter by them; but they are duties none the less, and even more important to *us*, for we hold our *position* by them—and we set an example and keep up the social tone.

"To do this, as I said before, you must marry. You *must*, you know."

"But," said Moorhead, "whom should I marry?"

"Whom? Why, there are plenty — *plenty* who would do you the greatest credit.

"There's Elsie Kent, for instance. People said once that you would surely marry Elsie Kent. Why didn't you? Why don't you?"

"Between ourselves, I don't think I was ever very fond of Elsie Kent," said Moorhead.

"*Very fond!* Just like your roving, romantic disposition! As if *that* mattered! Please try to remember that you are *not* a troubadour; *not* a rustic swain, *not* a turtle-dove, but the head of a good old family, with two big houses to keep up, and duties and responsibilities that belong to your position.

"Men who wait to '*fall in love*,' as you call it" (Mrs. Bradlee's marriage had been notably a love-match, but she held it exceptional), "generally end by marrying some unsuitable person—some girl they find in some unheard-of place" (Moorhead was not man enough not to wince and feel guilty), "or some person of whom nobody knows anything, who doesn't know her *proper* place and can't learn her *new* one, or some adventuress, perhaps.

"I have the greatest faith in your judgment, if you choose to exercise it; but you are too impulsive and rash and boyish!"

The two smiled at each other. It pleased Moorhead to be credited with impulse, and Mrs. Bradlee to think she knew people through and through and could not be deceived in character.

"I suppose you are right," said he; "but I know no one whom I feel inclined to marry."

He was thinking of Elsie Kent and the other girls of Mrs. Bradlee's coterie, and had forgotten for a moment; then, as the thought of Leonora came to him, he turned very red, looked down, and added, indistinctly, "that is—"

"What?" said madam, looking sharply at him with her bright little black eyes; "you said, 'that is—' I think? 'You don't know any one you feel inclined to marry — that is.' What is? or rather, Who is? *Who is she?*" the lady continued, leaning forward to look into his eyes, and touching his hand with the tip of her fan.

Moorhead grew more and more confused.

"Come!" said Mrs. Bradlee, sharply, giving herself up to the pangs of curiosity. "I never knew you bashful and shy before, and I've known you all your life. You're engaged. And something's the matter, or you'd have married, or at least announced your conquest. Perhaps you *are* married."

"No!" said Moorhead, eagerly, glad to have something to deny. "I'm *not* married."

"That's to say, you *are* engaged!" said Mrs. Bradlee, her eyes sparkling with excitement. "You don't deny that you're engaged? You can't deny it. You *are* engaged!"

Moorhead could not deny it. Had there been time, he probably could have argued himself into the belief that all that had passed between him and Leonora did not constitute an actual formal engagement, their marriage being to be only on condition of Mr. Willoughby's return to civilization; and then he could have denied without a blush or a downward look.

But he hadn't time.

"You have guessed it, Cousin Sarah," said he, meekly.

She drew back with a little smile of triumph that faded into an anxious expression. "Well?" said she; and after a moment's silence, during which she sat with her eyebrows raised and the tip of her once very pretty nose on high, added, in a coaxing tone:

"Tell me all about it. What's her name, for instance?"

"Willoughby."

" Well enough as far as it goes. There are Willoughbys, and, of course, Willoughbys. And where
does she live ?"

" In the most beautiful spot on earth."

" Yes, of course. And what is it called ?"

" The Valley of the Yawmish."

" The Valley of the—what did you say ? How very
romantic ! And where is this valley ?"

" 'Way out in the woods—under the Olympics."

" The Olympics—are mountains, are they not ? In
Siberia, isn't it ?—no, I mean Alaska ?"

The footman came in with a card.

" No, I'm very particularly engaged. Sorry, Peters.
'Mm—'way out in the woods. How ever did it happen ?"

" I tumbled off a mountain, and the loveliest girl
on earth found me, took me home, nursed me, and—"

" Loveliest, of course. Every girl is loveliest to
such a man as you are when no other is in sight.

" Nursed you, did she ?"

" Yes. Well, as I began to know her better, I found
she was all she looked, and, if possible, more."

" How did she happen to be living there ?"

" Born there."

" Full of sweet sylvan graces, I suppose ? Good
gracious ! Had she any relations ? What kind of
people are they ?"

" A father, a very superior old gentleman, not that
I liked him. They—they had a butler."

When Moorhead left Mrs. Bradlee's he was in a
very uncomfortable state of mind. He had tried to
be loyal to Leonora, but as his first thought had been
then, as always, Charles Norman Moorhead, he had

tried to defend his engagement by excusing and jus-
tifying himself for entering into it. This had made
his tone apologetic, which was not a compliment to
Leonora.

Mrs. Bradlee had taken the position of one who
accepts an apology. She had graciously conceded
that it was excusable and natural enough in a young
man of what she was good enough to call his "ardent
temperament," but had more than hinted that it was
a great misfortune.

He had expatiated on Leonora's beauty and splendid mental endowments ; her scholarship and exquisite taste.

She had laughed a little, and acknowledged that
his admiration of the only girl then in sight was a
thing to be expected, and had implied that the circumstances were such as to stimulate imagination to
the utmost and magnify each grace a thousand-fold.

He had grown a little indignant, and become really loyal for a while, and had shown more enthusiasm
in praise of his choice than he had felt for some time
before.

She had laughed at him good-naturedly, and said
that she had not meant to doubt his taste, but only
to suggest that where there is no standard of comparison the very best taste may be at fault.

Then she had sighed and said quite plaintively :
"Of course, it's irrevocable. You can't escape it
now," and had looked at him with pity.

"Engagements," she had continued, "are *never
broken, of course!*" and had looked at him sideways.

He walked home, thinking it over. The more he
thought, the more indignant he felt at the worldly

old lady's attack; the more indignant he felt, the
more her arguments repeated themselves to him; the
more they recurred, the more sound they seemed, in
spite of all he could say to the contrary.

From that time there began to grow up in his mind
a feeling that perhaps Leonora's loveliness *was* partly
due to the glamour of her surroundings, or *lack* of
surroundings; that perhaps it *would* have been different had there been others with whom to compare
her; perhaps it *was* impossible that one born and
bred in the backwoods could possess all he had seen
in her; that perhaps she *might* be out of her ele-
ment elsewhere; that perhaps, in short, he had made
a mistake. Then came the reflection that, as Mrs.
Bradlee had said, however that might be, it was irrevocable.

This preyed upon his mind. Every day he saw a
pretty girl or so here and there; and he was not un-
susceptible. Mrs. Bradlee told several people.

XIII

Moorhead went to Mrs. Bradlee's party, and, having been greeted by his hostess and escaped from a *débutante* in whose victorious path he had been cast, retreated to an alcove, and looked about for some way of passing the time.

The house had been made gay for the occasion, and wore the air of a solemn old personage decked by his daughters for a feast, and all the more glum by contrast with, and the sense of, his festal attire.

Among the stately sticks of furniture grew palms and rhododendrons in conspicuous pots, and seemed, as well they might, stiff and ill at ease in each other's company; and there were elaborate devices of flowers painfully like those that are admired of the funeral reporter, and called by him "floral tributes."

All that could well be lighted was lighted, and the carpets were sombre, the pictures on the walls were sombre; there was an effect of too much glare in too much gloom.

There was an abundance of costly, heavy ornament; articles very beautiful and curious in themselves, but suffering from their environment, having the look of being set on show, giving a shoppy aspect to the rooms.

The gas-fire blazed in pale merriment among its iron logs, and the air was stuffy with the flowers and millinery and upholstery. There was also music behind the ill-assorted plants. He stood looking over the throng and dividing the people into two classes— those he knew, who would bore him, and those he did not know and did not care to take the trouble to meet.

His glory as an explorer and author was beginning to pall upon him; he knew he might be expected to talk of his experiences, and hated the thought.

How many people had Mrs. Bradlee told of his engagement? Would people ask him questions about it?

Something tickled the tip of his ear.

It proved to be the swan's-down fringe of a fan, whose owner, as he looked up, shrank playfully back from him, clasping her hands, with a look of mock terror in a pair of wide blue eyes.

"Oh—but forgive me!" said the lady. "I had no idea you could seem so fierce and touch-me-not-ty, or I should never have dared—*indeed* I shouldn't. Is that the look with which you were wont to quell the fierce bears and things of the Western wilds in their native haunts? The look that frighted the stern savage from your side and made him run away and forget not to take all your things with him? H-m? Is it? Pray take it off and be amiable, Charles—or Norman you call yourself now, don't you?

"I hoped you would have forgiven my waking you up—for old times' sake; but, of course, you have forgotten—"

And the large eyes rolling upward, as in despair, were followed by the corners of the wide laughing mouth.

"Forgotten? Indeed I have *not*, Nelly—Mrs. Merivale, I mean. A man doesn't easily forget the cause of so many happy and so many painful times!" said he, rising and seizing her hand and looking eagerly into her face as he spoke.

She withdrew her hand.

"I think you have learned many things from your bears and savages. One of them is 'shaking hands,'" said she, with a very becoming frown and pout. "Happy and painful times, you said? I forgive you the happy ones—which you had no right to—for the sake of the others—which you deserved! Eh?

"But now tell me what have you really been doing all this weary while, and why you have not written, sir? Give an account of yourself!"

"How *could* I write? I had no permission," said Moorhead, who was lazily submitting to the lively lady's assumption of authority and found himself beginning to enjoy it immense.

"How *could* he write? Hear him!" said she, appealing as it seemed to invisible and attendant Graces of her own to judge him.

"No *permission*, indeed! You should have written to *ask* permission, then, if for nothing else!"

"If I had dared write," said he, "it *would* have been for something else also, I imagine. There are people so blessed with the power to grant favors that one can hardly see them or think of them without asking!"

"'People!' I don't know that I like that," said she. "Are there many?"

"I only *assumed* that there might be others. I only *know one*," and he bowed before her.

"That's better," she said, "and so — you'd have asked favors, would you?"

"Indeed I should. Would it have been of any use?"

"Ah! who knows what might have been? What leads you to dream that it *could* have been of any use? Not I, surely. And yet — as you *didn't* write and *didn't* ask—who knows?"

There was a pause, while she looked unutterable possibilities at him out of big dark-blue eyes under a heavy fringe of lashes.

He had forgotten how beautiful she could be *when she tried,* and thought he had never seen her forehead so white, her hair so richly clustered, her lips so full and sweet.

It is probable that he never had. She had meant to look well that evening, and was one of those persons who carry out their intentions.

"Besides," he said, as an after-thought, "you were married, you know."

"Oh," she answered, "how *absurd* in you! Why, anybody could see—everybody *knew*—it was only temporary!"

Then, seeing a shocked expression on his face, she added a mitigating clause or two in a voice of grief:

"There, you've misunderstood me!" and she looked deeply hurt. "Have I got to explain every little thing I say to you?" (fretfully). "You used to understand me" (reproachfully, with a little sigh for bygone days). "Well, I didn't mean, of course, that *I meant* it to be temporary at the time—"

"Oh," he protested, "I never—"

"Yes you did!" said she, sharply. "Your face

said it, if your tongue didn't. You see I can read you like a *bill*, or any other disagreeable document—just as I always could.

"Well, as I said, I never thought of it at the time, or while it lasted, as only temporary, of course! What I did, I did to please my friends, and took to myself all the credit of making a lifelong sacrifice.

"I did not see, as every one else did, that poor Mr. Merivale had but a little while on earth, or, of course, I wouldn't have married him, because I should have seen that it would look as if I did it for money. Some people think that now."

She looked at him defiantly, as if to dare him to express such an opinion ; but he only said, meekly enough :

"Of course not. I always knew and said you married him blindly, because your people urged you to—and in a way coerced you to it."

"Oh, you always said that, did you ? How sweet of you !"

"But," said he, "that's all over now."

"Yes, all over," she answered. "And it seems like a dream, as if it had never been at all."

"I'm glad of that," said he.

"But you," said she—"to return to our original and more agreeable topic — how has it been with you ?"

"Oh, I—I've—drifted."

"But why did you not write ? It wasn't for lack of permission, you know. That was the very lamest and flimsiest excuse. Haven't you made a better one by this time ? Come now, tell me : Was it because you were vexed ?"

" Yes," said he, " if you call it '*vexed.*' It's rather
a weak term for the feeling of a man who has just
seen the girl he has fancied *everything* to him married all of a sudden to an—but we won't say anything
about the late lamented Abner Merivale.   Yes, I *was*
vexed !"

" I'm glad of that, Charley," said she.   " I'm glad
you were vexed, because it showed that you cared a
little.   And now tell me : You have consoled yourself,
of course—*men always* console themselves.   How have
you done it ?"

Mrs. Merivale was a peculiarly fascinating woman—
more so than even when he had thought her the only
girl on earth.

He had begun to enjoy himself immensely ; had
reached the stage of tender reminiscence, and was by
no means prepared to tell her about Leonora.

" How have you consoled yourself ?" said Mrs. Merivale again.

" I—oh, how *could* I console myself ?" he asked.

" Ah !" said she, searching his eyes for a confession.   " Who *is* she, then ?"

" There's no one !" said he, lying freely, and was
about to say more, but she rose with a short laugh
and a mocking glance, turned to one Timmons, who
had been waiting at a respectful distance, impatient
to speak to her, nibbling such of his downy mus-
tache as he could get hold of ; took his arm and
walked away.

" So he says ' there's no one !' she thought ; " and
what does he mean by *that?*   Does he mean me to
think there has really been no one ? As if I didn't
know all about this highly romantic engagement of

s

his? Or does he mean it's broken off, like one or
two others he's had for fun, and that there's no one
now? Anyway, I don't like his trying to conceal it.
It shows it was in earnest, and that he still cares
about it, otherwise he'd tell. Well, never mind; if
it's not broken it will be now. He's hooked. But I
sha'n't feel sure of him till I've made him confess
and do penance; and *then,* if he's still engaged to the
Wild Lady of the Woods, I'll help him out of his
scrape."

They had begun to dance. Moorhead was fond of
dancing; but to-night he stood the saddest of wall-
flowers, watching the young widow as she tripped light
and lithe and clinging about the room in the arms
of various men, whose faces wore each and all a look
of unmitigated bliss while they were with her.

She gave him not a word or look, and he dared not
seek her; he was afraid of himself. Mrs. Bradlee
saw him standing and staring, and found time to
scold him for his uselessness and boobyism and intro-
duce him to several new girls, and to renew his acquaintance with Elsie Kent. But it was true that
he had never cared for Elsie Kent, and she and the
others, who all liked attention and could get none
from him, got rid of him with equal ease and comfort.

He thought all through a long, wakeful night of
Nelly Merivale.

He struggled feebly against the spell. He remembered his duty, and tried to compare her with Leonora. Then he knew for the first time how he had
forgotten Leonora.

He could not remember clearly how she looked. He

knew that she was tall and graceful and very fair to look upon, but thus much he knew of many girls.

He could not remember the tones of her voice, nor her smile.

She was only the very shadow of a memory to him; and Nelly Merivale—what a living, glowing reality! How eagerly his mind turned, in spite of itself, to her charm of look and speech and manner!

Perhaps he had really loved her, once—at all events, he had thought so. Thought so?—he knew it. He had forgotten it awhile, but he knew it now; and her new charm for him wrought with the old boy-love to make his mind completely subject to her.

He belonged to her—he had always belonged to her! Leonora was a mistake.

A strong, well-disciplined mind may pass through such a crisis as Moorhead underwent that night without harm or change, and spring elastic back to its old faith and honor not a whit the worse for temptation resisted, and stronger than ever in its sterling loyalty.

But when a mind has always been subservient to the moment's wish, undisciplined, trained by custom to yield and not to withstand, to indulge the fancy and not to rule it—how can it be trusted?

It may happen to a man to be so long away from the woman to whom he has given his love, be she maid or wife, that her very face and voice are forgotten; nor is it likely that he will not see many a face that he admires meanwhile. That is no shame to him in itself.

But if he *be* a man, he will look in his heart and find her name graven there as on steel, and he will remember that he is hers and be proud of it. His pride will conquer any foolish fancies, his honest love will be the stronger and his honor the brighter for the trial, and he will have the more faith in himself and the more delight in being worthy of her.

But if he is a poor, self-indulgent weakling, with a heart like mush, that takes every impression and holds none—why, then, the sooner she is rid of him the better for her.

Moorhead meant to do right because it was the thing, but he was as weak as water.

He persuaded himself that all this sudden turmoil in his thin blood, stirred up by Nelly Merivale, arose from the fact that she was his first love, and that it was his duty to her, to himself, and to Leonora to write at once and tell her he had made a mistake.

But there again he was weak. He dared not do it. He thought of her as pining for him and lamenting his enforced absence, and he could not bear the idea of breaking her heart. It was horrible—dreadful—awful! He might sacrifice himself and give up Mrs. Merivale—but no; he felt so little inclined to give her up that he told himself it would be wrong to Leonora —it would be deceiving her—to remain true to his engagement and keep his promise.

Being in this highly moral and creditable pose of mind, he was rewarded with a luminous idea. Perhaps he could persuade Leonora to break off her engagement to him without letting her know that he was trying to persuade her. So he arose in the morning and wrote her a long letter—the longest he had written for a year or more.

He told her how unworthy he was of her; how his conscience troubled him for having taken advantage of her inexperience to win her love; how she did not love *him*, but only what she imagined him to be; how she never would have promised to marry him had she known him for what he was; how that same conscience would not let him rest till he had told her so. But one thing he dared not tell her, and that was —the truth.

He waited in eager anxiety for her letter. When it came it hurt him sorely, for it was cold as ice and true and faithful as Leonora's self, and all it said was this:

"My dear Norman,—

"You say you are unworthy of me, and that I would not have promised to marry you had I known you well.

"It may be so. What I *would* or *would not* have done can make no difference; what I *did* remains, and my word is sacred.

"So I only tell you—for your own sake and mine—whatever these faults and shortcomings may be of which you speak so vaguely—cure yourself of them, as you are in honor bound to do, even as I am in honor bound to keep my word to you.

"Leonora Willoughby."

Only a little while before such a letter would have won him back to his allegiance, but he had counted on a different answer. He had been rather proud of his sneaking epistle, regarding it as an act of able and kindly diplomacy, and had expected in return some reproach or complaint, which would have enabled him to write a most magnanimous letter offering to release her from her engagement if she wished it. And even if she did not wish it, he had felt sure that he had taken a step towards estrangement. He had certainly painted himself black enough to encourage such a hope. Meanwhile he had given himself up en-

tirely to his infatuation for Mrs. Merivale, and Leonora's influence over him and power to bless had become lost to him.

Being but a poor-spirited fellow, especially in his
present state of mind, he was unable to appreciate
her steadfast truth and downright virtue, which he
felt only vaguely and uneasily as a reproach to his
own weakness. He was conceited enough to imagine
that her words proceeded from a blind love for himself, which could not or would not regard the bad
traits which he had so more than frankly confessed—
mean enough to hate her faithfulness, since it stood
in the way of his own inclination.

He was even so small of spirit as to despise *her* for
not despising *him!*

But he pitied her, too — he hated to give pain to
her, and, above all, to himself. He dared not confess
his breach of faith, and meanwhile sought for some
roundabout means by which he might escape with
what he considered credit to himself.

XIV

MOORHEAD could think of nothing to say in reply to Leonora's letter, so he did not write, and found a thirsty solace in much wine and as much as possible of Mrs. Merivale's society.

After the very first she kept him at a distance rather, with a pretty air of offence that teased and piqued him; till at last, having pursued her to a cozy corner, he made full confession to her.

"I knew it before," said she. "But you did not tell me the truth. You said there was no one."

"No one but you, I meant," said he, "and that was true. There is not, never has been, never will be, any one but you—for me."

"Then your engagement is broken?" she asked, in a careless tone.

"Don't call it an engagement," said he. "It was a mistake—a dreadful mistake."

"It's not broken, then?" said she.

"Well, no—not exactly that; but, of course, it's impossible."

"So I should have supposed from what little I have heard of it. Pardon for my frankness, please; I'm only agreeing with you, you know. Have you told this Miss—Yellowby—"

"Willoughby."

"Ah! Willoughby—I beg her pardon. Have you told Miss Willoughby that it's impossible?"

"N-no. That is—not exactly—I—she—it seems to me it ought to come from her."

"Very likely—in the first place. But you see it *has* come already from you—not to her, but to others—to me. When you tell me your engagement to Miss Willoughby is impossible, you ought to tell *her* at once. You can't go about telling other people that your engagement to a girl is impossible and not tell her, you know."

"It isn't the thing for a man to break an engagement, exactly."

"Bah!"—she snapped her fingers with a pretty upward gesture—"*that* for the Thing and all its worshippers! You good people here make me weary of life with your *Thing*. You all bow down to it like a lot of darkies round an idol—only the idol's better, because it exists. What does it mean—to you? Nothing in particular. It's useful, perhaps, as an excuse for not doing what you daren't do for fear of unpleasantness—for fear of comment from others.

"What do you mean by the *Thing?* That which looks best, in general, in the eyes of the set in which you move, perhaps, if you mean anything.

"You wouldn't like, for example, to have it get about that you—a man—had done anything so unconventional as to break an engagement with a girl. It wouldn't *look* well. You haven't the least objection to letting people know you don't care for the girl you've promised to marry, while you are still engaged to her and she still trusts you. Why? Because that enables you to pose as a man too *honorable* to tell her the truth, even though your polite fraud is a living lie that may well make her life and yours wretched, and give amusement in time to all the gossips and scandal-mongers.

"To pose, in fact, as a martyr to that same precious Thing and be canonized by its worshippers.

"In short, 'Norman Moorhead broke his engagement himself'—fancy a man breaking his engagement!—doesn't *sound* well, does it? So you say, 'It's not the *Thing.*'

"But, 'Norman Moorhead, poor fellow, is engaged to a girl he doesn't love, and is too true a gentleman to break the engagement, and she *won't* break it, and all the time he's in love with some one else. Sad, isn't it? And so romantic—and so good of him. The way he bears it is simply angelic!'—sounds well, eh?"

Moorhead had nothing to say to all this.

"You see," she went on, "I know you pretty well. I've known you since you were a smooth, well-behaved, proper little boy.

"Do you think I have forgotten the model child who wouldn't do this and that because it wouldn't please mamma, and who had no objection whatever to getting his scapegrace brother Tom to do it and be unmercifully thrashed for it?"

"You're very hard on me, Nelly," said Moorhead. "I think I'll say good-bye, for the time being."

"It'll be good-bye for the time to come, as well," said she, "unless you wait until I have done. I've a little more to say to you."

"Very well," said he.

"Just this. Do you remember what you said to me just now? That *I* was the only one? How do you dare to come and make love to *me*—*me!*—when you're still engaged to that—girl?

"Is that the *Thing* you're so fond of talking about?

"Now you may go. And in future be good enough to let me be. I want nothing more to do with you."

She knew she was quite safe in saying this, and the answer she had expected came.

"Oh! Nelly, forgive me. I—"

"Mrs. Merivale, I am called."

"Don't be so unkind. I beg your pardon. What I said to you wasn't the—was wrong—and impertinent. Please don't say you won't see me again!"

She looked at him a minute, and let a softer look come to her eyes by degrees—a thing at which she was very good—then said:

"I shall have nothing more to say to you until you have broken your engagement.

"This is not a case of '*Thing*,' but of '*Right and Wrong*'! The next time you venture to speak to me I shall ask you if you have written and broken it off. You can tell her it was all a mistake, and that will settle it. When you have done that you may come and see me—if you care to."

"*If* I care to!"

"That will do. You haven't written yet, you know —and you may go now. Charley," she said, suddenly changing her cold manner for one almost tender, "I don't part so easily from an old friend. I won't deny that this has hurt me; and what I have said, I have said for your own good, as well as in—well—in self-defence, if you will. Good-night."

Moorhead had been unable to appreciate the words of Leonora, but all Mrs. Merivale had said to him had seemed the voice of Virtue in the language of Eloquence.

Her words had hurt him too, but he submitted gratefully, and felt it a high privilege and luxury to be scolded by her.

Had he heard what she said a few hours later he might have changed his mind, but even then he would perhaps have found some blissful interpretation for her words, for his infatuation was more violent than ever.

He went home and sat down to obey her.

He thought when he took up his pen that he knew exactly what to say to Leonora; but was it a lack of ink or a bad pen? The words would not come.

" Dear Leonora," he began. No, " Dear Miss Willoughby "—under the circumstances— No—" Dear Leonora."

He tore these up one after the other. After he had settled that question, not at all to his satisfaction, he forced himself to write a plain, straightforward letter.

How cold and blunt and brutal it seemed! He destroyed it and wrote another, which seemed too mean and sneaking to suit him.

Then another, which, all things considered, was too tender. The next seemed ridiculous and flippant. He fortified himself with brandy and soda, and more brandy and soda, till he could hardly read what he had written.

It was two o'clock. He was too tired to write. His eyes and his fingers ached. He would put it off till morning, when his head was clear.

XV

While Moorhead was trying to write, Mrs. Merivale sat in her own boudoir in her little flat on Commonwealth Avenue.

She wore a dainty undress—whatever that may be—and was surrounded by all the extravagant appliances of luxury.

She looked tired and somewhat older than she had when she was talking with Moorhead that evening.

Her complexion was not quite so perfect, and the dimples had apparently narrowed and lengthened till they almost might have been mistaken for incipient wrinkles.

Nevertheless, she had the self-satisfied look of one who has worked hard and done well.

Another young woman, whose manner was a close, and dress a distant, copy of her own, sat near her.

Their relation was intimate. They had been schoolmates awhile, though otherwise very differently placed in life.

Mrs. Merivale's father, generally known as Joe Trask, had usually been in debt and out of pocket because of his sporting proclivities, and, having no credit at any young ladies' boarding-school, could not afford to send his daughter to one until old Abner Merivale, having met her, suddenly became very kind to the Trasks and paid for the expensive part of her education.

Meanwhile she had established a sort of school intimacy with Alice McNally, a carpenter's daughter.

Afterwards, when Nelly Trask had been "finished," Alice, having imbibed at the high-school ambitious ideas and a tendency to look down upon her own people and yearn for a more luxurious existence than her home was likely to give her, called upon her old school-mate, and, finding her in the lap of luxury, expressed a bitter discontent with her own lot.

Miss Trask was about to become Mrs. Merivale and to go abroad.

She was not enthusiastically fond of Abner Merivale, and felt that it might be more than useful to have a companion, bound to her by gratitude and entire dependence, for an ally in case of emergencies. She offered to take Alice with her, and the girl had proved a most invaluable lieutenant in all her battles and skirmishes.

Mrs. Merivale was a schemer and needed some one with whom to discuss her plans, who would sympathize, co-operate, and say nothing.

The two had managed Abner Merivale entirely to the bride's taste during what little of his life was left, and since had conducted many a triumphant little campaign against the world.

"Alice," said Mrs. Merivale, "give me my pick-up, will you?—there's a good girl!"

Alice brought from a rosewood cabinet a dainty flask and liqueur-glass and set them by her.

"Thanks! Where's yours?" Alice brought another glass and filled both.

"There—now we're cozy. Sit you down and let's chat a bit. Do you know, I've been wondering lately what we were to do ? The late Mr. Merivale's fortune would have stood *anything* short of Monte Carlo; but that nearly emptied the coffers, you know."

"I know," said Alice. "Well, is there anything on ?"

"Yes; it's all plain sailing now; nothing to do but work the Back Bay a little longer—be good—avoid slang—have a fad or two—(mine's Esoteric Buddhism at present, *and* the Zuñis, with a vague, inexpressible connection between the two)—take in a lot of dreary teas—show a becoming respect for Bostonian institutions and ancient landmarks—talk intelligently about the Norumbega theory, the pictures at Doll & Richards's, and the Symphony Orchestra—agitate the subject of a new Music Hall—and there we are. Not so bad fun, either—playing propriety !"

"Not when one's only *playing* it," said Alice.

"I agree. You've heard me speak of Charley Moorhead—now called C. Norman Moorhead; used to be Charley, to distinguish him from Tom, who is also Norman — Charley Moorhead, who was so blue and glum after my marriage ?"

"Is it he ?"

"'He is it,' as we used to say when we were wee things, and played games where one was chosen for the useful and stupid part of the game. He's chosen —elected."

"Does he accept the office—vote for himself, in fact ?"

"*Does* he ? He's gone clean daft at the prospect— can hardly keep away. Engaged to a girl, but she's 'way, 'way out West — a backwoods missy in some impossible place—and I've made him give her up. Sorry

—hate to interfere with her enjoyment of life; but we had to have him, didn't we, Alice, dear?"

"Rich?"

"He? Beautifully! Richer than I ever dreamed he'd be—or he might have been No. 1, instead of poor dear Abner, I'm thinking, Alice."

"Yes, we do need him," said Alice. "How soon will it be, do you think?"

"Oh, *very* soon—it's *got* to be, you know. First, because I can't *stand* this Back Bay business, and these poky people with their intellectual fads, *much* longer; secondly, because stories 'll be floating in from over across, and it's on the cards *they* may not care for *me*, though, so far, I'm a tearing success; thirdly, because people are absurd and unkind enough to want their money for value received.

"I suppose I might get a loan from little Timmons, at a pinch, if it's absolutely necessary; but I'd rather not, Alice."

"That little boy with the downy upper lip?"

Mrs. Merivale nodded.

"No, I should think not. Why, that child, to judge from his looks when he's with you—he'd be so proud to have lent *you* money that he wouldn't be able to help going about and bragging of it. Don't do it. I can stand off these people with bills a little longer."

"You're not bad at that, Alice. How do you do it?"

"Give 'em more orders. They're so imbued with the desire to sell things, they forget all the things they've sold and *not* been paid for, in the delight of making one new sale and the anticipation of being paid by-and-by."

"So they do, as a general rule," said Mrs. Merivale, laughing. "And while I'm in with the lot I run with now, they'll keep on selling and anticipating, I think. So much the better for them and for us. It won't be long before everything's right."

"I shall be glad—glad when you're free from all this anxiety and worry, poor dear. It isn't good for you!" said Alice, affectionately.

"So shall I."

So Mrs. Merivale, to her confidante; but afterwards, alone, she spoke to herself as follows:

"It's strange, when I think of it, that I could talk so to Alice—of him. Partly force of habit, I s'pose; partly because I can't bear to let her see that I—that I—really—care for him. But I'd take him if neither he nor I had a cent to our names. And as for that wild Western girl, she'd better not stand between us. I wonder if he's written that letter yet? Of course he has. Well—he'll come to-morrow!"

Moorhead called next day and found Mrs. Merivale at home.

"Have you written?" she asked, with an inward flutter of excitement and an indifferent air.

"Yes," said Moorhead.

He had been totally unable to write that letter yet, and had meant to say so frankly, submit to her blame, and ask her advice; but when she said, "Have you written?" it suddenly occurred to him that he could say "Yes," quite truthfully, with reference to the former letter in which he had declared himself unworthy, thinking that Leonora might be led thereby to cut him adrift.

"You have—as I told you?"

One prevarication follows another easily.

"Yes," said he, again telling himself that she had told him to write a letter breaking the engagement, and that the one he had formerly sent was written with that end in view.

"Do you mind letting me see the answer when you get it?"

"No, indeed," said he, "or, at least—there may be things in it that I ought not to show even to you."

"You'll let me know when you get it, will you?"

"I will."

"Very well," said she. "Good boy."

"That means I may stay and see you awhile? And you won't send me away altogether?"

"Oh—yes—you may stay if you care to."

"If I care to? Nelly, if you had any idea *how* I care to!"

"Do you really care so much?"

The rest of the conversation, which lasted some two hours, was much in the same strain. It dwelt on the old times before her marriage, on reminiscences of past scenes, on the delight of the present, and grew in passionate eagerness on Moorhead's part and graciousness on Mrs. Merivale's, till at the end of it they found themselves vowed to each other.

After that Moorhead came every day, and brought flowers and gems and costly gifts, and the useful Alice was able to say incidentally to the tradesmen that Mrs. Merivale was soon to marry Mr. Moorhead, on the strength of which duly authenticated statement they were willing to wait.

This blissful state of things lasted a little while, and then came a stormy scene, when Moorhead was

9

obliged to confess that he had not written the letter, and to explain his prevarication.

Mrs. Merivale sent him out of her presence.

"What is the matter?" Alice asked that evening, when she found Mrs. Merivale brooding long with her head on her hands and her elbows on her knees.

"He has not written," said Mrs. Merivale.

"Why should he, after all?" said Alice.

"It can mean only one thing," said Mrs. Merivale. "He is still fond of her."

"Suppose he is?" said the practical Alice. "He's going to marry *you;* then much good may his fondness do her. You don't want it. It would only bore you—after a bit. Better without it. One can't have everything."

"But I will," said Mrs. Merivale; and then in a fright she sent for Moorhead back, lest she had gone too far in sending him away.

He found her in a new mood when he came. She had determined that, come what might, she would not lose him, and, angry as she was, controlled herself, and was grieved, and gentle, and sweetly forgiving.

"Charley," said she—"you see I must call you by the old name—you have done me a sore wrong. I trusted and believed you. And you—what have you given me in return? You have dishonored me by making me promise to marry you when *you* still remained promised to some one else. Now, to me, betrothal is a sort of marriage—a sacred tie. You have nearly broken my heart. And yet—poor fool as I am —I am willing to trust and believe you still. Tell me again that you love me and no one else."

"I do," said Moorhead. "You know I do. Else

why should I try to make you believe it ? If I cared for her should I not have been content to be as I was —hers ?"

"As you are—hers, you mean," said Mrs. Merivale, very sadly.

"No !"

"Then, why will you not break that engagement ?"

"Nelly, I thought I loved her — once. She was the only girl there—we were much together."

"Oh ! spare me that !"

"When I saw you the memory of the old time and the first love came over me, and I knew it was you I loved. I could not resist—I *had* to tell you.

"I would tell her so—I *wish* to tell her so, and have it all over between us—but when I try to write to her —and I *have* tried—I can't do it. She was kind to me—she saved my life. I can't bring myself to wound her in return.

"Yet I must. It would be doing all three of us the greatest wrong if I should marry her. But how *can* I—a *man*—deliberately write to her and tell her, when I have taught her to look forward to the future I have promised ? I simply can't. Sometimes I feel—oh, Nelly, it's maddening ! Use your woman's art to help me and tell me some way out of it !"

For a second the words "Hang yourself—and so much the better for her and me !" were on the tip of her tongue, but she restrained herself. "Give me time to think," said she, in a weary tone, "and I'll try to help you. Now go. That's all I can bear for to-day. I'll send word when I want you."

After he was gone she said to herself, "Poor fellow ! What a weakling he is ! He cannot do an un-

pleasant thing.   And yet—I can't let him go."   And
then she added, hardening her heart bravely, " I
mustn't forget that this is business with me as well as
pleasure.   As Alice says, ' we need him.'   And, after
all, the weaker the better to manage.   Well, I'll try
to make it easy for him, poor boy."

In two days she sent for him again.

XVI

Mrs. Merivale had a plan.

The discovery that Moorhead had not enough strength of mind to write and break off his engagement, that he still felt grateful towards Leonora, was ashamed of the part he was playing towards her, and afraid of giving her pain, threw her into perplexity and deep dismay.

She had no objection, on principle, to his being engaged to two people at once, provided she herself was the one to be married and cared for; but she sorely feared the extent and effect on her own plans of his feeling for Leonora. She had determined to marry him, and to settle down to a peaceful, conventional existence, and she was fond of him. She was anxious that no influence should mar her plans or diminish his affection for her. Leonora was an unknown quantity.

Mrs. Merivale did not feel quite sure of her own position, even after her marriage should have taken place. She knew that her life abroad had not coincided with the sacred Thing which was Moorhead's religion, and she constantly feared the arrival of reports of her conduct, magnified in travelling.

People would be shocked, Moorhead's pride in her would be hurt; he would not hesitate to throw her over before marriage—and after marriage, if there were any other influence to draw him away from her; he would very likely put her on an allowance and go off to seek sympathy somewhere else.

Then, naturally enough, she wanted her husband all to herself.

She need not have been afraid of reports from abroad, for she had never succeeded in attracting the attention which she fondly supposed had been accorded her. She had been simply a very silly girl, reckless and extravagant in her first freedom, and delighting to pose as fast. Every one who had noticed the pose had seen through it and smiled, or been momentarily annoyed at its folly. No one remembered it. Its only effect was its reaction on her own state of mind, for she had come to imagine herself a scheming adventuress with a past, in need of rehabilitation.

So she had come back to her first love, succeeded in infatuating him and stealing his easy affections—a part quite in keeping with her own estimate of her character—and now found herself in a situation which, from her point of view, was dramatic to a degree. She had spent much of her time—as perhaps most people do—in acting out little comedies under the impression that they were tragedies, and had become an accomplished amateur schemer under the cherished delusion that she was a wily adventuress, such as infests the mind of the novelist.

Her plan was worthy of the occasion, and had it not been supremely absurd would have been most excellent, in that it involved, at a considerable sacrifice, the ultimate earthly happiness of all concerned.

Leonora was to be made happy—without Moorhead.

Not for her own sake, but because Moorhead, rightly or wrongly, was full of the idea that she was devoted to him and that he was depriving her of all hope in depriving her of himself. Therefore it was necessary to remove his impression that she was pining for him.

Moorhead was to be made happy in his Nelly, his first love, and his said Nelly in him. Leonora once off his conscience, Mrs. Merivale had no doubt she could be eliminated from his heart. That sensitive organ once free from external influences, she was sure that she could manage him to her own taste.

The sacrifice was to be pecuniary and was to come out of the worldly goods of Moorhead. Mrs. Merivale was averse, as a rule, to the sacrifice of worldly goods, but as the price of a woman's dearest possession —her own way—she did not mind giving up Moorhead's property even to the half any more than she would have objected to spending it for any other article that might have pleased her fancy.

There was also a fourth person to be benefited. All that remained was to convince the necessary persons of the feasibility of her scheme. If they would but see it as she did all would be well.

She bent all her energies to this task. When Moorhead came in obedience to her summons he was delighted.

She was arrayed for conquest and welcomed him with a sad forgiving dignity, tempered judiciously by a tender feeling for himself and sympathy with his troubles.

Here was a glorious creature whose only thought was for him. This flattered his self-esteem, and in ten minutes from the time he entered the room he

was ready to believe in anything she said, to do anything she told him, to think anything she wished.

She knew the signs of the lover's mood : the head a
little bent forward—the meek, upward glance—the
pleading set of the lips—the soft, lingering clasp in
which he held her hand till she took it away—the ab-
ject humility of manner, which was so unlike his usual
style.   All the signs of victory were plain before her.

She watched him narrowly while she talked for
some twenty minutes of other people's affairs, and of
what was doing in town, giving him no chance to
speak of what was uppermost in his mind, and saw his
increasing impatience with great satisfaction.

"Now," said she to that inward confidant who sym-
pathizes with our mischievous intentions, "he'll do.
He's in a mood to throw reason to the winds and do
whatever I tell him.   As for Tom—but never mind
him yet ; one thing at a time."

She stopped in the easy flow of her discourse and
looked at Moorhead in a way to delight his heart, by a
suggestion of mutual understanding.   There was a
proprietorship, and authority too, in her look that
pleased him beyond measure.

"Well," said she, "you do not seem altogether interested in what I am saying ?"

"You promised to help me," he said.

"Did I ?   Oh !—yes, I said I *could* help you—I can
if you'll do as I tell you.

"But I want obedience.   Otherwise I can do nothing.   I'm not one of those people who care to give advice for the sake of talking and then be laughed at for
my pains.

"So if you'll mind, you can have my help, such as

it is ; and if you are not sure that you will—why, you may go to some one else whom you can trust. I think you owe it to me to trust me, Charley, for you've hurt me sorely."

"I'd trust you with my life and happiness," he began.

"Very good," said she, "only you happen to have given all that to some one else to take care of—and you must get it back first, it would seem.

"The simplest way, as I said before, would be to write and ask for it—say it was a mistake, and that kind of thing. But you won't do that—it is hard for you, and I won't ask it of you."

"I do not want to be unkind to her," said he. "What I want to do is to get it back without hurting her. *She* ought to break the engagement; I can't. And I'm sure, with all your tact and delicacy and intuitive regard for people's feelings and knowledge of human nature, Helen, you ought to be able to find a way."

She almost laughed aloud at his compliments, but repaid him in kind.

"Well," she said, softly, "I honor your unwillingness to give pain ; it's like you — though you have made *me* unhappy, and I will do what I can. Only, if my plan should seem at first extravagant and absurd to you"—("It won't," said he)—"you must remember that I, a woman myself"—("And such a woman !" said he)—"understand women better than you can ; yes, and I know something of men, too, to my sorrow ; and you are not to fly off at a tangent, but give heed to what I say, and believe that I have thought it out carefully for your—for *both* our sakes;

Charles, and am not giving you careless or unreasonable advice. In fact, you have put your case in my hands, and you must obey me or I cannot manage it."

Promise? Obey her? He was delighted through and through. Obedience implied ownership, in a way —he belonged to her.

"Suppose," said she, "that your unfortunate engagement need not be broken off at all, but simply be put in the way of dying a natural death, to the mutual satisfaction of both parties? What should you say to that?"

"I'd give anything—"

"Would you? Remember that, for you'll have to give something.

"Do you remember the details of Miss Willoughby's personal appearance very well?—so, for instance, that you could draw an accurate picture of her if you were an artist?"

"No, I don't. Her face seems to have faded out of my memory. I have a general idea of how she looked, but not an exact one."

"How long is it since you saw her?"

"About three years."

"Ah! Now suppose Miss Willoughby had a sister."

"Yes."

"Suppose that sister was about her height and complexion, and very much like her in every way."

"Yes."

"Suppose you knew nothing of that sister's existence?"

"Well?"

"And that sister were to come to you now and say, 'I am Leonora,' and were to remind you of things that happened when you were there, and which no one had known but you and Miss Willoughby: would it ever occur to you to doubt that she *was* your Miss Willoughby, and might you not have married her believing her to be the same?"

"Why, yes. I suppose so—certainly. Why?"

"Wait a minute. Let's suppose again. What shall it be this time? Suppose a certain young man, who shall be nameless, had a brother who was generally considered the scapegrace and black sheep of the family.

"Suppose that a report—never mind what—got about, concerning this brother and reached the father's ears, and made him so angry that he turned the scrapegrace brother out of his house and made a new will.

"Suppose the model brother was quite able to contradict this report and prove it false, but did not, and allowed the father to die believing it?"

Moorhead had turned very red, and white, and red again. "How?—what makes you say that, Helen?"

"How do I know it, you mean? Oh, never mind! I'm just supposing a case. Attend, please, and not interrupt."

"Very well," said Moorhead, looking, however, very ill.

"Then suppose the model brother to be very well-to-do, and the scapegrace to be on the verge of starvation and running to rags—all because of the model brother's silence and the consequent testamentary dispositions."

"Nell!" he cried, "you are *unjust*. The reason I said nothing was because—well—because I felt myself to be the best fitted to represent the family and keep the property together as it had been kept for generations — and I didn't want to see Tom make ducks and drakes of his share. I would have seen that he got all he wanted—I should have felt that I held it in trust for him. I offered him an allowance at once, and he was angry and unreasonable and quarrelled with me, on the very day of the funeral, though he didn't know the reason of the will. Imagine quarrelling at such a time ! And I haven't heard from him since. I have always taken it for granted he was getting on well enough, or I *should* have heard. You are unjust to me, Helen."

"Will you kindly remember that I am only supposing a case, and keep still and give your mind to what I say ? What do *I* know about you and Tom and your affairs ?

"Now, suppose that the model brother, having far more than he needs, and being blessed with a peculiarly tender conscience so that he cannot bear to be the cause of suffering, should see a way whereby he can make amends to his brother with great advantage to himself ? Do you think he'd do it, Charley ?"

"If you told him to, I don't see how he could disobey !" said Moorhead.

"Oh ! Well, suppose the model brother, who, after all, has his faults and weaknesses—who hasn't ?—to have become engaged, by reason of his affectionate nature, to two ladies at once.

"Why should he not make up with the scapegrace, who by this time has certainly had enough of starvation and rags and will listen to reason if properly put to him (there's everything in the method of approach)?

Charley, get him home, give him the best of everything, *except* the society of marriageable girls, from whom he must be kept clear; and when he's had a fair taste of enjoyment offer him, not an *allowance*, which he won't stand, but independence and comfort for life, and beg a favor of him in return. He'll accept, and he'll grant the favor if he's properly managed."

"The favor is?"

"To marry a girl who, by the account of a well-known connoisseur in girls who has had every opportunity to form his opinion, is among the most beautiful of her sex, highly educated, talented, of sweet disposition, an even temper, and who must be, from her peculiarly lonesome position, somewhat easy to win—namely, Miss Willoughby!"

"Tom marry Miss Willoughby! But how can he?"

"Stupid! By-the-way, were you telling me the truth when you happened to say the other day that you had never mentioned Tom to Miss Willoughby?"

"I certainly never said a word to her about him."

"Mm. Sore subject, perhaps. Now, *why* do you think I put all those suppositions about a possible sister of hers? You admitted that you might marry her, did you not?"

"Yes."

"Well, this is a parallel case, isn't it? Only stronger. Tom goes out—*as you*. Ten to one she doesn't know the difference. Feed him up and he's awfully like you. I know, because I saw him a little after I got home; and even then I thought for a moment it was you, and wondered what on earth you were looking so seedy for.

"Time makes great changes; lapse of memory would

account for others. A beard would account for still more difference in looks.

"Coach him up on all that passed between you. You weren't there long. You can teach him what you remember. What you don't remember isn't necessary for him to remember either.

"It seems absurd at first, perhaps; but when you come to think it over it's feasible enough—eh?"

"But Tom will never do it. He'd never consent to masquerade under my name—"

"Stupid again. What are you generally called, Charles or Norman? It's been C. Norman lately, hasn't it? You never cared much to be called Charley, and you were called so to distinguish you from Tom? What did she call you — in moments of tender ecstasy?"

"Norman," said he, flushing, and looking vexed.

"Exactly. You're C. Norman Moorhead and Tom's *T. Norman Moorhead,* eh?"

"Yes."

"Well, what's to prevent his going as Norman Moorhead, just as you did?"

"It's true; he can, of course. But he won't—"

"I grant you, that's a difficulty. But it isn't by any means insurmountable. I know his character, and I can lead him by it. I don't mind doing him a good turn either. If *you do exactly as I tell you* you shall get him home, and have him out there and offering himself to her before very long.

"But it—it's such a *queer* thing to do. It seems such a swindle!"

"Look here, my friend—don't accuse me of planning a swindle. I won't have it, Charles.

"Listen. When you went out there she would have fallen in love with you just the same if your name had been Thomas instead of Charles? Now suppose, all other things being as they were, you had been some one else than the person you called yourself—would that have made any difference? No! Then suppose Tom goes out—it's he she sees, not you. She accepts him as he is—on his own merits. He makes love to her and she returns it. Does she love him any the less—or any the more—because she thinks he is some one else?

"The idea that he is you simply acts as an introduction to her good graces.

"If there's any difference in you two so striking that she objects to him, she won't marry him.

"In such a case he can absolve her. If there's no difference that she is able to see, I don't see how she's to suffer by it. Do you?"

"But it must all come out some time," said Moorhead, somewhat bewildered, "and then—"

"And then? She simply finds that the man she loves as her husband is not you but some one else. But he's none the less the man she loves. If a girl loves one brother, thinking he's another brother, it doesn't alter the fact that *he* and *not* the other is the one she loves. Does it?

"If she finds she loves Tom well enough to marry him, it doesn't matter what his name is, does it?"

"But—" said Moorhead.

"But what?"

"It's passing off Tom for me."

"Oh! Now I get your idea. You think it's passing off inferior goods for superior—a worse man for a better. That's it. I'm not sure that I agree with you. Tom's a sterling right good fellow. Is that it ?"

"No," said Moorhead.

"Then how is Miss Willoughby injured ?"

" Perhaps, then, you'd rather marry him yourself?" said Moorhead, testily, dodging the question.

"I ? No, Charley. Perhaps, if I'd only a casual acquaintance with you, the result of a few weeks of mutual isolation in a romantic spot, I would rather marry Tom. But you forget. I loved you long ago, and have, to my sorrow, ever since. It's no passing fancy with me—no romantic impression. I know your faults, and I love you in spite of them. You are everything to me—as I am to you."

Moorhead was silent awhile. He was quite deeply touched by her devotion, and all she had said seemed plausible enough.

Certainly, if Leonora should care for Tom enough to marry him, it would be Tom she married and Tom she loved. Every one would be benefited. His own conscience would be free of Tom and Leonora; they would be happy, and Nelly would be pleased. Nelly would be Mrs. Moorhead. At that thought he looked up with a smile like that of a child who has been led into obedience by the promise of some coveted indulgence.

" Do you really think this will work, Nell ?"

" If you do as I tell you it shall ! I am so sure of it that, to prove to you *how* sure I am, I'll tell you what I will do. If you will promise to try it now, and be guided by me, I will let you formally announce our engagement—at once !"

He jumped at the bait, and before he had gone had taken her orders and promised to obey them to the letter.

"What a fool a man is—when he's in love !" said she, after he had gone.

"What do *I* care whether the plan succeeds or not ? She *may* possibly marry Tom. But one thing I am sure of—to go out there and make love to her is just the hare-brained prank that will appeal to Tom—and I can remove all his natural scruples on the point of honor, fraud, and so forth. I see my way clear, and if he goes out there and offers himself—as he shall—it necessarily puts an end to all intercourse between Charles Moorhead and her forever and a day—which is all *I* want. Good of me to let him announce the engagement. If the worst comes to worst it's a broken engagement, and one more or less does no harm. But he'll have to marry me now."

XVII

A MAN sat in a musty office 'way up in the top of a big ramshackle building.

Three chairs of doubtful stability, a green table, a threadbare lounge, a pair of shelves with a few second-hand law-books, were the furniture of the room.

The sound of many quick footsteps coming and going on the floor below, the rush of elevators, the roar of the busy street outside, added to the lonesomeness of the place, for no one ever came to this room except the man in the chair.

He had sat there day after day, year in and year out—not to attend to his business, for he had none; not in the hope of getting any, for he had given that up long ago ; not to study his profession, for he had studied it for years with no return, and knew everything in those books by heart ; but merely because he had nothing else to do—unable to find employment or to afford pleasure—glad of a refuge where he could hide his shabby raiment and thin hopeless face from the people.

At night he slept there.

The office was his home. He was only a tenant at sufferance, long in debt for rent ; but the owner of the building would not press him, and let him stay. He could not have let that office if he had turned the tenant out ; those about it were empty, and he knew that he could get no more out of him in one way than another, "so," said he, "why disturb him?"

This delinquent lived by his pen, or rather kept death off at the pen's point. It was hardly living.

He went out sometimes at night, and prowled in the streets watching the people, and once in a while a face or an incident would impress itself on his mind. Then he would go and brood over it in his solitude and write a morbid story about it.

Now and then he could sell one of these stories. Then he would get a loaf of bread, a little dried beef, and a bottle. A five-cent loaf lasted him nearly two days. In fact, he was slowly starving.

He had not sold any stories for a long time, and his money was all gone. He had been two days without food. He could think of nothing new to write—his mind was in that state when it preys upon itself and finds no nourishment, so he sat and waited for the end.

A quick, sharp tread came along the long corridor from the stairs; a letter came tumbling through the slit in the door.

He got up slowly, went with a weak step to pick it up, and started when he saw the address.

"Strange!" he said. "Why does he write now?"

He opened it and took out a letter—and a check.

The letter was as follows:

"WELLWOOD, MASS.

"DEAR TOM,—

"You wonder, perhaps, at my writing to you after so long a neglect.

"You will attribute some selfish motive to me, and you will be right—the motive is selfish enough.

"The ties of flesh and blood are strong, and do not let one go so easily. I am lonely, and own that I have a hearty longing to see my own brother.

"I have treated you ill, Tom, and I wish most earnestly to make amends.

"Come and see me. I hope you will not take it amiss, from your brother, that I enclose a check for your expenses — for I *must* see you, and it may be you do not feel that a visit to me would be worth the price of the journey.

"Come, and let us be brothers as we were.

"With love,

"C. Norman Moorhead."

Thomas Moorhead read the letter and tore it across. He was about to tear the check also, but stopped and thought a moment. His imagination was conjuring up a feast. He saw himself sitting in a cozy supper-room at a little table spread with snow-white cloth. Before him lay a plate with a great porter-house steak, thick and juicy, and mushrooms about the steak.

The savor seemed to arise to his nostrils. A pewter mug of stinging musty ale stood beside the platter.

He looked at the check again, and picked up and pieced together the scraps of the letter, which he re-read with a look that softened from wrath to doubt, and from doubt to wistfulness.

Then he put on a seedy hat and went down to a lower floor.

There he stopped and looked doubtfully at several office doors.

People coming and going glared suspiciously at the shabby raiment and sharp, pale, eager face.

After some delay he entered an office and waited there, while the incumbent — a fat, pursy real-estate man, gorgeously apparelled — described the glories of certain property to a probable buyer.

By-and-by the customer departed. The agent turned to the new-comer, and said, genially:

"And what can I do for you, Mr. —— ? Land for sale, eh? Money scarce at present — sell a lot — get some new clothes and a shave and a square meal, eh? Ha, ha!"

"I have an office on the upper floor," he said. "Thomas Moorhead my name is, you may remember. I came to ask if you would cash a check for me."

The agent gave him a sudden, quick, sharp look which meant, "You don't play *that* on *me*, young man!" then asked, with his accustomed jollity and effusion of manner, "And how large a check?"

"Fifty."

"My *dear* sir! So *sorry* to disoblige—haven't got it with me! Just enough left to get home with—*so* sorry! Good day!" and bowed him out forthwith.

Tom went to another office.

A tall, shrewd-looking, iron-gray man greeted him with a cold stare. He had hoped that the junior partner, a pleasant, easy-going, kindly fellow, would have been there, and would have withdrawn, but a sharp "Well, sir?" stopped him.

"I wanted to see Mr. Torrey," said he, in his weak voice, "but—"

"Mr. Torrey's out. His business and mine are one. What is it?"

"I only wanted to ask him to cash a check."

"H'm! Be identified at the bank it's drawn on and cash it there."

"It's on a Boston bank."

"Oh! Then deposit it in your own bank and draw against it. Good day!"

He tried another—a bustling, red-whiskered individual.

"Don't cash checks! Busy!" was all the answer he got.

He went back to his office, and lay down on the threadbare lounge.

He was exhausted and discouraged, and had been made to feel like a beggar. He did not care to repeat his experience at other offices, and saw little prospect of doing better that afternoon.

So he lay all night sleepless and growing weaker, with his check in his pocket and no means of buying food.

Next morning, with a sip or two from the dregs in the bottle to strengthen him, he set out for the office of a paper to which he had sold a story—a slight acquaintance with an assistant editor had been the result.

"Hullo! Another MS.?" said the editor.

"Yes."

"Fiction, I suppose?"

"No, though everybody that's seen it seems to think it's fiction of the most improbable kind."

"M-m-m—I fear we shouldn't be able to use it. What we want is fiction in the garb of fact—not fact that looks like fiction. Truth is seldom very marketable; highly improbable truth is for the scientific and agricultural periodicals only—sometimes also for the newspapers. However, leave it, and we'll have it read in due course and let you know. Why, what's the matter?"

The visitor had dropped into a chair, and during the editor's remarks had grown visibly paler. It was evident that he was extremely weak.

"Oh, nothing much," said he; "tired, that's all."

He took his check out of his pocket and held it out with a shaking hand.

The editor examined it and smiled.

"Am I to understand that this is a *contribution?*" said he.

"The price is stated," said Tom.

"In short, you'd like this cashed?"

"I—I wouldn't have bothered you," said the contributor, "but the fact is, I know nobody in this city, long as I've been here, whom I can ask. I've sat in my office and made no acquaintances. I knew one or two, but they have fallen off. Now, for two days and more I've been without food, and this has just been sent me by a relation. Last night I tried to get it cashed and failed; I've been all night with this upon me, unable to get a bite. Now if you'll oblige me, I'll gladly wait while you wire to that bank, if you wish, to see that it's all right."

"My dear fellow," said the editor, "I won't keep you so long. Just endorse it, and sit there a minute."

He ran down to the cashier's office. "Cash this, please," said he.

"All right, I suppose?" said the cashier.

"I'll endorse it myself, if you prefer," said the editor, and did so.

"There," he said, a minute later, putting the proceeds in his visitor's hand, "your contribution is accepted, and there's the remuneration. And remember, in future, that when you find any difficulty in disposing of that sort of article it always takes here, and brings more a line than any other kind. Bring 'em to me for personal inspection. Don't mention it. I've been in the same fix myself many a time, in the old days. I know what it is, and all about it."

The assistant editor's mind was running on the time when he too had been shabby and friendless, and, as he said, he knew.

"Now look here," said he, "it's time for lunch. I'm going with you, if you don't mind. I nearly killed myself eating too fast once, when I was in the same cheerful predicament, and I'm to look after you. We lunch together—Dutch treat. These little experiences hurt; but they're our stock-in-trade afterwards, you know. Write it up and make a yarn of it, eh? and sell it."

The feeling of money in a long-empty pocket is a wondrous restorative. It is sad to realize how much one's strength may depend on the mere presence of that talisman which opens the hearts and storehouses of men to the possessor—and how little in comparison is the effect of intrinsic worth on one's self and others. One would think that conscience itself spoke to a man according to his means, and upbraided him sorely with the shame of an empty pocket. But that is probably because too many of us insist on carrying what we call our consciences in our pockets.

At all events, Thomas, who a few minutes before had been almost ashamed to speak to his fellow-beings and had carried himself after a guilty fashion, now freshened in his aspect like a plant in a shower after a long drought.

He squared his shoulders and held up his head— his eye brightened, and he looked the world in the face with an aspect of cheerful self-respect that made even his shabby garments seem things of his own choice dignified by his upright presence.

He accepted the assistant editor's offer with grateful courtesy. They went to a neighboring quiet lunchroom.

Tom looked ravenously at the bill of fare.

"Roast turkey—" he began.

"Pardon me," said his companion, "we begin with soup, and not too rich at that," and ordered consommé.

"You mustn't rush headlong at substantial fare," said he. "Just leave the ordering to me, will you?"

After the soup came raw oysters—then eggs, soft-boiled.

"There," said the editor, "that's all you can have for the present; in an hour beef and beer. Now I must leave you. Good luck to you. Write it up, eh? Send you another check—and cash it for you, too, if need be. Good-bye."

"Now for some trousers and a shave," said the *nouveau riche*, prodigally. "The coat may remain *in statu quo* — not because it *can*, but because it *must*. These shoes will last, with new lacings, till I get there. Well, it'll be good to be at home again. I wonder what Charley is up to, anyway? Somehow I can't but think he really means it."

He went back to his office, stopping on the way to buy the necessary articles. Once he stopped doubtfully before a bootblack's stand; but, ashamed to submit such a disreputable *chaussure* to the critical eyes of the Professor of Calcear Polition, bought some blacking instead and performed the function for himself in privacy, having due regard to rips and worn places, and inserting a piece of law-calf (taken from the one remaining cover of *Byles on Bills*) in the sole of the right shoe, through which the ball of his foot had gradually made its way to Mother Earth.

He locked his office door, put upon the outside the businesslike legend—

"Out of town—will return hereafter,"

and at three o'clock, with a large valise of withered and empty aspect, boarded a train, whereby he arrived that evening at the village of Wellwood.

XVIII

WELLWOOD was a pleasant little New England vil-lage, with its elm - arched street, its bit of common where the boys played ball, its trim little white houses with green blinds, its railroad station, smithy, post-office, and general store, its rival meeting-houses, and great area of outlying farms.

Some miles out of it the Moorheads had long had broad lands and a great house, that had been their summer home from generation to generation.

"Well, Tom, at last!" cried some one, cordially, as the new-comer stepped off the train, and a well-gloved hand rested on his shoulder with possessive good-fel-lowship.

"Hullo, Charley! I came, you see."

"It's good of you, Tom. I've missed you lately—but we'll talk of that at home. Good heavens, old man, how you've changed!" Charles cried, with a look of dismay which Tom observed and set down to his credit. "That's genuine, apparently," he thought. "Seems really troubled at my looks. Perhaps he means what he says, and did actually want to see me again.

"Yes," said he, when they were side by side in the carriage that was to take them home; "as you say, I've changed. The practice of law ages a fellow—takes away the blush of youth. Anxiety for the wel-

fare of countless clients has doubtless sharpened my
features; the constant atmosphere of courts of justice
and the conduct of important trials have imparted solemnity to my visage; the responsibility of managing
large and weighty trusts—these things, Charley, crush
out youth and make a man elderly before his time."

" Where's your baggage ?" said Charles.

" Here," said Tom, holding up the starved hand-
bag. " Should have brought more, but hadn't it."

Charles looked at the lean and hungry bag, then at
the polished coat, frayed of braid and button.

" I fear," said he, looking a little pleased, Tom
thought, " practice is less profitable than laborious.
What is your specialty, old man ?"

" Don't know yet," said Tom. " General practice,
so far. Still waiting for client. When a client turns
up I shall find out."

" Ah, well, you were never cut out for a lawyer,
Tom. We'll try and find something for you to do.
Dear old boy, it's good to see you again !"

They rolled along behind a handsome pair of grays
over a road that wound in and out between low hills
and sunny pastures; through pleasant, feathery woods,
and over brooks fringed with willows; past bright,
level meadows and neat farm-houses that stood white
among their elms and maples—homely scenes full of
present sweetness and old memories for both the
brothers.

Here were pools they had fished or swum in, or-
chards they had robbed, woods where they had shot,
windows they had broken; even old Joel Bently,
whom once, as Indians, they had pelted with the eggs
of his own setting-hen from the bushes by the road,

and who now glowered at them from his barn door as they passed, for he had never forgotten the loss of his eggs and personal dignity.

Tom, whose spirits were rising fast, recalled the incident. "How was it that I got the thrashing for that and you escaped?" said he, trying to remember. "You planned the whole thing, you know, Charley, and got me into it."

"You were rash, Tom. You were always that, you know. I had my *alibi* prepared beforehand."

"You generally did," said Tom. "Look there! I believe that's the same old turkey we slew and cooked in the woods and ate!"

"That was twelve years ago."

"Never mind; account for it as you will, it's the same good old turkey to me, and I ought to remember, for I was the poor wretch that got caught and identified with the crime, as usual. My memory is keen."

So was that of Charles. He thought, not without a certain self-complaisance, how he had put that turkey's feathers on Tom's clothes and adroitly drawn paternal attention to their presence, knowing that Tom would say nothing of his share in the matter, and that justice, satisfied with a victim, would look no further, and would leave himself in peace and safety. But he only said:

"You were careless, Tom. The feathers gave you away."

"Yes, the bird is revealed by his feathers, the carpenter by his chips, the man by the company he keeps."

"Meaning me?"

"Not at all. The turkey."

So they went on, indulging in reminiscences, from some of which the coachman, if he had heard, and had been addicted to the summing up of evidence, might have gathered that Tom had been a merry, mischievous, harum-scarum youth, always in trouble, and Charles singularly successful in escaping his deserts at Tom's expense. Yet it was Tom who dwelt most fondly on the recollections.

Some six miles from the village they turned between two massive gate-posts of granite up an avenue arched with old elms, between broad lawns, set off with well-grown trees and shrubs, to the *porte-cochère* of a yellow colonial house, whose overhanging front was supported on eight tall pillars.

A man in livery opened the door to them, and Tom stood in his boyhood's home for the first time in five years.

When he had removed the dust of travel and had put on some of his brother's clothes, which hung rather loosely on his emaciated frame, the two sat down to a delicious dinner.

It was the first time in years that Tom had really *dined*. He had eaten when he could, but dining and mere eating are as widely different as verse and poetry. He did ample justice to the meal, and his brother watched him with pleasure.

"We're quite alone, as you see," said Charles, as they lit their cigars after dinner.

"Naturally," said Tom. "Who would think of showing off his disreputable brother? Not you, Charley."

"Now, it's not that, as you know, Tom," said Charles, with a proper touch of indignation in his voice. "I have some people coming soon. But I thought I'd like to have you to myself a few days first. It's been a long time, and I've been much to blame for not looking you up before. But I've been drifting here and there, and somehow I've always imagined you prosperous and busy at the law. By-the-way, it's lucky those clothes are a bit loose for you now. They'll be tight before we can get new ones made if that appetite of yours holds."

"Yes," said Tom, cheerfully, "the law gives a fellow an appetite if nothing else."

"Tell me more about the law, old chap."

"Really," said Tom, "I haven't seen much of it. I've hunted it, and fished for it, and lain in wait for it; but, up to date, it don't bite. I never wanted to go in for it, you know."

"Then why did you do it?"

"To please the shade of our uncle. It was always a dream of Uncle Tom's, you know, that I should follow in his footsteps. He left me his library on condition that I would. Then father got the idea, by collateral descent, from Uncle Tom. He thought the library a grand start in life. He said it was too good to be lost; that there had always been a lawyer in the family; that it was a pity it had been left to me, because you would have made a better one, except that you were perhaps a shade too scrupulous; but that I must learn to live up to it, otherwise it would lapse into Uncle Tom's estate.

"I said, 'Let it lapse!' Then mother, almost ready to cry, said it was a shame to speak so and thwart Uncle Tom's dearest wishes, when he had always had his heart set on my being a lawyer because

I bore his name, and that if Uncle Tom knew of it it would cause him the deepest grief.

" I had my theological and psychical doubts as to whether Uncle Tom would care, but it was plain that mother really *did* care ; so I held my peace and submitted, and passed the rest of my existence burdened with that library and trying to live up to it."

" You haven't been practising all these years ?"

" No, no—not quite. I had a little money to begin with, and wandered about in the West—seeking practice, of course. I didn't find it. If there's a place more overrun, swarming, and infested with legal luminaries than the East it is the West. Office-rent is higher there, too. I couldn't get a place to store the library in. I was paying storage on it in the East, and didn't care to add the expense of shipping it till I should find some use for it.

" Meanwhile the funds steadily ran out. One morning a big bill came for storage, with a notice that if the bill was not paid within a certain time the books would be sold.

" I overhauled the exchequer, and found I'd enough to pay it and a few dollars over.

" Out of regard to family feeling, and the shade of Uncle Tom, and a sense that if it must be sold I'd better sell it myself, I paid, and then went with a light heart to look for a job, meaning to earn enough to go East on.

" I'd always had a theory that an able-bodied fellow who was willing to do *any* kind of work, no matter what, could always make his living somehow. I found my mistake and nothing else—living meanwhile on dry bread.

" ' Had any experience ?' was the invariable answer to my request for employment, and my undeviating reply was ' No !' Whereupon I wasn't wanted.

" One man said he'd try me if I had good references. I hadn't. But at last I got a job as a roustabout on a Columbia River boat. Then I earned enough to come part way East with, thrashed the captain of the boat for value received, and started.

" Got as far as Wyoming. There I struck a sheep-ranch, where I stopped overnight. It was run by three brothers—strapping big collegemen with athletic records, and about as much knowledge of sheep-raising or any other practical thing as I had of preaching.

" They wanted a fourth man to play whist with winter nights and make up a set of tennis in summer, and, incidentally, a herder ; so they employed me.

" The life was not so bad, but the ranch broke, for they lost sheep right and left, not knowing how to take care of 'em.

" So they decided to go home, and paid me off, and I came East. I'd saved quite a bit—wages are high out there, especially when one plays good cards and tennis with his employers.

" With what was left I hired an office, painted a shingle, and sat down to practise.

" Couldn't afford much of an office.

" Mine was high up-stairs ; nobody ever came there except to collect rent, which they didn't, as a rule, get.

" Lived on proceeds of the library, which I sold, a few volumes at a time. Second-hand books don't bring much, and soon the library and proceeds were

11

gone. Wrote a story or two, but didn't make much at that. Can't lie freely; my mendacity was crippled in early youth. Made enough to buy dry bread, so I lived on that with intervals of nothing. There you have it all up to date."

"Poor old fellow," said Charles, affectionately. "You *have* had a time of it. Why *didn't* you write to me?"

"Why, you seemed to wish to be regarded as a stranger, Charley. Your offer of an allowance the day we parted—well, I suppose now that you meant it all right, but your manner was — unbearable! You see, I was nettled at being so left out in the cold; and at the same time I was awfully cut up about our mutual loss, and at our father's having been unwilling to see me at the last; and in my state of mind it seemed to me that you were so elated at the will that you hadn't a feeling to spare for him or for me. And when you came out with your offer, that seemed to rub it in somehow."

"Thank Heaven, he *doesn't* suspect me of having worked against him!" thought Charles. "Well," he said, in a forgiving and conciliatory tone, "no more of that now. We'll just devote ourselves to having a good time and getting into condition, eh? And please remember that I'm your brother, and that all I have is yours—at all events, until you are on a good, solid financial basis of your own."

Every day Tom's natural affection for Charles, great originally, became strengthened by constant kindness and the interchange of pleasant sentiments, and the result was that he was ready to do almost anything for Charley.

XIX

Time went on, and Tom was still with his brother, enjoying himself immensely. The hollows in his cheeks were no more. He was clad in the best. He rode, fished, sang, boated, and helped his brother in the ordering of improvements and the management of the estate. He would have been entirely happy but for two things. First, he did not quite like visiting as a profession, and he had no other means of support. He occasionally told Charles that he thought it time to look about for work—that he felt himself a burden.

This was just what Charles wanted. It was the effect Mrs. Merivale had desired him to produce. But he would not hear of it from Tom.

"Who feels the burden," said Charles, Socratically—"the man who bears it or another ?"

"The man who bears it, to be sure," said Tom.

"Good. Now you say you feel yourself a burden. Therefore you bear the burden, and are a burden to yourself, for no one else feels the weight you talk about. Don't complain of your own burden. There's logic for you. I could go on, and prove to you in like manner—"

"Spare me !" said Tom.

"That's just what I can't do," said Charles, laying his hand on Tom's shoulder and smiling. "I *can't* spare you yet. You are all I have, you know, and, seriously, if you insist on regarding yourself not as a brother but as a matter of business, I can't get on without you at present. I should have to pay a lawyer—I beg pardon, any *other* lawyer—untold sums to do what you are doing for me in the way of deeds, leases, advice, and so forth. But we won't put it on that ground, boy. Can't I have the pleasure of my own brother's companionship awhile without his talking nonsense about 'burdens'? In a time of trouble, too!" And Charles sighed, plaintively.

This was the other matter that had marred Tom's pleasure. It was clear to him that Charles had something on his mind that distressed him. He was often abstracted, moody, and silent—rallying with an effort, it seemed when spoken to, and wearing a becoming but unaccountable melancholy.

Tom was thoroughly affectionate, and very grateful to his brother. He had quite got over the idea that Charles wanted to get something out of him in return for this sudden kindness; indeed, what was there to get? "A time of trouble, old man?" said he.

"Yes," said Charles; "I'm not over-happy, to tell the truth."

"I thought so," said Tom. "Now, my dear boy, tell me all about it."

"No, no; I won't bother you with it, Tommy. It's nothing much. None of our earthly troubles are, when you come to think of them. After all, why *should* a man have happiness, if there be such a thing? What good would it do?"

"The deuce! it *is* something serious," Tom thought. "Look here, Charley," he said, "don't talk any more of that. You call it 'philosophy.' I call it 'rot.' Let's have facts and not absurd generalities. Come, tell me; and let me help you, if I can."

"Help me! I'd tell you in a moment if you could by any human possibility. But you can't, and so I won't bore you with a lot of uninteresting details. Come, let's run out and get some air."

They went out and walked together up a winding rocky road on to the hills, lazily, in the heat of a sunny summer afternoon.

A farm-house stood alone on a high barren place, in accordance with the plan steadfastly adhered unto by the early New-Englander of building in as inaccessible a solitude as he could find, and then approaching it by a devious road, going every now and then over the crest of a hill to take his bearings.

They stopped here, attracted by a well with mossy stone curb and old-fashioned sweep and bucket, and were greeted by a stout old dame, who sat before her door knitting.

"Well, if 'tain't the two young fellers from the big house down below! What's brought ye away up here — afoot, too! — such a hot day? Ye must be pretty spry, both on ye; but I guess the hill took it out'n ye some!"

"It did," said Tom. And he emptied the tin dipper that stood on the curb.

"Land!" said the old woman, "to think o' seein' you two ag'in! How you've growed!"

"Garrulous old toad!" said Charles, muttering impatiently.

"An inconsistent metaphor, dear boy," said Tom. "The toad is seldom, if ever, garrulous."

" Then why can't she keep still like the others, and let us alone ?"

" You're touchy this morning," said Tom, and turned courteously to the old woman. " Yes," he said, " we have grown, but that is not our fault. We would have continued gladly in the form and garb of boyhood, but time has not permitted us."

"Wal," said the old woman, beaming at him for his kindly manner, "I don't know what you're a-talkin' about with all them words, but you've told me one thing pretty plain—I was jest a-goin' to ask ye which one of ye was which ; I couldn't hardly tell ye apart first off, but now I know. *You're* th' one they useter call Tom : always real pleasant an' affable an' social an' a-pokin fun ; an' the solemn, sour feller, *he's* Charley. Ain't ye, now ?"

This incident and speech seemed to have an unaccountably cheering effect on Charles. Instead of sneering at what he would have generally called "the impudence of the creature," he looked hard at his brother, and answered, pleasantly, " Yes, we're a great deal alike, aren't we ?" standing beside Tom for comparison.

" Wal, yer faces ain't so *very* like, but I'd know ye apart when I see ye together," said she, critically. " His'n"—pointing a fat finger at Tom—" hez more life in it than your'n, an' don't look so kinder *dolly*, but yer motions an' height an' build are pretty near the same ; an' I guess if I see either one o' ye alone I wouldn't hardly know which one it was—not till I got to know ye good."

Charles patted his brother on the back. "It's a compliment to both of us, madam," he said, cheerily.

" Wouldn't ye like to buy some fresh eggs ?" said the old woman, taking advantage of the mood of her public to find a market; and Charles bought a dozen then and there, and gave them to Tom to carry home.

All the way he was unusually merry, and Tom, delighted with his spirits, did his best to keep them up. The next morning, however, Charles was moody again and so remained. Sometimes Tom, looking up, saw his eyes fixed upon him with a queer, calculating expression, and when they met his glance they turned away.

XX

THOMAS MOORHEAD came down one morning and found his brother sitting at a table with his face on his arms. He did not move as Tom came in, and the latter stood, doubtful whether to speak to him or go away.

When Charles finally raised his head his face was so sad and rueful, and his tone as he said "Good-morning" so woe-begone, that Tom did not answer at all, but held out his hand in sympathy. Charles grasped it, pressed it warmly, and said—nothing.

"Why, what *is* the *matter*, old fellow?" said Tom.

"Oh, nothing more than usual."

"Now, my boy," said Tom, almost angrily, "we've had enough of this. What's the matter? You must tell me. It's something very serious to affect you as it does, and I can't bear to see you so moping and blue. Out with it!"

"I ought not to have made such an exhibition of weakness," said Charles, "but you took me rather by surprise. It is not so very serious, perhaps—at least, it might not strike a stranger so—but it's life and death to me."

"I'm no stranger," said Tom; "I'm the nearest friend you have, and what is serious to you is serious to me."

"You'd laugh at me if I told you," said Charles, shaking his head mournfully.

"You ought to know me better, Charley."

"All right; if you *will* have it, here it is. I didn't mean to bore you with my affairs. I'm engaged to two girls at once!"

"The deuce you are!" said Tom. "I knew, of course, you were engaged to Nelly — Mrs. Merivale, *née* Trask — and thought that was enough. But I didn't know there was another. My poor boy! Women are the very Old Nick incarnate! *I* know *that!*" Tom's knowledge of women was culled chiefly from his dealings with one or two landladies and washer-women to whom he owed money, and, like most men of such experience, he had very pronounced views on the subject. "*They are the very Old Nick!* But I never thought *you'd* get trapped. Break with 'em both and begin over! You can stand a breach-of-promise suit or two."

"Thanks for your advice. But they are not that kind," said Charles, with a slight sneer. "Breach-of-promise suits are not in their line. And as for breaking with them both, I won't break with Nelly, and I don't see how to break with the other. If you knew her you would understand."

"How did you ever come to do it?" said Tom, sorrowfully.

"It's a long, dismal story," said his brother. "You know Mrs. Merivale?"

"Yes; used to know her—Nelly Trask; she married old Merivale for his money."

"Well, Tom, before she did that—she was *forced* into it, mind, by her scheming old mother and her brute of a father, poor thing!—she was practically engaged to me. Suddenly she went off without a word to me about it." (Charles had never known that Mr. Merivale had been educating Miss Helen while he himself was making love to her.)

"Now she has come back ten times lovelier than before — sorrow beautifies some faces wonderfully; and as soon as I saw her I felt as fond of her as ever. I knew I had never got over it.

"We talked over old times, and I learned how she had been dragged and driven to the altar.

"When I saw her I was engaged already to another girl, and then I knew that my other engagement was a sheer mistake. Certainly no man has a right to marry any woman when any *other* woman can make him feel as Nelly Merivale made me.

"She told me too, Nelly did, in the sweet innocence of her heart, that she still cared for me, though of course while Mr. Merivale lived she had done her best to get over it; that she knew it was wrong, but that she had never been able to help being fond of me; that in her wretchedness, after her cruel marriage, she loved me in spite of herself, and turned to me for comfort.

"Of course I could only meet that avowal by one of my own, and before I knew it I was engaged again. I wouldn't undo it now, for I feel that Nelly and I belong to each other, and that under the circumstances I have no right to marry any one but her. Have I?"

"Why, no, I suppose not; still, it *would* seem that the other girl has a sort of *lien;* but then, according to your account, Nelly Trask's original *lien* would seem to take precedence of hers, unless, indeed, the mar-

riage to Abner Merivale acted as a *waiver* of her claim
on you ; but then, on the other hand, a *waiver* must be
sua sponte—of one's own free will—and the marriage
was not *sua sponte*, but under a sort of *duress*—coer-
cion, so to speak, by her father and mother. Yes,
I'm inclined to think that, according to your statement of the case, dear Nelly's prior claim holds good
as against the other's subsequent one. But how are
you to make the other see that ?" said the legal brother, stroking his chin and raising one eyebrow.

"Ah, there it is !" cried Charles, in a voice of
misery. "How am I to break it to Leonora, who is devoted to me too, and has waited—is waiting—patiently for me till our marriage becomes possible. What
shall I do? It's disgraceful ! pitiful ! maddening !"

Charles was not a bad actor, and indeed he had but
little need to act. It *was* disgraceful and all the rest,
and he felt it keenly. His face could be expressive
enough when he chose, and now it was such a picture
of woe that the tears of sympathy almost came to the
younger brother's eyes—not at the facts, which were
commonplace enough, he thought, and somewhat absurd, but at the anguish of the man who related them.

"Tell me about the other girl," said Tom.

Charles described Leonora almost as well as she deserved to be described—as well as he could, in fact—
and enlarged on her love for himself till Tom began
to sympathize strongly with the lonely, lovely girl
breaking her heart in the wilderness for this faithless
brother of his.

"Charley," he said, "how could you do it? I see
that you have no right to marry her if you really love
Nelly Trask, or even if you only think you do. But

why—*how* could you do it? Are you sure you're fonder of Nelly?"

"My dear Tom, how could I know? I *am* fonder of Nelly, yes, but I didn't know it then. It seemed all right at the time. Nelly had seemed irrecoverably lost to me, and I had made up my mind to forget her—*had* forgotten her. It wasn't till I saw her again that I knew what a mistake I had made. I may be a brute, but I can't help it any more than any other brute. It was all wrong, but I didn't know it; how could I?"

There was little said after that. Tom was astonished. He had had no idea that his brother was a man of so much feeling, and was deeply touched by his sorrow and by the humility with which he owned himself in the wrong—a thing he had never known him to do before.

That night Charles wrote to Mrs. Merivale:

"DEAR NELLY,—

"I am carrying out your instructions most successfully, and I think you'll acknowledge ably. The results are, so far, all that could be wished.

"Tom is living on the fat of the land, and blesses me as a most affectionate brother. I think he'd almost cut his hand off to do me a service, he is so grateful.

"He was really in a most wretched condition, starving—in fact, a disgrace to the family—and my letter, it seems, with its timely enclosure, just saved him.

"So besides being naturally fond of his dear brother, he almost worships me as the being who has brought him from misery into luxury and pleasure.

"He *is* like me. A woman in the neighborhood, the other day, could hardly tell which of us was which.

"I have—reluctantly, of course—told him my sad story, and while he does his best to console his poor erring brother, and would, I think, do anything to help me out of my scrape, it is plain that he has deep sympathy for Miss Willoughby. I have taken pains, as you suggested, to enhance this sympathy with harrowing descriptions of her forlorn plight and glowing accounts of her beauty, and I'm not exaggerating when I tell you that he's actually falling in love with her on hearsay.

"I will propose the scheme to him at once unless you have something further to suggest. I only wait your reply—eagerly, as I do every word from you.

"Strange as it seems, I think he will go in for it.

"Now, does not your servant deserve some reward? May I not come down and see you soon?

"Ever devotedly yours,

"C. NORMAN MOORHEAD."

Mrs. Merivale laughed when she read the letter, and repeated her favorite aphorism: "What fools men are! Both of them twisted round a woman's little finger, and one of them congratulating himself on the fact as evidence of his sagacity and acuteness. A rare diplomat, this Charley of mine! Yes, mine he is, absolutely; and he'll make a good husband. 'Come up and see me?' I think not, my friend. I shall see enough of you by-and-by. You are about the most agreeable man I know, to be sure; but as sure as I let you come you'll wax sentimental. Also, you're in your most self-congratulatory frame of mind."

Mrs. Merivale was not at her best. She was still recuperating after a long season, and taking great care of her roses, which were not far from fading. So she did not wish Moorhead to see her, and sent him a dainty note:

"MY DEAR CHARLEY (or C. Norman, if you like it better),—

"You certainly deserve, as you say, a reward, and I deeply regret that all I can give you at present is my thanks for taking my advice and my congratulations on having done it so extremely well.

"I am almost famished for a sight of you—*you know that!*—but one is not altogether one's own mistress, you know, and I am promised at the Egertons' for a couple of weeks. I'm *so* sorry, Charley! If you had only written sooner! You can't come to the Egertons', but be patient—and—by-and-by!

"Besides, there's another reason that makes it absolutely *impossible* for you to come.

"What *are* you thinking of? The idea of leaving Tom at this critical juncture is *too* absurd. He needs all your attention, and it's my positive *command* to you—I don't give one often, you know, but when I do I *mean* it—that you stay with him till he starts on his mission westward. It is imperative that you do so. You *will*, won't you? When he has gone you may come.   Good-bye, from yours,

"NELLY."

"P. S.—*Yes*, tell him, by all means, at once, and lose no time in coaching him up, so that he may start as soon as possible, for I won't marry you while that engagement lasts—and, Charley, I'm tired of waiting! Now do as I tell you. Preserve a deep and unbecoming melancholy before my brother-in-law elect, enlarge on your sorrows, and extract from him, if you can, a *wish that he might be able to help you.*

"Say it's impossible— Or—no!

"Did I say I was going to the Egertons'? I won't. You shall see me, but you needn't come; I'll go and see you. Invite some people; invite me among them. Get Mrs. Bradlee, your cousin, to preside and matronize — I know she's dying to, or will be directly she hears of it—and have her send your invitations.

"I'll come, and I'll manage Thomas; leave him to me, bless him!

"*Don't ask any pretty girls.* It is of the greatest importance that he should be unattached and uninterested here.

"Ask the Wymans — he's safe with *them* — and a few staid elderly people — friends of your ancestors — poor relations — anything of that kind.

"Do it *now*.   "N."

Wherewith she called on Mrs. Bradlee, and made herself so agreeable that that lady was filled with pleasant memories of her own charming youth, highly approved of the sweet, modest, young lady—a widow, and yet a mere child !—and inly complimented Charley on his good taste, and rejoiced that he had escaped from that backwoods entanglement.

XXI

Mrs. Bradlee was delighted, as the astute Nelly had prophesied, to matronize Wellwood. She was well pleased too at the list of Charles's guests. They were all old friends, as Mrs. Merivale had proposed, "of his ancestors," and she felt that the young head of the family was showing a highly proper respect for the last generation. She suggested, indeed, a few young girls and their mammas, but Charles called her attention to the fact of Tom.

Tom was a dangerous ineligible — wild, penniless, attractive. He wished to keep him away from girls —for his own sake and theirs—till he had succeeded in putting him on a sound and solvent basis. It would not be the Thing to present such an unknown quantity as Tom at Charles's own house to maidens who, it was to be hoped, would do better for themselves.

"Quite right and very thoughtful of you," said Mrs. Bradlee. "Still, if Tom could make a good marriage—"

"It is not to be thought of at present. He is too flighty," said the affectionate brother.

Mrs. Bradlee went down to Wellwood, issued the invitations, and the guests arrived.

Everybody behaved well. The ancestral friends played whist, took tea, and drove about in state.

Mrs. Merivale was Mrs. Bradlee's right hand, and went about making everybody comfortable. She treated Tom with a shy reserve very becoming to a sister-in-law elect, who felt herself, as it were, on probation. She seemed constantly trying in small ways, wistfully, to win his approval.

"Well, Tom," said Charles, one day, "what do you think of my choice?"

"A lovely woman, sweetened by sorrow," said Tom.

"What does he say?" Mrs. Merivale asked, afterwards.

"He says you're a lovely woman, sweetened by sorrow."

"Oh, he says that, does he? He's right," said Mrs. Merivale. "Then he's ripe for plucking. I'll speak to him to-day, Charley."

She found Tom smoking in a secluded spot. He laid aside his pipe and mentioned the beauty of the afternoon.

"Mr. Moorhead," said she, hesitating, "I know you don't want to be bothered, but I wish to ask your advice—and help."

"I'm all at your service," said he.

"Charles — your brother — has — of course he has spoken to you of our — our engagement," said she, shyly.

She looked down, and her manner had the effect of a blush. Then, without raising her head, she slowly turned her large eyes upward towards his.

"Yes," said Tom, "of course he has. He is highly to be congratulated."

"There!" said she, "you have that same mysterious tone that *he* has" ('Tom had not been aware of

his "mysterious tone"), "as if something were *wrong*
about it. Something *is* wrong—I know it, I can *feel*
it; but I'm all in the dark, and can't see what it is.
Our engagement *ought* to make him happy, and it
seems to have saddened him. He's a different man—
moody and melancholy. He never used to be that;
and he won't tell me what the matter is. It's that I
came to ask you about. I feel *sure* it's something
connected with our engagement that makes it so. *Is*
it? I'm so anxious for his happiness! I'd break it
off in a moment if I thought that better for him.
Do *you* know what it is that makes him unhappy?"

"I—er—do I—*is* he unhappy?" Tom faltered,
wishing himself back in his extremely quiet and peaceful office, or anywhere rather than here.

"You know what it is!" said the lady. "Oh! you
can't deceive me. People don't hesitate in that way,
unless they are thinking what to say. Is it money
troubles?"

"He's not troubled about money," said Tom.
"Nelly—Mrs. Merivale—please don't ask me any
more questions. Ask *him*. I'm sure he'd tell you
everything—"

"Then there *is* something. I *knew* it. And you
say it's not money. I wish it were, for *that* wouldn't
matter. Is it—is it—any other woman?"

"Really—my *dear* Mrs. Merivale," said Tom, turning very red, "*I* can't be supposed to know what is
the matter."

"*There*," said she, "it *is* another woman! If not
you'd have answered '*No*,' just as you did about
money troubles. *Who* is she? Tell me what it all
means; I have a *right* to know. Is he—does he be-

long to some one else ?   Has he promised himself to
some one else ?   Tell me ' No,' or I shall believe that
he has !   Yes or No ?   *Can* you look me in the face
and say ' No' ?"

"I can't talk about it," said Tom.   "You must
ask him about his own affairs.   How should *I* know
anything about them ?"

"Thank you.   You've told me all I need know, I
think," said she, very sadly.   " I won't pry into his
affairs further, for they are mine no longer.   Forgive
me for intruding upon you with questions ; but I was
so anxious *for him*, and he would tell me nothing.   I
had a right to ask, and hoped to help him in his
trouble, whatever it might be ; but I had not dreamed
of such a thing as this !   Good-bye, for I am not likely to see you again."

She turned, bowing her head and putting her hand
upon her forehead, and hurried away—a pretty, touching, graceful picture of Beauty in despair.

"Good heavens !" said Tom.   " Now, how the devil
did she get that piece of information out of me ?   I
didn't tell her a *word!*   Women in love have the most
wonderful intuition !   Poor old Charley !   He'll catch
it now !   Serve him right for not telling her himself.
Poor boy !   What will he do ?"

Mrs. Merivale came laughing to Charles Moorhead
in the library.

" Mr. Moorhead," said she, coolly, " our engagement is at an end.   I find that some one else has a
prior claim on your valuable affections."

"Why, Nelly, you don't mean, *really?*" said Charles,
puzzled.

"Don't be silly !   Never mind what I *mean*, which

has nothing to do with it; what I *say* is the point! You must tell your brother what I have just said; also tell him it's *his* fault for letting me know about it. Also, fly into a rage with him and tell him he's ruined your life, and then mope and sulk and look desperate."

"Did Tom tell you about it?"

"No. But he thinks he did. Oh! He's *too* good. I've just been with him. I came before him in the grove, meek, shy, sad, all but tearful, and spoke with him of our engagement. He was kind enough to approve of me. I asked him what was the matter with you. He wouldn't say, so *I* told *him*, and now he thinks *he* told *me*. Now it's *your* turn.

"Just go and tell him I came to you and said our engagement was at an end. I *did*, you know. Tell him he had no business to meddle, that he ought not to have told me a word about the other girl. Don't forget to say that your life is ruined; or, no, you'll make a mess of it. Wait and give him the note I'll send you."

She ran out, and presently came Alice McNally with the following production:

"Mr. C. Norman Moorhead :

"*Dear Sir*,—Your brother has told me of your engagement.

"Let me congratulate you. You need not let anything you may remember having said to me stand in the way of your marriage to the lady who is, I doubt not, in every way worthy of your devotion.

"As I go home to-day, and shall not see you before I go, I will say, Good-bye.

"Sincerely,

"H. A. MERIVALE."

Another note was enclosed :

"DEAR CHARLEY,—

"I'm off to-day. Sorry to go, but it will give color to the proceedings. Will see you in half an hour and give you further instructions.   Yours for keeps,

"NELLY."

The next day a gloom had fallen upon the house at Wellwood.

Mrs. Bradlee was vexed and puzzled by the sudden departure of her fascinating guest, who had taken an early train with one of those explanations that do not explain.

The host was preoccupied and openly dismal. The guests sat about and gossiped and promulgated theories, with much lifting of eyebrows. They enjoyed it, themselves.

Tom was thoroughly wretched, looking rather guiltily at his brother, who shot angry glances at him now and then, but avoided speaking to him.

At last Tom, feeling that he ought, plucked up courage to go and find his brother alone.

"Well, Charley?" he said, and Charles handed him the letter without a word.

"I can't tell you how sorry I am, Charley," said Tom.

"You needn't; I don't see that it makes any difference."

"Of course not," said Tom. "But I didn't think I told her. I don't see how she got it out of me. I tried to avoid talking of the matter. But Mrs. Merivale insisted, and put her questions in such a way that they brought out an answer whether I would or no. Even silence was an answer to her. If I had such skill in cross-examination, Charles, I'd be one of the best lawyers in—"

"Never mind about that. A man whose life is ruined doesn't care much about other people's professional prestige," said Charles, bitterly.

"Why not write, break off with the other girl, and then tell Mrs. Merivale. I'm sure—"

"Oh! Nonsense! I can't. It's not a man's place to break an engagement. I've given her every chance, and she won't. I'm bound to it, that's all."

"Perhaps it's better so. From your description of that Western girl, she must be as much the superior of Nelly Merivale as a—"

"That will do," Charles broke in. "I don't care to hear any comparisons between the two, or any comments on Mrs. Merivale;" and he turned away and hid his face.

"I wish there were any way in which I could make amends. I'd give my life to do it, old fellow!" cried Tom, deeply distressed. "You have taken me out of misery, fed and clothed me, and made me myself again; and now I have brought only trouble upon you in return. But what can I do?"

"I'll tell you what you can do," said Charles, in what seemed a sudden fit of passion. "Go out and marry her yourself; or else hold your tongue, and don't bother me."

"Marry her myself!" said Tom, with a bitter laugh at what he thought a bitter jest. "It's likely she'd marry *me*, when she's in love with *you!*"

Tom fully believed in the superiority of Charles. The latter suddenly turned to him and laid his hand on his arm.

"Wait a while, Tom," said he, more kindly. "Something has occurred to me—I must think it over. You say you wish to help me. I believe you can, if only you will; I'll tell you later. Now let me think. Would you mind letting me be quite alone awhile?"

"I'll do anything and all I can to help you—you may be sure of that," said Tom, and went out and walked in the moonlight, waiting his brother's pleasure, and determined to make any sacrifice for his happiness.

"Though how on earth he thinks I can help him out is more than I can see. But I'll do it, whatever it is, if only to show him I'm willing," said he to himself.

All day long Charles seemed brooding over something, but rather less dismal. The friends of his ancestors watched him with interest, Mrs. Bradlee with perplexity, Tom with deep anxiety.

In the evening, when the guests had gone, Mrs. Bradlee said to Charles: "Do you mind my asking what you have done to Nelly Merivale, or what she has done to you? It doesn't take much perspicacity to see that something is wrong. You ought not to let such things appear."

"My dear cousin," said Charles, "I wish I could tell you all about it, but I can't. And yet I don't know why I shouldn't. It's just this: she's found out about my other engagement."

"Well, I really don't see why she should be so particular. She's been married once, and why your having been engaged—why, you've been engaged to other girls, too; and she knows about that, because she spoke of it to me, and didn't care. I don't understand it. Perhaps she thinks this backwoods maiden just one too many."

Mrs. Bradlee began to wish that she had never told any one of Charles's escapade, as she considered it.

"Yes, she's been married once," said Charles, ruefully. "But that's over, and this engagement is not."

"What!" cried Mrs. Bradlee, almost screaming. "Do you mean to tell me you didn't wait till it was broken off?—that it still exists?"

"Yes, that's the trouble, you see."

"But what are you going to do? You *can't* give up Nelly for that doubtless perfect but impossible person out there?"

"I don't intend to."

"Then, what *are* you going to do? Write at once and say it's impossible."

"I can't. I've tried and can't bring myself to do it."

"Good heavens! How did Nelly find out?" said Mrs. Bradlee.

"She says she noticed something queer about my manner and got it out of Tom."

"But now, what can you do about it, if you don't write? You surely don't mean to go on and marry Mrs. Merivale without telling that girl anything about it, and let her go on thinking she's engaged to you?"

"I couldn't if I would. Nelly won't have it." And he divulged to her the Utopian plan with regard to Tom, without, however, mentioning Mrs. Merivale's part in it; merely stating that he intended to set Tom up for life in worldly possessions, and should make his marriage to Leonora a condition.

The old lady laughed aloud. "Fiddle! Stuff and nonsense!" she cried. "Do you really think—do you

think for a moment that he'll do it? Or that she
will fall into such an absurd trap?"

"I shall try it."

"Oh! I wash my hands of you; no, I'll say nothing about it; but I'm done with you unless you write
to that girl like a man, at once, and tell her the truth.
I never heard of such a childish scheme. *What* will
people say when it all comes out?"

"You—you surely won't tell?"

"Tell—no, boy, I'm too much ashamed of you to
speak of it or even think of it."

Mrs. Bradlee stayed till the guests had gone, and
went away leaving Charles to his own devices.

XXII

CHARLES came late at night to his brother's room, and sat down on the bed.

"I want to talk to you, old fellow," said he. "You can help me if you will."

"*If* I will!" said Tom. "Just tell me how!"

"What I am going to propose may not seem exactly sensible to you at first. But when I tell you that I have looked at it from every possible point of view, examined it in every light, and found it reasonable and practicable, I am sure you will try, at least, to do it for me. I think you owe it to me to try, Tom."

"There's no doubt of that, Charley. And if I didn't I'd try anything that offered a chance of making you happier."

"Then, this is the position : Nelly would marry me, I'm sure, if this engagement were broken off. In fact, she as good as told me so.

"Now, *I* can't break it. A man doesn't do that. And if I might. I simply haven't the heart to write to that girl and say I won't marry her.

"Yet if I do marry her I am doing a great wrong to her and Nelly and myself. You see that, don't you?"

"Yes."

"And I'm also doing wrong now in letting her think I shall marry her when I cannot."

"Yes."

"Then, the only way is to have her break the engagement of her own accord.

"Now, Tom, it's three years since I've seen her, and I hardly remember her face.

"If another girl, very much like her, came to me and said, 'Don't you know me? I am Leonora,' and reminded me of things that had passed between us, I should think it was she. It is reasonable to suppose that her remembrance of me is even less distinct, for she has a very striking face and presence. I have not—that is, not so striking as hers.

"Now, Tom, you know how a beard changes a man. How often you fail to recognize a man who has grown a beard since you have seen him last!

"You know that you and I are much alike in height and shape and action; that we both have the mother's eyes and the old gentleman's nose and voice, eh?"

He waited for Tom to answer, but Tom did not understand.

"Well?" said he.

"Tom," said his brother, "if you go out there and see her, you'll fall in love with her, as I did."

"That is not unlikely," said Tom. "I am only too easy a prey, as a rule."

"I doubt if you could find a better wife in the world, Tom. If Nelly had not become necessary to me long ago—but she is—"

"But suppose I went out and made love to her— that seems to be your idea as nearly as I can make out? She wouldn't throw you over for *me*, Charley. And, if she did, *I'm* in no position to marry!"

Tom had begun to think his brother was crazy to

make such a suggestion, but did not like to say so. So he reasoned with him instead.

"Great obstacles, dear boy," said Charles, "but not insurmountable. In the first place, you need have no fear about money matters, if that's what you mean. *I'll* take care that you are in a position to marry, as far as that goes. The question is : If you should see her and grow fond of her and she were willing to marry you, would you marry her ?"

"Why, yes, of course ; *if* I grew fond of her, I suppose I would."

"Have you any reason to think you wouldn't fall in love with her ?"

"Why, none in particular. Dare say I should."

"Well, now, listen ! All you've to do is this : Grow a beard. Imitate my manner. Go out and see her. See if she doesn't think you are I. If she does, don't contradict her.

"The beard and lapse of time will account for any change in looks ; time again for change in manner. If she notices a difference still, lay it to the fault of her own memory after all these years. I was only there a little over a month, you know. I can tell you enough of what passed between us to enable you to talk to her of old times. What you don't know she'll think you have forgotten. If you make mistakes, she'll think either you or she has forgotten. But I can prime you on all material points—"

"Look here, Charley, do you mean to say that you really, seriously ask me to do this ? Why, man, you're crazy !"

"You won't try it, then, Tom ?" said Charles, very sadly, in a tone of deep disappointment.

"But—my dear boy, you *can't* be in earnest."

"Will you do it or not, Tom?"

"I'd do anything I *could*, Charley, as you know."

"Oh yes, I know. You *would* do anything, and you *won't* do anything."

"Anything in reason, of course; but—"

"'Anything in reason, *but*—' is the usual answer of a man who doesn't care to be obliging, but wants it understood that he does!"

Tom looked hurt, and said: "Wait a bit, Charley. I don't say that I won't do it. But I think I see a better way out of it than that."

"What is it, then?" said Charles.

"Never mind yet. Give me a little time to think about it. A man can't undertake a step so important both to himself and others without careful consideration."

"I don't see why not. What better prospect have you to offer yourself? I offer you wealth and ease, a home, and independence; and the only condition attached is that you marry a lovely woman. By doing so you still make me your debtor and remove a great trouble for Nelly and me. It's worth trying. Plenty of fellows would go out there gladly enough just for the trip and the chance of meeting such a person as Leonora Willoughby. Once you see her, I'll trust you to make love to her fast enough."

This latter view of the matter began to appeal to Tom. But he said, "I can't decide at once."

That night he wrote Mrs. Merivale a most pathetic letter, setting forth the sorrows of Charles in a piteous manner: telling her of the proposition his brother had made to him, as proof that Charles was infinitely fonder of her than he could be of the other, and asking her to be kind to Charles and use all her influence with him to make him break off his other engagement.

By return mail he had her answer:

"MY DEAR MR. MOORHEAD,—

"I will not conceal from you the fact that I am more delighted than I can tell to know that your brother's words to me were not idle, and that his professed attachment to me is real. I am fond of him—why should I deny it?—though when I think of that poor 'other girl' my heart misgives me, both because I am sorry for her and because her circumstances warn me to beware of my own; for how can I tell that the love that failed her will not fail me also? Yet I own that I should be willing—foolishly, perhaps—to trust it if your brother were free.

"But from his point of view, which I share, it is impossible for him to ask her to release him from his promise. She must do so voluntarily if at all. And how can she be brought to do that unless she can be made to care for some one else?

"Now, if you are 'fancy-free,' why not at least try the experiment your brother proposes? She is, from his account, a very beautiful, delightful girl, worth knowing, anyway. Go and see her. You needn't marry her if you don't want to. If you find she mistakes you for your brother, I see no reason why you should not let her think you are he for a while. If she gives *you* the love she thought was *his*, why it will be *you* she *loves*—not *him*, but *you*, no matter who she may think you are. Then who is hurt? Not she, for she will have the man she loves and be spared a mortification; not you, for you will have a lovely bride and wealth to give her; not Charles, for he will be free to marry the woman he has chosen.

"Oh, if I were a man and before me such a quest, with beauty and wealth and the welfare of some one dear to me at the goal, not a scruple nor a difficulty should hold me back a day; and if there were uncertainty about it, it would add to the charm!

"Try it and win, and my blessings go with you in your attempt to bring us happiness.

"Yours affectionately,

"HELEN MERIVALE."

"Holy cake!" said Tom to himself, "I believe I'm prejudiced! I never should have supposed that any one would entertain such an idea for an instant. I almost thought Charley had taken leave of his usually excellent senses when he proposed it. But really he's generally as level-headed a chap as I ever knew, and he recommends it; and now Nelly Merivale, *née* Trask, who is also level-headed, and a very nice, sweet girl into the bargain, seems to think still more highly of it! They're the very best kind of people, both of 'em, and know what's what better than I do, and neither of 'em sees anything out in my going and passing myself off for Charley on the girl he's engaged to—*one* of the girls, I should say. To be sure, I haven't seen much of people for some years, and perhaps I've lost track of their little ways. Maybe I've grown quixotic too, and apt to grind a point of honor too fine. In thinking things out by myself too long, I may have invented new standards that other folk can't see. The thing looks impossible to me, but that don't matter so much. If it's all *right,* why, 'gad, I don't want any better *fun* than to try it. I like the way she puts it: Quest, with love and boodle — no, 'beauty and wealth'—at the end, and wouldn't she try it if she were a man and only had the chance! If Miss Willoughby don't take me for Charley, and sees right through it—why, it won't hurt her any more than to have him write and break off, or marry Nelly without saying a word; and those seem to be the only alternatives. If it *does* hurt her, by the Lord Harry, I'll console her! If she *does* take me for Charley— Well, it's queer, but, as Nelly says, no one's hurt. I'm in for it!"

"I'll do it, Charley," he said. "I believe I was foolish to back out."

"Tom," said his brother, "on the day you marry her you shall have this house, the Aiken farm, and thirty thousand down."

"Go slow," said Tom. "I've not seen her yet; and, mind, if I'm not fond of her I don't marry her. Moreover, ten to one it won't work. But I'm in for it, and I'll do my best."

Tom, having once made up his mind, was as eager and full of anticipation as a child with a new game. He was all impatience, and wanted to be off at once; but there were other things to be done first.

"The first thing," said Charles, "is to write, and accordingly I have written. Look here:

"'MY DEAR LEONORA,—

"'Shall you be glad to see me soon, I wonder? Is not Mr. Willoughby getting tired of the woods? Surely he is not the only person to be considered. Don't be surprised if I appear in the charming valley before the summer is over. I hope and beg that you may be persuaded to leave it. It is a pity—a shame!—that you should waste your life there.

"'How do you like my new hand? I have always written with a fine pen before, and have just been trying a stub. How it changes one's writing!

"'No more at present. I am very busy and very tired.
　　　　　　　　　　　"'Lovingly,　　　NORMAN.'

Now, Tom, copy that, will you? The Norman does as well for you as for me, you know. And try to come pretty near my writing. Then write several more letters before you go, gradually working back to your own proper hand. That will make the stub account for any difference she may subsequently notice between your writing and mine. Now mind, this letter is from *you*, not from me. There's nothing in it to say it's from me. You are in my place, as regards Leonora, from this time on."

" I see," said Tom, and copied and sent the letter. He devoted himself diligently to studying his part and growing a beard.

Every day Charles spent some time in going over with him the details of his life in the valley from the very first, and being of good memory he soon knew all Charles could tell him. He also learned to imitate his brother's peculiarities of speech and action, till Charles was somewhat annoyed at his proficiency. He dropped a certain swagger he had had, he eschewed slang, and spoke and walked with eminent correctness. The whole thing had begun to strike him as a colossal joke, and Tom was one of those persons to whom a joke is dear and sacred, and who will take any pains to carry one out successfully.

One day he ordered a carriage and drove off to a neighboring town, when he stopped before a house at which Charles sometimes called, but where he himself was not known, and sent up one of his brother's cards.

Mrs. Brand was at home.

" Dear me, Mr. Moorhead," said she, " how your beard has changed you! I should have known you, though. No one else bows just like that."

Tom sat down, and, having carefully conducted his

13

brother's manner through a series of conventionalities, among which was a touch of indignation at the allusion to his beard and bow, took his leave undetected.

"Charley," said he, when he got home, "will you do me a favor? Call on Mrs. Brand to-morrow."

" Why ?"

" Oh, nothing! There's a little surprise for you there, that's all!"

" What is it ?"

" I can't well enter into explanations. It's remotely connected, however, with your prospects in regard to Mrs. Merivale."

Charles went.

"Ah, this is an unexpected pleasure!" said Mrs. Brand, observing her caller's clean-shaven chin with interest. " So you've parted with it! I must say I like you better with it than without."

" I beg pardon ?" said Charles, mystified.

" Oh, you needn't apologize," said Mrs. Brand. "A man may do as he will with his own. All the same, I think you'd do well to let it grow again."

" Really, I—er—cannot imagine to what you refer, Mrs. Brand!" said Charles, turning quite red.

" How deliciously funny of you! But truly I'd no idea that an allusion to your beard would hurt your feelings, as it seems to have done," said she. " It's plainly a tender subject, and I'm interested in tender subjects. Now tell me ; why—*why* have you parted with it ? Forgive a woman's curiosity—"

A light dawned upon Charles.

" Oh, my beard ! To be sure—yes—quite so—just a fancy—I—" said he.

"Ah! Now I know! Of course. How stupid in me!—you wanted a really candid opinion about your appearance with and without—before and after—so you came yesterday with it and without it to-day. Thanks for your faith in my taste, and you've had my opinion!"

Poor Charles could hardly conceal his wrath. He hated personal remarks of any kind, and the imputation of having called twice in two days on Mrs. Brand, whom he was inclined to patronize, one day with a beard and one without, for her opinion, was terribly galling. He did not attempt to explain, however, but stayed out his short call, with an awkward stiffness of manner and evident ill-temper, which, combined with the foregoing circumstances, made Mrs. Brand think he had turned extremely queer.

"Did you see Mrs. Brand?" Tom asked, with much interest, on his return.

"Yes, Mrs. Brand was at home."

"Did you—enjoy your call?"

"It seems to me high time for you to go about your undertaking," said Charles. "I am obliged for this signal proof of your ability to succeed in it that you have just given, and feel no need of further demonstrations."

"I am fully prepared," said Tom, mocking his testy manner, "to conduct it to a successful issue."

Two days later he set out, delighted with the novelty and excitement of his adventure, with plenty of money in his pocket and a sense of having done a good thing; for his brother and the pretty widow were friends again, and let him understand that he had brought about that happy result.

Now, when Mrs. Bradlee heard that he had gone she was very angry, and rated Charles and Mrs. Merivale for a pair of silly children ; told them that if she had ever supposed they seriously contemplated such a ridiculous plan she would have prevented it if she had been obliged to have one or both of them confined as *non compos* — which she was good enough to say might easily have been done under the circumstances.

XXIII

ONE day in July a boat was steaming slowly down Puget Sound from Vancouver. It was raining—a rare occurrence at that season—and the passengers saw only occasional glimpses of the dark shaggy headlands. The wind shifted. The clouds broke and rolled away in masses. The shores began to appear, gleaming in the wet farther and farther inland, and great blue masses showed in the distance above the green; the clouds rose higher, and one by one the peaks shone out, and all was glorious with light and color.

Tom, sitting at the bow, saw a splendid white cone of rich outlines rising far into the clear blue, and asked a solemn-looking man in a tall hat and a suit of black what peak it was. The man came close and whispered in his ear, "Sh! it's Mount Rainier; but you'd better not name it till you're safe in Seattle, if that's where you're bound ?"

" Yes, I'm going to Seattle," said Tom ; "but why not ?"

"There may be Tacoma people aboard," said the other, looking apprehensively about him. " They call it Mount Tacoma, and they won't have it called anything else. They think it belongs to Tacoma, and want all the credit themselves. Likewise, when in Seattle don't call it Tacoma, or you'll get into trouble."

"I see," said Tom.   "What's the penalty?"

"Personal violence among the lower classes, social .extinction among the higher.   In the tribunal, contempt of court.   Among the old settlers I'd be afraid to say what might happen."   And the stranger, solemnly regarding Tom, chuckled internally from the depths of his gravity.

"I take it you're a Seattle man yourself, sir?" said Tom.

"I am proud to say that I am, sir—Druby, of Seattle."   And he produced two cards, one of which was edged with black and bore the legend:

SOLOMON DRUBY,

Undertaker and Florist.

The other:

SOLOMON DRUBY,

Attorney and Counsellor at Law,

Notary Public.   *Justice of the Peace.*

Real Estate Agent.

"An harmonious combination," said Tom.   "You can draw a man's will, bury him, settle his estate, and dispose of his realty."

"Exactly," said the other; "and since you are coming to our city I shall be glad to be of use to you in the one capacity, and, should occasion arise, will serve you in the other with becoming regret."

"Thanks," said Tom; "I'll remember.   Do you conduct both branches of the profession in the same office?"

"I find it convenient to do so," said the other, "as a recent case will illustrate: A man died in a boarding-house, and, after waiting a more than sufficient length of time for his friends to come and claim him, the landlady, at the request of the other lodgers, handed him over to me. I gave the case all due attention, and the funeral was on for the afternoon. Meanwhile Darnley—a mere scavenger, sir, who *calls* himself an undertaker—had somehow found out where he belonged, and wired his relatives, asking for the job, and offering to do it at a price for which no man with any self-respect would care to be buried. They gave him the job, and while I had gone for my hearse he came with his and took the body away. My assistant ran straight to me. It took me just one minute and a half to draw a writ in *quantum meruit,* suing estate of deceased, two more to put it in the hands of an officer. We gave chase, and, just as they were entering the cemetery my hearse dashed up. We attached that corpse *in transitu* for my services. The relatives had to give in and pay up, and I buried that man with as much respect as if I had never put an attachment on him. And there he lies. That's what I call *hustle!*"

As the undertaking attorney finished his funereal tale the boat rounded the promontory, called West Seattle, where a great lone tree known as "The Old Siwash" stands, with the semblance of a pack on its back, looking down upon the harbor, and came out of the bright green of the sound into Elliott Bay, blue with the fresh waters of the Dwamish, the port of the Northwest.

Beyond the bay stood the city, spread over a long, high hill. Along the water-front lighters, laden with brick and lumber, were puffing slowly, steam-wheelers from every part of the sound were coming and going, and screaming tugs were plying to and fro among the ships that lay at anchor. The shore presented the appearance of a great encampment on the site of a newly sacked town. All along the lower shore, above a forest of blackened piles, a vast assembly of tents, great and small, stood among ruins that still smoked and skeletons of buildings—some charred and broken; some new and growing; while on the ridge and upper slope were terraced streets of a variety of houses— pleasant cottages among their trees and vines, some clad with ivy, some resplendent with the owners' taste in paint, and rough, bare, unpainted shanties, or "shacks," that stood above the chips and shavings of their making.

Immense pile-drivers were busy all along the water-front and far out in the shallows of the bay, and scows laden with lumber lay beside them. There were throngs of people idling about, and other throngs pushing their hasty way among them. A babel of noises, whistles screeching, engines puffing, planks falling, loads dumped out on the sounding wharves, pile - drivers, hammers, creaking derricks, howling dogs, roaring teamsters, the trundling of heavy trucks, and among them all hardly a sound that was not harsh and discordant.

"What do you think of it?" Druby asked, proudly, waving a glad hand at the mass of rubbish and confusion.

"*Think* of it! How *can* a man *think* in all this wrack and row?" said Tom.

"There," said Druby, pointing to a tall brick building on the edge of the ruins, towering over the low white tents, "is the Boston Block!"

"Yes?"

"That's what. That, sir, is the building that saved the city. That edifice was built and conducted on conservative principles. The fire came tearing up Second Street. The Boston Block greeted it with a cold stare— Ever been in Boston?" said Druby, catching Tom confidentially by the coat.

"I have," said Tom.

"Well, you know the way them houses on Beacon Street, and the folks in 'em, stare when a feller's a bit lively?" •

"I have noticed it."

"That's what they do. Well, as I was saying, that fire was painting Seattle red—cleaning out the town. It came a-roaring up Second Street and met that Boston Block, and started in to caress it. The Boston Block greeted it with that same cold stare and turned a chilly side to its advances. The fire, sir, never got over the snub. It got discouraged, and quit right there. But it got in a sight of work before. That's what it did."

"So I see," said Tom. "Will Seattle ever recover from the fire?"

"Recover!" Druby shouted, indignantly. "Man, it's the biggest boom Seattle could have had. O boys! O *boys!* what a boom! Can't you see *that?* Why, look here, the burned part was a ramshackle old lot of shacks and tenements that reduced the value of the land they stood on fifty *per cent. !* Who would buy land with such buildings? No one! Who would pay rent for 'em worth touching? No one! What business could succeed in such shanties? None but that of the dive-keeper and the Chinese laundryman.

Yet the owners wouldn't tear 'em down; the property had been so unprofitable they wouldn't lay out a cent on it. The city was perishing, sir, of stagnation—dying of that fungus growth of mould and rot. Here was the most perfect harbor—the *only* harbor, sir, of the great Northwest—the one port of the richest corner of earth's surface—that's what it is—you hear me! —going to wrack and ruin because of a lot of rusty old shanties in the hands of men who wouldn't pull 'em down. What happens? Fire comes as from heaven, sir, and turns those miserable hotbeds of impecuniosity into smoke. The owners must build or sell to those who will. A new city will spring glorious from the smoking ruins. What do *we* do? *We* take advantage of the general turnout to get in on the ground-floor. First we get the public eye. We press the fire into our service as an advertising medium; it advertises the name of Seattle in letters of flame all over the nation. People who had never heard of the place before, and never would have otherwise, see a full account of the glad disaster in the papers, and they ask, What is Seattle, *where* is Seattle? Then *we* rise up and answer. Seattle, sir, is the great, new, model city —the home of Enterprise—the cradle of a young and mighty Prosperity! Seattle is the place where things are to be done as they *ought* to be done! Seattle, purged by fire from the mistakes of former time and from all that is undesirable, is now being rebuilt on the newest and best lines of modern improvement! Seattle is *the only* place where everything is up to date! *Where* is Seattle? Seattle, sir, is in the richest piece of country in the world—the port of the boundless cedar forests of the Northwest, where the nations come and trade for shingles—of the untold mineral wealth of the Olympics and Cascades—"

"I didn't know there had been anything discovered in the Olympics and Cascades," said Tom.

"I said *untold*, I think," said the orator. "Untold, sir, was the word I used. That's what I said—you heard me. The vast grazing lands of Eastern Washington; the unfailing fisheries of the sound; the rich agricultural regions of the Skagit and the Dwamish Valley—all these pour out their abundance through Seattle, and the ships of the Old World go nobly laden from her harbor, leaving gold behind them. Seattle is, in short, the Queen City of the Northwest. We tell them that, sir, and then we show them our plans —broad, busy streets, stately edifices, gorgeous emporiums, big business blocks. Why, sir, within ten days after the fire began the plans were made, and pictures of the buildings exactly as they will stand, ready for the eager public."

"I see," said Tom. "But where do you get the money for all this?"

"Money! Already thousands of lots are being exchanged for Eastern capital—already the contracts for the new buildings are sealed; and on that spot where the ashes are still smoking whole blocks are already let to men of enterprise, who stand in with the Fates and the Future—who know a good thing when they see it, and will push it along!" Here Mr. Druby, carried away by his own eloquence, smote his chest, and, taking a dramatic backward step, nearly fell over the rail.

Tom, not blessed with prophetic eye, could only see, as the boat steamed slowly in towards her wharf, a mass of litter and confusion—of scorched timbers and new lumber, of white tents and gray smoke, and a swarm of people like ants upon a hill.

"You have the true real-estate agent's gift, Mr. Druby," said Tom, "of describing what you wish and believing what you say."

They disembarked, and Tom lost sight of his acquaintance in the crowd, though he could still hear him shouting that he knew of a comfortable lodging which he highly recommended. The traveller allowed himself to be hustled—for it was growing dusk, and he had no time to look about him—into a sort of barge or omnibus, which took him to a hotel far up the hill in the unburned part of the city.

After a good supper he went to the post-office. He had written to Leonora, telling her when he meant to come to Seattle, and begging that Moloch might meet him there, if possible, and guide him through the forest, and might post him a letter stating where he could be found.

There was a letter for Norman Moorhead, to be held till called for:

"DEAR NORMAN,—

"I have your letter. Moloch cannot meet you. Come at once, as best you can. We need you.
                              "LEONORA WILLOUGHBY."

Pondering what this might mean, he went back to the hotel, and fell asleep as soon as his excitement would let him.

XXIV

MOLOCH, to whom his young mistress was everything in life, thought she had changed a great deal since her lover's departure. He had been accustomed to watch her since her first childhood; his chief study had been the art of understanding her unspoken thoughts, that he might forestall her wishes. He had thought that he knew her well; and, like all men who presume to flatter themselves with the belief that they know a maiden's mind, he found himself at a loss.

When Moorhead was gone she became passive, and subject to moods of abstraction and absent-mindedness. She went out and spent long days in the mountain solitudes. He listened for the sound of her rifle, and seldom heard it; he saw her return in the evening slowly; and then, instead of coming with sparkling eyes to tell of the day's hunting or the new places she had found in the mountains, and give directions about the game, she would put her rifle in a corner and sit listless with her brown hands folded, looking up at the peaks. Sometimes she took to her books, and read hard and diligently awhile; but soon she might be seen sitting with her chin upon her hands and her books lying unheeded, while the pages turned at the will of the wind. Then she would take her rifle and wander aimlessly in the woods again. She grew moody, too, and impatient, and for the first time in her life was easily vexed; frowns came instead of bright smiles, and bitter words sooner than laughter.

Then, after a time, she seemed more at peace—less restless, but no happier. Her face was calm, and the proud set of her lips seldom changed or softened. She was pale, and her eyes deeper and darker, by contrast, than ever; but the eager fires seemed pent in their depths, and no longer came dancing out to meet the light.

She grew thinner a little, and so seemed taller, and this, with her slower movements, added to the splendor of her presence, giving her a rare stateliness to be wasted on her father, who thought only of his books and fishing, and on poor Moloch, who would have given half his life to know what was the matter and the other half to help her.

He thought at first that she was pining for her lover, and ventured to speak of Mr. Moorhead as often and as pleasantly as he could, speaking of his return, and proposing little plans to be carried out " when Mr. Moorhead came back "; and it was then that his mistress, who had never had an unkind word or look for him before, began to show that her temper was not invulnerable, and gave him to understand by tone and manner that she did not care to hear from him of Mr. Moorhead's return.

He gave it up, grieved and astonished, thinking she must miss the man sorely indeed if the mere mention of his name hurt her so keenly.

He had been one day at Seattle, and had found a letter for Leonora. All the way home he gloated over it, thinking that this at last would bring his little girl some gladness, and looked forward to putting it in her hand and seeing the light of pleasure on her face.

But when he gave it to her, beaming himself in anticipation, he was bitterly disappointed.

She only seemed annoyed, then resigned, and took the letter away.

Moloch made a pretext for coming near while she read it, and there was no mistaking her look. It was not mere annoyance this time, but sheer sorrow, and that day and the next she seemed more than passively unhappy.

The old servant put his own interpretation on this, and was wroth. He thought the letter had hurt her— that Moorhead had written something that grieved her—was faithless or unkind, and he cursed the man who had stolen the joy from his lady's eyes, and swore that he should account for it one day to him.

She gave herself up to hunting, followed her game far to the wildest places of the mountains, and slew for the sake of slaying.

Moloch begged her one day, when she came home exhausted, but still excited and eager to be out again, to be more careful, and she laughed at him.

Even her father began to notice her long absences, her scant words, and sad looks. "Leonora," said he, "you go too far and hunt too hard. You must remember that you are a girl, after all, and that home is your place—not the woods."

"It's *all* home to me," said she: "the rocks and cañons and the still heights, the dancing, singing waters and the shadow of the woods — they belong to me, these places, and I to them, and the higher and deeper and stronger, the more lonesome and desolate they are, the better I love them all!"

"Then you wouldn't leave them—yet?" he asked, rather wistfully; for he loved them too, though his promise to his dying wife that he would take Leonora away was always on his conscience, and he hoped that he need not keep his word yet awhile, and felt guilty of breaking faith.

"No, no," said she; "not for all there is in the world besides! I read of it in these books, and for every good thing they tell of are ten evil."

"You are a wise woman," said her father, "and I am glad. I thought at one time that that puppy who was here had taught you discontent."

She laughed without much mirth, and Moloch, who came in just then with a dish of dewy salmon-berries, saw that instead of blushing, as a girl ought when her father, not knowing of her lover, speaks his name to her, she grew pale and looked straight forward with a set face—a fact which he set down in his heart's account against Moorhead.

He was sadder for her than ever, for he knew that she could not be always hunting and roving the woods and mountains, and wondered how it would be with her, whether she left them with a husband for the world she had learned from her father and her books to hate, or whether she stayed there in the valley till her friends were gone and age came to her alone in the wilderness. He swore to himself that he would live for her, old as he was, while she had need of him, for he was strong as a young man still, and in her service yet stronger.

So their life went on without event of mark, save

for such small risks to life and limb as Leonora ran when climbing in the mountain fastnesses—almost any of which would have lasted an ordinary girl a lifetime, had it left her any; but these she kept to herself.

She still wrote to Moorhead whenever Moloch went to the sound, and still received his letters, but with indifference, showing neither pleasure nor sorrow.

Winter came, and the forest was dark under a thatch of moist snow; the tossing river made fantastic imagery of ice with its spray that froze upon the rocks; the mountains were as a marble wall, and the snow lay deep in the valley; the elk came down and herded together in sheltered places, fearing nothing but the cold; and now and then a great black bear went lumbering along the river trail on his journey to the fishing in the open water, or a few timber-wolves howled their prayers to Famine in the long nights.

The old man, his daughter, and his servant stayed in the cabin beside great open fires—Mr. Willoughby smoking, and making rods and flies for the next summer's sport; Moloch quaintly carving in wood; Leonora busy at her needlework or painting; and all three reading a great deal.

Before, she had made the house glad with mirth and song; now all was very quiet, and seldom any one spoke. The master of the house was wrapped up in himself; the girl was too full of her own feelings, whatever they may have been; and the negro, bursting with questions to ask, sympathy to give, and advice to offer, must perforce hold his peace.

Outside the wind roared in the forest, the branches groaned and cracked and crashed in the storm, and

14

masses of snow and rock came roaring down the mountains, and the voice of the river was louder than ever
in its icy caverns.

The spring came with soft, warm rains, and the low
places in the valley were flooded till the sun dried
them again, and the wild beasts betook themselves to
the mountains, and summer was come again.

So the seasons passed, and the years; and the
fourth summer found the three still in the valley, and
no other with them.

XXV

ONE day—a hot, sweet, languid day—when all the air was still, and the innumerable murmurs of the woods were faint; when the great flies buzzed drowsily about, and the smoke of the distant fires hung lifeless on the dreamy atmosphere, Leonora took up her rifle and went out into the cool of the forest.

Moloch had strained his arm in handling a slippery log, and she went to gather an herb of which she knew that grows far up on the heights, when the heat of the unhindered sun and the freshness of the snow blend and make flowers spring among crisp grasses along the upland pools. She passed lightly up the elk-trail that led over the wall at the head of the valley to the inner range. Another of those highways of the forest creatures, leading from the woodland between the valley and the sound, joined it far up on the heights.

Leonora climbed steadily on till she came out of the woods, and reached one of those broad levels that lie beneath the peaks. There lay a little pool bright in the sun; about it a sweep of grassy open, hemmed in by the curve of bluffs, rocky and cavernous and shaggy with massed bushes wherever there was soil enough to give them life. The pool, which had dwindled much in the summer heat, had a broad edge of moist, oozy soil, and there were a multitude of tracks, for it was a favorite drinking-place for the beasts that inhabited the heights. There the great cloven elk's hoof, the dainty tread of mountain deer, the cougar's round, muscular paw, and the bear's foot, with its unpleasantly human aspect, had all left their traces; and one of the latter, unusually large, greatly took the fancy of Leonora, who had become, in the matter of ordinary game, the least bit *blasé*, just as any other girl might of the theatre, sweets, or admiration.

Looking carefully, she saw where the grass had been crushed under the broad heel and torn by the savage claws. Apparently the creature had been there for his morning draught that very day, and the chances were that he was even now stripping the salmon-berries from the thick brush somewhere very near, for the place was a paradise for a bear, where he would be likely to stay long unless urgent ursine business should have called him elsewhere.

She wet her finger in the pool and held it up to feel the wind. What little motion the air had came down across the bridge—a chance favorable to her approach in case the wary old thief should be in hiding there.

The keen delight of hunting took possession of her ; her eyes brightened, an eager flush came to her face.

She threw the cartridge of her Winchester into place, dropping the ejector carefully, to make as little noise as might be, stood a moment bending slightly, with lips parted and shoulders down, the right forefinger on the trigger and the barrel in her left hand, and stepped softly forward, pausing at every step to look and listen, and stooping low to peer under the bushes.

She had skirted the base of the ridge without success when she came to an opening in the bushes, which she knew well as the foot of a beast's trail, that led up to a broad shelf half-way up the ridge, where there was a bare patch of rock surrounded by berry-bushes.

"More likely there than anywhere," she thought, and the trail, scarred with the bear's claws, confirmed the idea ; so she went lightly up and crouched in the thick of the brush at the edge of the open—hardly breathing, eager and keen, ready with her rifle, with eyes and ears straining for any sight or sound of life. And presently— Was it the wind in the brush ? a stone that shifted on the slope ? a bunch of leaves that fell? a trick of imagination? There it was again —and, yes ! again — just across the clear space — a rustling, a snapping twig or two — the noise of slow steps.

Now she could see a bush move ever so little, and raised her rifle, tempted to fire at the place ; then better counsel prevailed, and she waited to see a vital part of her game.

She crouched, as still as a breathing being may be, with her rifle half-way to her shoulder, and her finger on the trigger.

For what seemed a long time there was not another sound or movement.

At last (for there is said to be a limit to almost every woman's patience) Leonora could bear it no longer, rose to one knee, and took aim at the place where she had last heard the sound, when out of the bushes on the other side came a tall man with slouching shoulders, rough-bearded and uncouth, stepping

softly, armed and ready. She rose, and as she did so
he also took aim as if at her!

The two stood a moment still with their rifles at
their shoulders and their fingers on the triggers; then
they lowered their arms. "Lord save us, girl! I
tho't ye was a bar!" cried the man, and burst out
laughing.

The ancient peace and gravity of the place were
broken; the echoes, that never had laughed before,
revelled in the sound and tossed it from rock to rock.

Leonora, however, was not so easily amused. She
was disappointed about the bear and frightened, partly at having so nearly shot at a human being, partly
at having so nearly been shot at, and also at the man
himself; for, little as she knew of people, she could
see well enough that he was not the sort of man one
would choose to meet alone in a lonesome place.

"Wal, I'm damned!" was his next remark, and he
looked it, after a fashion.

He was huge and bony and dirty; his garb faded
and weather-stained to the color of the brown pine-
needles on a storm-beaten slope; bits of twigs thrust
through the cloth took the place of buttons, or held
together the edges of rents. His boots also were a
dull rusty brown, and all broken; and from one of
them a pair of toes looked out, not modestly and shyly, as toes are wont, but with an air of bold and unbecoming disregard. He was hatless, and his un-
kempt hair, rusty and ragged as the rest of his
person, hung, like long strands of oakum, to his
shoulders.

"Good I didn't fire blind inter th' brush, pretty
girl!" said he. "I was nigh doin' it."

"So was I," said she, bravely and coolly, and almost wished she had done so; for he frightened her terribly, coming up to her with a long, slouching step, and knees that dipped as he walked, after the manner of a man that is of stealthy habit.

His face was hard and bold and hollow-jawed, and he stood near and stared at her with sharp, hungry eyes that gloated on her beauty.

Girls, it is said, enjoy being appreciated, and even at times admired, but not gloated over; and Leonora, who never, perhaps, had been afraid before since she was a little child, turned and ran through the brush, headlong, scratching her face and tearing her gown, till she tripped in a place where the rocks were many and sharp and the bushes thick between them. She had left the hammer of her rifle up, and as she fell it went off.

She heard the man crashing after her, and directly he stood by her side and grasped her hand to help her rise.

"No call to be afeard o' *me*, pretty girl!" said he, with some anger in his voice, swearing (and it may be well to say here that he *always* swore and cursed, and so save the trouble of reproducing the many varied and hideous expletives of which he was master). Leonora shrank from him in disgust and stood without his help.

The men in the wild places of America are, as a rule, more chivalrous and gentle towards woman, child, and weakling than their more civilized brethren of the cities. Nor is it strange, for the latter have the excuse that they see much of the less divine side of the weaker sex, by whom they are sore let and hindered in the streets, the cars, and the elevators—places in which the divinity of woman goes veiled and in deep disguise.

They are men in a hurry; and women with great umbrellas and long sunshades, women with trains and enormous hats, women with bundles, women with children, and, worse than all, women with questions, are ever in the way, wasting the precious hours and moments that are dollars and cents.

But the men of the great plains, of the backwoods, of the mountains and the ranges, whose life is spent much in solitude or in the company of their own sex and kind, are much in awe of woman in the abstract, as the type they remember of all that is best, and in which their own lives are sadly lacking. When she dawns upon them in person it is with all the dignity of a revelation.

But here and there among these men are exceptions—*among* them, and not *of* them; not the mountaineers and woodsmen and plainsmen, but outcasts, who know only the worst of life and of the community of human beings. Perhaps they have never had anything good to remember, perhaps they have utterly forgotten; but to them the world is a feeding-ground and nought else—everything in it either a prey or a thing to be feared, according to its strength or weakness.

It may be that the man Leonora met on the mountain was one of these, and, if instinct is to trusted, that may account for the fear and loathing that arose in her at the sight of him and the sound of his voice.

"Now I'm goin' ter fergive ye fer stampedin', an' see ye safe home," said he, and his voice was as evil as his looks. " Ben a time sence I've walked home with th' girls, an' never I thought ter find none here !"

He chuckled and looked sideways at Leonora, who had got out of the brush and went on without looking back at him, panting from her running and fall and fright ; red and angry-eyed, upright and stately, and beautiful beyond all telling.

He followed her.

"Are yer folks livin' hereabouts ?" he inquired. "Mebbe they could put a man up for a while. I'd pay fer lodgin' and find my own grub. I hain't ben under a roof fer —— knows how long, an' gettin' kinder sick er my own comp'ny."

" I should think you might," said Leonora, turning on him. " No, my people won't take you in. Go your way, and I'll go mine !"

" Wal ! That beats ——!" said the stranger. " But I'll see ye home anyways. Yer too pretty ter be let run loose around in these yer woods—sposin' th' bar sh'd git ye ?"

Leonora had passed beyond mere annoyance and fear, and was growing cool and pale now as she got her breath, with a dangerous kind of wrath.

Her only answer was to pump another cartridge into the chamber of her rifle, and hold it ready with the barrel near the breech in her left hand and her finger on the trigger, and a look in her eyes that stopped him, foot and tongue.

She turned her back and walked away, upright and alert, past the pool and down the trail, with an easy step, disdaining further notice, but listening to every step he took.

There was an appearance of readiness about her elbows and shoulders that affected him unpleasantly. The fellow watched her with an ugly expression, but did not follow till she had passed out of sight. There was a place were the elk-trail forked, and one branch went right down into the valley.

The elk, the only engineers and road-builders of the mountains, not liking the Willoughbys as winter neighbors in their visits to the lowlands, nor caring to go much to the valley since their arrival, had let this path get out of use and repair and had made another, passing in a wide curve along the slope to another good pasture of which they knew, where there were no girls with guns, no blackamoors armed with long knives and frying-pans to cut them up and salt them down, no old white-bearded gentlemen to fright them as they came down by the river and eat them before they could go home again. This branch of the trail was well broken into dust by their sharp hoofs.

Leonora, at the forks, gave one glance behind her, and followed the newer branch, taking good care to tread firmly at first, so as to leave her dainty tracks in the brown dust, and afterwards stepping more lightly or walking a little off the path when it was possible, that they might appear less often, by degrees, till finally she came to rocky ground, where no tracks could be left.

Here she turned into the woods, and hid in the undergrowth till the stranger, who had followed her tracks as she had supposed he would, came by. She could see him from her hiding-place as he passed at a dog-trot, bending forward to see the trail, with his ugly face all in a grin. When he was out of hearing she ran back, taking care to leave no tracks this time, soon reached home by the old path, and threw herself down on a lounge with a faintness she had never known before. As she thought the matter over, it seemed to her that she had been very foolish in running away, and was at a loss to account for her fear. The man was repulsive, to be sure; but he had not done or said anything to alarm her. He had been rude and uncouth—that was all. It was surely natural enough that a man alone in the forest and finding he had neighbors, should wish to know them. It could not be thought that he would not make every endeavor to do so. As for his following her, he evidently knew no better. She told herself that if he had not been such a repulsive - looking fellow she would not have been frightened; that his appearance was not his fault, perhaps; and that she had treated him in a very uncharitable manner, and blamed herself. Nevertheless, when the image of him running by, as she had seen him, occurred to her she felt a fear that would not yield to reasoning. She told Moloch, while she bound up his hand with the fresh leaves. He showed a great deal of white eyeball, and a kind of faint purplish tint came into his usual blackness; also, she felt the muscles twitch in his great forearms. But he only said, "Wish ma hand was well, Miss 'Nora." She told Mr. Willoughby.

"So!" he said, angrily, "no peace from sweet humanity even here! We must find means to make him go, if he stays about. Solitude is too precious a thing to lose." Then he laughed a little. "So he didn't see you home?" said he. "A Winchester is no bad chaperon for a young maid. None better. But, even so, you must not stray from home again for a while. However, I dare say we shall see no more of him."

XXVI

For the next few days Leonora stayed at home and helped her crippled butler with the housework. Her fears passed easily away. Nothing was seen of the stranger, though once she thought she heard the report of a rifle far away.

On the sixth day she was splitting kindling-wood at the back of the house, when her father and Moloch heard her give a faint cry, and came out.

"There he is—now he's gone!" she said.

"That man?" said her father, and he and Moloch went towards the place she pointed out—a gap in the woods—but though they sought a long time they could find no one.

"I'd like to catch that fellow! I'd send him about his business!" said Mr. Willoughby.

"Yo' be'n up early, Miss 'Nora!" was Moloch's greeting to her next day. "You ought'n' to done so, ef you'll excuse mah sayin' it so plain, Miss 'Nora. _I_ can split kin'lin's well enough—an' it ain't the kind of work for yo' pretty han's, Miss 'Nora."

"What do you mean, Moloch? _I_ haven't been splitting wood this morning. I'm just up!" said Leonora.

"Then it mus' ha' been Mr. Willoughby. I wouldn't 'a' thought it of him," said Moloch. "I take it real kind in him—but he needn' to 'a' done it."

But Mr. Willoughby denied all knowledge of kind-lings and refuted the interpretation of early rising.

Here was a strange thing: Moloch had found a large pile, newly split, by the kitchen door.

"It's that man again," said Leonora. "He saw me chopping yesterday. And he must have come and done this to show that he wished us well and meant to be neighborly."

"Confound him for his pains!" said Mr. Willough-by, "and damn all neighbors!"

"Hush, father!" said the girl. "I dare say he means well. But he *is* so frightful and hideous. I wish he'd stay away."

"How 'd ever he do it without wakin' anybody?" said Moloch, and, looking carefully, found a long mark on the ground, like that of a broad wheel.

Now Moloch kept on hand a supply of sections of fir trunk, cylinders of a foot in thickness and three or four feet across, and the mark was of one of those which had been turned on its side and rolled along the ground. Following the track, he came to a place near the river where the noise of the rushing water would have drowned the sound of the axe, and there were chips and bits of bark on the trampled grass. The stranger had taken the wood there in bulk, car-ried it back split to the door, and carefully piled it.

"He saw Miss 'Nora choppin', an' he done it as a kind a' hint to her he'd like to work for her," said Moloch to himself. "'Pears like he darm' to think he 'spire to be in love with Miss 'Nora."

Two days later a fresh haunch of venison was found in the morning lying at the door.

"Take it away and throw it into the river," said Leonora.

"I am not sure," said Mr. Willoughby. "While the human creature is not to be desired as a companion, it is sometimes indirectly useful. One does not hold intimate converse with the wolf or seek its friendship, but one need not on that account refuse its hide. When *anything*, however small, is to be gained from humanity, why, gain it, as a rule. Nevertheless, Moloch, do as Miss Leonora tells you. Chuck it into the river, but first chop it up and—you know the big pool just below the cañon? Bait that pool with the meat."

That night Moloch watched by the kitchen door, but no one came.

He watched again the night after, determined to have a word with the persistent benefactor, and just before dawn, when the mountains were dimly seen, a mass of deeper darkness against the dark sky—all but the highest peak, that was beginning to glow—and a few faint stars hung above them, he heard a step coming cautiously into the clearing, and the stranger appeared out of the dusk. When he was very near Moloch spoke.

"Mornin', sah. Yo' out early this mornin'!"

The man took a step back, startled by the unexpectedness of Moloch.

"Are yo' the gen'leman that's been so kind as to come an' split some kinlin's an' leave a leg o' deer?"

The butler spoke suavely and with respect.

"Why, yes! You're right, friend! It's me!" said the stranger.

"It was kind in you, sah. But it was kindness

frown away. I had ordahs to frow it in the ribbah,
an' I did. Yo' see, sir, my employah isn't in the habit
o' takin' gifts from nobody. What he likes is fo' folks
to let him alone. I'm perfeckly competent to split
all the wood an' git all the game, without troublin'
a stranger, sah. An' kind as my employah takes it in
you, sah, to cut up wood an' bring him meat, he'll
take it kinder yet if you was to go off an' not come
roun' here any more, sah—"

"Look here, nigger, who told you to say all them
words?" the stranger asked.

"Nobody, sah; but I've general an' permanent authority to negotiate with trespassahs with a view to
havin' 'em stay away," said Moloch, "an' my employah, he regards all persons comin' roun' here as
trespassahs."

"Wal, then, blackie, you c'n tell yer boss I didn't
cut no wood for *him* nor bring no game for *him*, nor
yet don't mean ter. I done it fer th' girl as lives
yere—an' shall do as much an' more. If I like ter
bring game yere I bring it, an' if I like ter split wood
yere I split it. These woods is jest as much mine as
his'n, an' I don't take my orders from no nigger, I
don't keer how black he is—not if he's as black as the
devil!"

"Complexion," said Moloch—"complexion, sah, am
a mattah ob taste, and has no bearin's on the present
discussion. All I say is, yo' kine intentions am dis-
appreciated an' yo' presence am unnecessary. As a
man of sense, yo' ain't agoin' to bring good game to
be frowed in the ribbah, nor yet to come aroun' where
yo' isn' wanted. Good-mornin', sah;" and Moloch
went into the house and shut the door behind him.

The stranger stood awhile rubbing his beard and staring at the house, and finally turned and sauntered away.

Moloch had been right in supposing that the venison and kindlings had been intended as love-offerings to Leonora — the one, perhaps, to kindle, the other to feed, a reciprocal feeling on her part. Doubtless the stranger is open to the charge of being precipitate in manifesting his sentiments, however they may have done credit to his taste and discrimination. But then his excuse was in his circumstances.

He was one upon whom society may be said to have had a stronger claim than upon most men, yet he had left it for its good and his own. The exigencies of his profession, which was that of obtaining a living by any means whatever except legitimate work, had driven him away, and society was still seeking, by means of her sheriffs and deputies, to bring him back to her maternal arms.

After a season of lonely wandering he had met Leonora, and, being no less susceptible than another, in his own way, had fallen a ready prey to her beauty.

He was deeply imbued with the opinion, beloved of the American blackguard and ignoramus, that "all men are born free and equal"; from which he deduces the idea that he, personally, is as good as any, and better than most.

Therefore this particular vagabond, knowing of no distinction in breeding, manner, and habit of life, saw no reason, since it appeared that he and Leonora were neighbors, why they should not become friends and more.

If he saw a difference between her and such a
15

woman as those to whom he had been accustomed, it was only that she was infinitely more attractive, and so infinitely more to be desired.

So he determined to settle near her home and win ,her, not knowing why he should be unsuccessful, nor why one settler should not be a fair match for the daughter of another.

He knew that he was ugly, and was proud of it; also that he was strong and large of stature, and that women care more for strength than beauty in a man.

He thought that he was a good shot and an expert trapper—what more could a backwoods girl want in a husband? He reconnoitred the valley, and found that the cabin was the only one there. He watched the place, took stock of Moloch and Mr. Willoughby, began his wooing with the friendly advances to which Moloch had taken exception, and hung about in the cover, hungry for a sight of Leonora.

Now, Moloch's warning encouraged him greatly, for he said to himself, "If that old feller in there the nigger calls his 'employer' is so shy o' strangers he's got a reason for it, and there can't be but one—same as mine.

"If he'll listen to reason, me an' him can pull together first-class.

"He needs a young feller about to help run the ranch an' stand by him in case o' trouble, an' I'm the feller! He'll be glad ter git me when he sees I ain't one to give him away. There ain't no reason but what, ef I work the thing right, I shouldn't be able to make it go. My act is to stand in with the old bird, make his acquaintance, shake his hand, let him know he ain't got nothin' ter fear from *me*, do his odd jobs fer him, give him a hide or a hunk o' meat now and then, and be good to him.

"I'll build me a shack up-stream thar whar they's a nateral clearin'—whar th' fish is swarmin' in th' water an' th' deer runnin' by, an' old bars eatin' huckleberries off'n th' rocks over th' back yard—an' I'll be his best an' only friend.

"The girl, she'll take ter me quick enough when she gits ter know me—bein' the only man about, an' a hearty one at that.

"It's a dead easy thing—an' in a year, or mebbe less, sure as my name's Andy Jimson, I'm in clover. That's what! And the girl's mine." Which, as his name *was* Andy Jimson, augured ill for the peace of Leonora.

"I'll lay for the old man an' have a talk with him," said Jimson.

Mr. Willoughby was easily found by the river. He was sitting and thinking his own thoughts, which, as we know, were by no means complimentary to his fellow-men, to begin with, when a large stone fell splashing into his favorite pool and sent his pet trout darting to shelter. The disturbance had been caused by Jimson, who was to be seen, much to the old gentleman's wrath, clumsily descending the opposite bank.

"Keep away, will you!" said Mr. Willoughby, angrily. But the intruder gave no heed, and, crossing where the stream ran shallow among the stones, soon stood by his side.

Mr. Willoughby got up, and the two men stared at each other a moment—the one with the mien of him who sees a trespasser disporting himself upon his lawn; the other with curiosity.

"What do you want here?" said Mr. Willoughby.

"How are ye?" said the stranger, extending his foul paw, of which the old gentleman took no notice.

"I have not had a diagnosis lately and cannot give you the information you are so good as to seek. *I asked what you wanted here?*"

Jimson did not quite understand the words; the manner was clear enough, but he was not to be put out by that, at the beginning of his undertaking.

He shifted his pose to the other foot, and looked sulky. "Fishin'?" he asked.

"No. Hunting elk!" said Mr. Willoughby. "Is that all you wanted to know?"

"There's a heap sight more I'd like to know," said the vagabond. "Live about here?"

"What business is that of yours?" said Mr. Willoughby.

Now, the evident wrath of the old gentleman at being addressed, and his unwillingness to answer civil questions, could have but one interpretation in the vagabond's mind, and strengthened his original opinion that Mr. Willoughby was in hiding, like himself, from the just vengeance of the law. This gave him a fellow-feeling.

"I don't mean you no hurt by askin'," said he. "I lead a kinder quiet life here, and like ter know my neighbors."

"How the devil should I know about your neighbors!" cried the old gentleman. "Go and ask *them!*"

"I reckon you're about all there be," said Jimson. "You and yer folks. Leastways, I hain't seen no others. I've settled here for a bit, an' my camp is just up the river near the gap."

This was more than Mr. Willoughby could bear. A stranger—and *such* a stranger—in his valley! To be sure, it was no more *his* valley, in fact, than another's. But Mr. Willoughby, during his many years of undisputed possession, had come to regard it as his own, and it never occurred to him to doubt his right to turn out trespassers. In short, he was in the habit of counting himself "monarch of all he surveyed," forgetting entirely that he had never surveyed it, and that a survey accepted by the State, accompanied by a claim filed in the Land-office, was necessary ere he could call it his own.

"Look here, my man," said he, "I want no neighbors. I'm not accustomed to argue. Get out of this!"

"I've got as good right ter be here ez you," said Jimson.

"Name your price and clear out," said Mr. Willoughby.

Jimson laughed. "Some day maybe I'll make a deal with you," said he. "Jest now I got my reasons, like you have, fer stayin' where money ain't so much good as leaves off the trees. An' now look a' here. I come here an' talk white an' civil ter you, an' you up an' answer me mean an' say, 'Clear out!' Tha's all right; I ain't kickin' at that, 'cause I see how yer fixed. When a feller's layin' low an' keepin' out er th' way, ez me and you be, he don't like ter hev no one come snoopin' round. His fust thought, when he sees a man, is: 'Is that chap a deputy-sheriff, an' is he after me?' That's likely what you're thinkin' 'bout me now. Wal, make yerself easy. I ain't no deputy, an' I'm keepin' out er their way too. I dunno what you done back in th' States, or wherever you

come from, but, judgin' from the way ye keep in the
woods, I reckon t'warn't nothin' short o' burglary;
an', what's more, I don't keer. I ain't a-goin' to put
no one on yer track. Now, you're a-livin' all alone
with a nigger an' a gal, an' I'm all *sole* alone. I kin
mebbe be useful to ye an' you ter me. My camp's
up th' river. Ef yer want anythin' done, jest let me
know; an' I hope ter see a lot more er you an' yer
folks, an' I shall alwers treat ye white. Now we know
each other."

Mr. Willoughby by this time was too wroth to speak.
He aimed a furious blow at the obliging stranger, but
was slow and stiff, and Jimson dodged it and passed
on, laughing and saying, "I don't fight with old fellers
like you be."

Now, it was not Mr. Willoughby's age that prevented Jimson from returning the blow—he had no such
scruples. "I'm willin' ter be friends wi' th' girl's
folks, ef they'll let me, while I'm a-makin' up ter *her*.
They may come handy. But ef they *will* quarrel an'
make me kill 'em off, th' old man an' th' nigger, what's
ter pervent me hevin' her an' th' hull outfit all ter
myself?"

After that he became persistent in his attentions.
He kept on bringing offerings to the door, and was
often seen near the clearing.

Mr. Willoughby's wrath increased as he realized his
helplessness. He could not invoke the law. Doubtless the man was a criminal; but even if the authori-
ties were looking for him, and even if they could be
persuaded to send out so far on a wild-goose chase
after him, Mr. Willoughby would not have his valley
invaded by a *posse comitatus*.

Nor would he resort to unlawful means. But he and Moloch both devoutly hoped that occasion might arise when it would become necessary and justifiable to shoot the intruder.

And Leonora — though she would on no account have wished any one ill — would not have heard the news of his demise with any deep regret.

It is bad enough (they say) to have an unwelcome and obstinate suitor at all. Under the circumstances it was a nightmare.

He left her in no doubt of his intentions, for he had succeeded one day in waylaying her on the trail near the clearing as she went to gather violets, and assured her of his devotion in lurid terms.

She had then spoken gently with him, and tried to explain the hopelessness of the case to his satisfaction.

He had taken her refusal as a matter of course, alleging that he thought none the worse of her for being shy at first—a customary and becoming trait in woman—but that he did not give up hope and meant to succeed in time. She had argued patiently, and he had grinned. She had tried the effect of bitter words, and he had said that he liked a girl none the less for a sharp tongue, and finally she had gone home to Moloch, who, forgetting his lame arm, had set out straightway in search of Mr. Jimson and had not found him.

She persuaded Moloch not to quarrel with him, for the butler's hurt placed him at great disadvantage — the man seemed a desperado — and "if anything should happen to you, Moloch," said she, "what would become of my father and me?"

Then one day Moloch went to the sound, taking her with him, well armed — for he would hardly let her out of his sight—and there she received the letter from Moorhead and left the answer that Tom found at Seattle, saying that she needed him and bidding him come at once.

XXVII

THOMAS MOORHEAD arrived at the mouth of the Yawmish, and had to find his way thence as best he could. There he dropped his first name, to be Norman Moorhead like his brother, slung his pack, shouldered his rifle, and set out to follow the course of the stream as the only sure way of reaching the valley.

The banks of the river were pathless and hard of passage, and the traveller made but slow progress. The river was his only guide, and he never allowed himself to go beyond the sound of its voice, even to avoid the obstacles that sometimes rendered its banks almost impassable, but took the country as he found it, toiling on over rough and rocky hills, whose stones bruised his feet even through the thickness of his heavy boots; through dense brush that seemed almost to stifle him in its damp and heavy foliage, or tore and pricked him with thorns and brambles; up slopes that were slippery with the dry and smoothly matted needles; on welcome stretches of clear lowland, or along the edge of a precipice up among the laurels, with the river hundreds of feet below; through places where the trees had fallen and massed their enormous bodies and locked limbs in tangled heaps; down deep ravines, where tributary streams crossed the way up and down, in and out; he climbed and slid, and walked and ran, waded, swam, and scrambled, and felt his pack grow heavier hour by hour as his unaccustomed shoulders turned sore under the chafing straps. His heavy boots, stiff with frequent wetting and drying, formed thick creases that pressed and galled his ankles.

At night he made his fire, ate, and threw himself down wherever darkness happened to overtake him, and dreamed strange dreams that ended in a sense of rolling down steep places into the water. He saw no sign of life, except a flock of the " meat-birds " that follow men about the woods for the offal of their game.

On the morning of the fourth day he came to a well-defined trail beside the river, and by afternoon found himself rounding the base of a high hill, which, he could see by a glimpse here and there, was the end of a long range. Another range stood parallel to this, and between them the river flowed in a fair land of alternate wood and meadow, out of a gap between towering mountains, and he knew that he was in the valley where he was to meet the mistress he had never seen and claim the bride he had never won. Should he meet her? What was she like? Beautiful, of course, but how? Would she really mistake him for his brother? Why not? How would she receive him? What had been the need that had made her urge him to come to her at once?

As he asked himself these questions, impatience overcame his weariness, and he went on painfully, limping away at a fair pace.

It was late in the day when he came to the clearing and saw the house in its pleasant garden, and an old man and young girl sitting on the veranda.

Now, up to this time his strange undertaking had seemed to him a sort of game to be played and enjoyed. The moment he saw Leonora he began to feel the reality and seriousness of what he was doing. His heart almost failed him. He yielded to a sudden impulse and turned back; then he laughed at the futility of it. "What am I turning round for?" he thought. "To go home? I would if I could. I only wish I were well out of this. But it's too late now—so here goes."

The people on the veranda did not see him as he came up. Leonora was reading aloud, and Tom heard with pleasure the sweet cadence of her voice and the delicate accent of her words:

> "With me upon this strip of verdure strewn
>   That just divides the desert from the sown,
> Where name of slave and sultan is forgot—
>   And peace to Mahmoud, on his golden throne.
>
> "A book of verses underneath the bough,
>   A loaf of bread, a jug of wine, and thou
> Beside me, singing in the wilderness—
>   Ah, wilderness were paradise enow!"

"So I should think, even without the 'jug of wine,'" said Tom, pleasantly. He had mustered up all his courage, since there was no turning back, and had determined to face the matter out coolly.

The girl sprang up, and her father rose slowly and looked puzzled and vexed.

Mr. Moorhead again, I think, is it not?" said he, with no warmth of greeting in his manner. "May I ask—"

But here Leonora, feeling that her father was about

to say something disagreeable, interrupted him and came forward, holding out her hand.

"Oh! father," said she, "how *very* good that your friend has come!"

"I don't see it!" said Mr. Willoughby, in a very audible undertone. "*My friend!*"

"Rest," said Leonora, giving Tom a chair. "I will come back in a moment. Father!"

She took the old gentleman by the arm and led him into the house.

"Father," she said, "what *could* be better? Ask your friend to stay; for surely at such a time as this, with that *creature* lurking about, I cannot well have a friend too many, and Mr. Moorhead has been your guest and is a gentleman. Ask him to stay, for my sake, father dear; you don't know how good it is to me, after all that has happened, to see a pleasant face."

"It may be you are right," said Mr. Willoughby. It's a pity—a great pity. But I am old, and Moloch is still lame of his arm, and a young man who knows our ways may be of use, especially if it makes you feel more easy, Leonora."

So in a minute he came out to Moorhead and greeted him with courtesy: "Mr. Moorhead, I am glad to see you again, and Miss Willoughby and I hope you can make it convenient to stay with us awhile."

"Yes," said Leonora, "we are glad to see you, Mr. Moorhead."

Tom was surprised at first at a certain coolness in Leonora's manner. He had expected and dreaded a lover's warm welcome, had begun already to feel ashamed of his false position, and yet had been afraid not to act the lover, and had nerved himself to play his part. He was much relieved at the lack of affection in her greeting, until he remembered that Mr. Willoughby did not know of the engagement, and then he wondered how it would be when he should find himself alone with Leonora. Happily for him he was too bodily weary to be nervous, and that saved him much distress.

The three sat together awhile, Mr. Willoughby exchanging cool civilities with the guest, and Leonora watching him with a critical expression.

At first, to his relief, she avoided meeting his eye, and looked bashfully down when he glanced at her— a thing he seldom dared; but when at last their eyes fairly met he had an unpleasant sense of transparency, as if she had been looking through into his very mind.

She spoke little, and he fancied there was distress in her voice.

"How do you do, Moloch?" said he, when the worthy butler made his appearance to announce dinner.

"Mr. Moorhead, sah. Ah'm glad you've come back *at last,* sah," said that functionary, with an air of reserve.

"Thank you kindly, Moloch," said Tom.

Tom—now T. Norman Moorhead—dreaded above all things the hour when he should meet Leonora alone.

His brother's plan had seemed to him at first both dishonorable and absurd. He would never have attempted such an imposition upon any one he knew; but until he had seen Leonora he had thought of her rather as a character in a play in which he was to take part than as a real being.

Nevertheless, he had thought of her so much that he had become, unconsciously, almost fond of her; and from the moment he saw her a deep respect and admiration for her began to grow upon him.

He slept little that night in spite of his tired limbs. How can a man sleep when he finds himself in love and in a most awkward position at the same time?

He lay wondering how she would treat him, and how he should conduct himself towards her; thinking what a fool his brother was to wish to give her up; half inclined to tell her the whole story; deeply averse to the thought of carrying out the fraud he had been so weak as to undertake.

When at last he slept, it was on the determination to disclose himself in the morning and tell her everything. But when the morning came he saw reasons why he should not. He thought of his brother's accusation of ingratitude, and how just it had seemed at the time; of Mrs. Merivale's convincing arguments, and the rosy light in which she had shown him the plan; of his own position when exposed to their anger and the scorn of Leonora herself — she looked capable of despising him very thoroughly; moreover, he could not bear to give up the undertaking itself, which, in spite of his self-contempt, had a singular charm for him since he had met the object of his quest.

He could wait—he could confess at any time; but having once confessed, there was no way to undo the effect. He would not be able to go home again to his brother—he would have seen the last of Leonora—he would have no mercy from either.

He felt like a man in a nightmare.

The lady of the valley seemed no more eager than he for the dreaded interview to take place.

He felt sure now that she had no suspicion that he was not her betrothed, but thought her strangely shy of him. She avoided being left alone with him with such success that the ordeal he dreaded was put off for two days. And yet it seemed to him that she did not regard him altogether with disfavor. Sometimes, again, he thought she did. There was a certain tenderness in her manner towards him, but it seemed of pity rather than of love, and so puzzled him not a little.

At length Mr. Willoughby, sitting at dinner, espied through the window a blue heron. The old gentleman hated blue herons because they destroy fish—a privilege he wished to monopolize; so he snatched up a rifle and set out after the bird, leaving Leonora to do the honors of the table.

Tom was seized with an inward panic. He could not for his life lay his tongue to a word, and he sat embarrassed before her in fear of what she might say. It seemed many minutes before she spoke, and then she said, simply and coolly:

"Norman, you found my letter at Seattle?"

"Yes," said he, "and came as soon as I might. I have told you why it was not sooner. Why did you write me so urgently? I hope I am not too late?"

"No, you are not too late. I wished you to come, because I am fairly persecuted by the man of whom my father spoke last night."

Tom heard her story with rising anger against the vagabond and sympathy for her.

"Now, at least, you'll not be imprisoned and besieged as you have been," said he, "for you have an escort."

Here Mr. Willoughby came back, without the blue heron.

"Did you get him, father?" Leonora asked.

"No, dear, I haven't your aim; but I frightened him terribly."

So that dreaded ordeal — the first *tête-à-tête* — was over. There had been no tender passages — nothing had been said about the engagement.

There was already a bond of sympathy between them—namely, Jimson. She understood Tom's genuine sympathy and indignation, and was thankful for a friend.

That afternoon she took down her rifle, and said, "Now, if you care for a walk, I'm going out, Norman."

Tom began to like his middle name.

"I'll be very glad," said he, and they went out together among the glories of the woods and hills. He looked into her eyes, heard her voice, touched her hand, and saw her grace in every little movement.

When they were nearly at home again Leonora suddenly laid her hand on his arm. He looked up, and saw the tall figure and ugly face of the vagabond close before them on the narrow trail.

"Say nothing to him—not a word," Leonora whispered; and as they walked on the man drew aside to let them pass, but glared out of the bushes with an evil look at Tom, who returned it with a cool stare.

"So that's your friend?" said he to Leonora.

"The man I told you about," said she.

"Hm!" said Tom.

The days went on pleasantly enough. Tom had given up the idea of confession, owning to himself that he had not the courage for it. He had been considering how he should bring his brother to his senses and back to his allegiance. But when they met the man in the woods, and Leonora held his arm, he suddenly felt installed as her protector, and liked it hugely. It occurred to him that he liked it too well to give it up.

So he said to himself, "If Charley's fool enough to throw away his chance, let him. He deserves to lose her. Now the only question is, can *I* win her? On my own merits? I want nothing better than that on earth. And I'll do it."

This resolution made him at once happy and miserable. He was tormented by the two worst tortures devised for man—Love and Conscience.

Conscience said, "If you persist in this fraud, your love shall be a curse."

Love said, "If you listen to Conscience, I'm off."

Moloch went to the sound.

After his return an unaccountable change took place in Leonora. Her father was surprised, Moloch delighted beyond measure.

She had never been in such high spirits before. She went about singing as of old. She laughed a great deal, sometimes without apparent reason. She showered small acts of kindness upon Mr. Willoughby and the worthy butler; and Moloch saw her go out into the clearing and catch and kiss each of the five ponies, then into the shed and kiss the cow.

Tom had his share of the change, but did not altogether profit by it. She was far less shy of him than

16

before; but that touch of sympathy in her manner was gone, and he even felt that he amused her without intending to—a most uncomfortable feeling, as every one knows.

He was not surprised, when he came to think it over, that she never spoke to him of their engagement. It was natural that she should wait for him to begin. But he was sure that *she* must wonder very much that he, whom she believed to be her promised husband, should never speak to her of love, especially since she must have got her ideas of that interesting topic from books, wherein love is made at great length and with much embroidery of words. But he could not bring himself to speak of it, nor could he abandon the hope of speaking by-and-by.

However, there are happily other things to talk about, even for a man and maid, and they got on well together, on the whole. The more they were together the more bitterly ashamed of himself he became. He could hardly look her in the face, and when he approached her it was with a sense of meanness that made him very humble indeed.

He hoped that she saw only the humility and not its cause. He also longed for an opportunity to save her life, or do battle for her in some way, so that he might establish an existence of his own in her eyes, and not be forced to hide in his brother's personality, which, he began to feel, was too small for him and not good enough for her.

He was in hopes that Jimson—the vagabond—would turn up and do something outrageous, that he might have at him in honor of his lady; but Jimson stayed away.

"Norman," Leonora said to him one day, "it seems to me that you have changed a great deal." He looked at her, and then his eyes dropped before hers.

"I hope I have," said he.

"Sometimes," she went on, "I find it hard almost to believe that you are the same person."

They sat silent for a moment, and he felt uncomfortably that she was looking at his face.

"The years make great changes," said he, "and so does a beard."

She laughed. "Yes, but a beard does not change a man's whole being—does it? His manner and way of thinking and feeling? I did not think even the years could do all that, and yet—you are so different."

Moorhead suffered inward panic, but struggled hard to seem all calm without.

"Improved, I hope?" said he.

"I won't say that," she replied; "only changed. You used to seem so fond of yourself when you were here before. That was bad. Now you seem—well—anything *but* proud of yourself, almost ashamed."

Did she know—had she begun to suspect? He gave a quick, frightened glance at her face, but it told him nothing. It was just serenely beautiful.

"Oh! You needn't be afraid," she said; "*I* don't care. I don't like it, of course. Still, I think I liked the other less—what you were before, I mean. There's hope for a man ashamed of himself. But when he's proud of himself there's not, I think. Yes, on the whole, perhaps you have improved—not that it matters!"

He began to believe that she had found him out;

but though he was much beside her that day she gave no further sign of knowledge or suspicion.

Meanwhile the man of the woods was not seen, and Leonora was not so much afraid of him. It was seldom out of Tom's mind, however, and the thought of him, though it brought forth no charming image, was pleasanter to the poor fellow than the thought of himself, whom he had come to regard as no better than a rogue.

He took long walks alone, and, in secret places, devoted himself to certain gymnastic exercises of his college days. He hung his roll of blankets to a limb, and punched it, right and left, by the half-hour.

Moloch saw him and told Leonora.

"Dear me!" said she, "I wonder why he does that? Did you offer to help Mr. Moorhead, Moloch?"

"No'm," said Moloch; "no, Miss 'Nora."

"Then do so at once, please."

Moorhead declined the offer of aid. "I am just trying to soften them a little," said he, knocking the bundle up among the leaves, "and now"—meeting it as it came back with a tremendous right-hander that sent it over the branch from which it sprang, and wheeling to stop it with his left as it fell on the other side of the limb—"I'm done."

"Now, what am Mr. Moorhead's purpose?" Moloch wondered, and Leonora also exercised her imagination in vain.

They lived to be enlightened.

One morning, very early, Leonora thought she heard voices. One was Tom's, and he spoke sharply and to the point.

"Get out of this!"

The other was gruff and harsh and surly—she shuddered as she heard it—and what it said was abusive and blasphemous.

By this time she had on a wrapper, had hurried to her window, and was peeping out.

There was her unwelcome suitor, the vagabond, uncouth, lowering, and savage, trying to tower with his slouching bulk above her friend Mr. Moorhead, who for his part refused to be towered over, and stood alert and cool, looking unusually pleased.

Mr. Jimson was scowling his ugliest; Mr. Moorhead was smiling gayly, only that there was something peculiar behind the smile. She had never seen that look before, but knew by instinct what it meant—fight, and the joy of it.

She felt afterwards, when it was over and there was time to think, that she ought to have roused her father and Moloch to prevent possible bloodshed; but she was so absorbed in what was going on that it never entered her head at the time.

"Then look out for yourself!" Tom was saying, quietly, drawing back a little at the same time, and resting his weight on his left foot.

Suddenly his laughing eyes flashed—lightning out of clear sky—and his left arm shot out.

It was a beautiful blow. Leonora could see that, but she wondered at the effect, for she did not know how much went to make up its perfection: how the left foot was raised an instant to the other knee; how the head went a little down, the shoulder swung forward; the right hand held itself ready, guarding chin and wind at once; the right foot pushed hard from the ground; the muscles tightened from breast to groin; and the whole weight and force of back and loins, chest, head, and shoulders—the whole muscular force of foot and calf and thigh, body and arm—concentrated in an instant on that one clinched fist that caught the fellow's chin and drove his head back on his round shoulders.

Before he could reel backward came the right hand upon his neck, hurling him dazed against the logs of the wall; but he had a hard head and staggered forward, wasting his wind in curses, and swinging his arms like the sails of a windmill, beating the empty air with blows that seemed fit to crush a skull or throw a shoulder out of gear.

But Tom had sprung lightly back, landing in position to strike: left hand well up; right just below and behind the left; weight on the left knee, and right foot poised on its ball.

A slight movement to one side, while the big fists flapped harmless about the back of his head; another straight, quick blow, in the body this time, and Tom stepped forward, the right foot coming up behind the left, still ready for another.

The objectionable suitor gasped and grunted, staggered backward, and put his hand behind him.

"Look out," cried Leonora from the window; "he's got a knife!" But before the words were well out of her mouth, or the knife from its sheath, came the terrible right again hard on the man's jaw. His head struck the wall, and the knife flew sideways from his hand and stuck in the ground.

Tom's face was set and stern now, and glorious (Leonora thought) with a right wrath. He moved like the flash of a sword. The sight of the knife had made him mad with a cold wrath. Left—right; left —right: the blows told heavily on face and body.

Leonora wondered that the other man could live through it. Indeed, any ordinary man must have fallen before now; but this one, calloused by hardship and a brute's life in the forest, had the toughness of a beast, and lacked the quivering, sensitive nerves that are the prey of a clever boxer.

Again and again Tom struck him at the juncture of neck and jaw, expecting at each blow to see him drop.

Suddenly he rallied, maddened with pain and the closeness of defeat, and, swinging his great fist with all his might, landed a round blow upon Tom's head close to the temple.

Tom reeled away, shaken in every muscle, and stood there a moment dazed and quivering; but none but a practised boxer could have told the state in which the blow left him, for the well-trained feet kept their firm position, the hands took their places, and he stood, to all appearance, as firm as a bronze statue of Self-defence.

On came the other, mad and exulting, and flung himself upon his foe.

Again the left foot rose, the left arm straightened with the whole weight of the body behind it — a mechanical movement without much force of its own, but accurate. The adversary supplied the force; his head, rushing forward, met the fist just as the arm stiffened.

Suppose an upright post, with a crosspiece reaching out from it horizontally at about the height of your chin. It is a harmless object. But quarrel with that post, become enraged, try to strike it, hurl yourself bodily at it, and let your chin strike the end of that crosspiece.

The post has exerted no force, and yet you will find yourself rolling on the ground with a head full of pain and flashes.

That is the effect of a straight counter, such as Tom gave Mr. Jimson.

It struck him full on the forehead and down he went. He was up again in an instant, and rushed at Tom, who had recovered strength again, and met him with a right-hand blow in the midriff.

Then Leonora saw the savage-looking fellow double over, and heard him groan and gasp, trying to catch his breath.

As he bent forward, Tom stepped a little aside, lifted his chin with a quick upward stroke of the left fist, and put all his force into a tremendous blow with his right, just where the jawbone joins the neck. The man tottered, fell heavily, and lay like a log.

"Oh, you have killed him!" Leonora cried.

"Not at all," said Tom.

"Killed whom? Killed what?" Mr. Willoughby called, from his room; and Moloch came out barefoot.

"You done well, Mr. Moorhead, sah. Is he daid?"

"No," said Tom. "He'll get up and go away soon. And he won't come here again."

When Jimson came to, the three men were standing over him, for Mr. Willoughby had arrived hastily clad.

The fellow rose with a sidelong movement and

slouched away, looking back over his shoulder as he went.

"*What* did you hit him with?" Mr. Willoughby asked, smiling at Tom with the first cordiality he had shown him.

"Nature's weapons."

"Well done, sir! But you ought to have used a club. No club could have been too hard or too heavy."

Then the door opened, and Leonora came, pale and anxious, all in a flutter, and held out her hand to Moorhead, saying, "You are hurt!"

"Not the least, thank you," said Tom, holding the little hand as long as he might.

"But he gave you a dreadful blow!"

"Did he? One doesn't notice much at the time."

"But you must have hurt *him* terribly; he behaved, at last, as if you had shot him."

"Deceitful and reprehensible of him," said Moorhead. "I didn't."

"I have read in the papers about fights—prize-fights—but I had no idea they were so frightful to see. I'm glad you are safe!"

"I am sorry you saw it, Miss Willoughby."

Now this was not true. T. Norman Moorhead had never been so glad of anything in his life.

"So am I," said Leonora, beaming upon him. "It was dreadful—horrible!" she added, smiling with genuine pleasure. "But oh, I'm afraid that horrid creature will do you some injury!"

"Not likely," said Mr. Willoughby. "That kind of animal is generally cowed by a thrashing. Besides, Mr. Moorhead seems able to take care of himself."

"*Why* did you do it ?" Leonora asked.

"You said you didn't want him about.   And then he was impudent."

"Oh ! What did he say ?"

Moorhead smiled—a restrained smile.   "I think I won't repeat his remarks, if you please. I haven't his vocabulary ; and if I had, the result might not be edifying."

"Oh !" said Leonora.

When they were alone together afterwards she said, "Thank you !" and looked as if she meant it.

"Not at all.   I enjoyed it," said Tom.

XXVIII

AFTER the fight Tom felt that he had a real claim of his own on the lady's acquaintance, apart from that his brother had made over to him.

He saw that she still looked curiously at him from time to time, as if he puzzled her; but when their eyes met there was a far more kindly light in hers than there had been before. It was plain, too, that he had completely won the heart of Moloch, and the sense of having a sound friend by, of whatever complexion, was a comfort to him. He was recovering his own individuality by degrees, and grew bolder in his own boots.

One day he was watching her little brown fingers as they moved deftly over her needlework, she sitting on one of her favorite logs and leaning back on a curving arm of vine-maple, he lying on the moss at her feet.

"Leonora!" said he.

It was the first time he had called her Leonora. Before the others she had been Miss Willoughby, of course; and at other times, not quite daring to say Leonora (which had become a very sacred word to him), he had called her "You."

Her eyes darkened as she looked down at him and she dropped her work.

"What right—" she began, and stopped and turned

her face away, for his was more earnest than she liked.

"What right?" said he, daring to be reproachful. "Why, surely I may call the girl who has promised—" and *he* stopped and looked away also.

He all but forgot, at times, that it was not he but his brother to whom she was engaged; because he felt engaged to her himself, knowing that he belonged to her, whether she would have him or no. When he remembered, he could not bring himself to say, "who has promised to marry me." He had not told her a lie yet, and did not mean to. He had allowed her to think, if she would, that he was *C. Norman Moorhead,* but he had never before come so near claiming actively his brother's identity; so he could not finish what he had begun to say.

"Well?" said Leonora, turning sharply upon him. Her face had a grieved and anxious look.

"Nothing," said he. "Of course, if you don't wish it I won't. But I thought—"

"You thought?" said she, and waited with parted lips and eyes full of question.

Moorhead was very busy tearing up bits of moss and laying them by.

"You said something about a promise?" she suggested.

He told the truth, as far as his speech went. "I had no right," said he; "I beg your pardon."

Then, if he had only known, the anxiety went out of her face, and there came to it a gleam of indescribable sweetness and forgiveness. Forgiveness for what? Time may tell. If not, perhaps Leonora will tell herself. Meanwhile her face was pretty to see, as when, on a spring day, light and shadow chase each other about among the flowers. Pleasure came next, and mischief, and her eyes laughed, but he did not see them.

"Please explain," she said, very coldly indeed. "I do not understand. You" (with immense dignity) "used my name!"

He was still busy with moss.

"You see," he said, "you have called me Norman —once or twice."

"Oh! Have I? I beg your pardon most humbly. And you want to be revenged by calling me Leonora. I am very sorry, Mr. Moorhead. I won't call you Norman again. It shall be Mr. Moorhead — *always* Mr. Moorhead, and, if you please, *Miss Willoughby.*"

"As you will," said he; "I will not offend you again."

So they dropped the subject and talked pleasantly of books.

He wondered what her objection was to his calling her Leonora. Certainly his brother had always done so. Perhaps it was only one of those fancies maidens are said to cherish suddenly. He had not offended in any other way—so far as he knew.

Perhaps it was better so. At all events, she was quite gracious in other respects — *so* gracious and sweet and kind that his conscience hurt him more than ever.

If he could have heard what she said to herself afterwards he would have wondered what she meant.

"A few days ago he proved himself a *man.* Now he shows himself a gentleman. And he has a conscience. But then—how *could* he? How will it end?"

After this his experience with womankind as exemplified in Leonora was strange and various, and he learned to marvel at the elasticity of her mood.

Sometimes he felt himself an accepted lover, admitted to his brother's rights, and suffered shame accordingly; sometimes a mere acquaintance, and suffered as with mental cold and hunger; sometimes a sort of dog or other possession of no great value, to be made careless and thankless use of and generally ill-treated; and this, by contrast, he enjoyed in a humble way, because it seemed akin to his true position; he had learned to take a snub from his lady as a favor.

Leonora seemed happier than she had ever seemed before, and was very good to her father and Moloch.

One evening, at dinner, she turned suddenly to poor Tom, who was trying to eat soup neatly without looking at his plate, because he had other use for his eyes, and said:

"Mr. Moorhead, do you remember the day you shot at the elk?" She had rather avoided reminiscences heretofore, for which Tom had been thankful, as he knew that they were the weak point in his position, in spite of his brother's teachings.

It happened, however, that Charles had told him all about the "elk," so he answered, glibly, being careful to say nothing literally untrue:

"Happily it was not hurt. It was one of your cows that had strayed into the woods."

She looked a little surprised, and then laughed. "Never mind," said she. "It *was* a bad shot; but it's as well you missed, since it happened to be the cow. But when you saved me from that wounded bear, that made up for it bravely, didn't it?"

Now this was very strange — strange and dreadful. Charles had never said a word about the wounded bear, or any other bear in particular, and he certainly would not have concealed through modesty any incident redounding to his personal glory.

Tom felt a pang of jealousy that Charles should have been so privileged as to save Leonora, and of rage that he had left him in ignorance of the fact. What *could* he say? He certainly did not remember.

So he hedged, inanely:

"It is sometimes easier to shoot a bear than a cow."

"Is it?" said Leonora. "I didn't know."

Mr. Willoughby stared. It seemed to him that Leonora was developing a vein of flippancy quite new to her, and he did not like it.

"*I* knew nothing of Mr. Moorhead's shooting at my cow or saving my daughter," he said, crossly. He was thinking what else might have taken place without his knowledge, and that perhaps Leonora had better see less of the young man in future.

Before the fight he had looked upon the guest as a mere puppy, and had never considered the possibility of his daughter's taking a fancy to him; but since that event he had felt more respect for Moorhead, and the change in Leonora's manner troubled him. He feared that she was too well pleased with the young man's victory over the uncalled-for Jimson.

"Never mind, father mine," said she. "The safety of your daughter weighs against the fright occasioned to your cow."

"But I can recall neither cow nor bear," said Mr. Willoughby.

"The bear is *beyond* recall; the cow is where she

belongs, and does not need it," said Leonora. "And
surely you have not forgotten, father, how you fell
into the deep eddy just above the rapids, when you
were after that very large trout, and how Mr. Moorhead pulled you out at the risk of his life. *You* remember, don't you, Mr. Moorhead?"

Tom began to see now how futile it had been for
Charles to try to teach him the events of his stay in
the valley. Here three incidents had been mentioned
—one he knew of and could talk about, guardedly;
the other two either his brother had neglected to tell
him, or he himself had utterly forgotten.

"You remember; do you not, Mr. Moorhead?"
said Leonora again.

She was leaning forward waiting his answer, and
Mr. Willoughby was staring at him with an expression of amazement, which Moorhead attributed to his
own delay in answering.

"He—Mr. Willoughby—was very wet!" he said, des-
perately. Then, inspired by the sudden thought that
Moloch had told him the river was unusually high, he
added, "The water was much lower then."

"Sir!" said Mr. Willoughby, sharply, unable to
retain his wrath any longer, "Leonora! what do you
mean? Pulled *me* out? *I* was very wet? What *do
you mean, sir?*"

"I was only trying Mr. Moorhead's memory, father,"
said Leonora. "It's a very good memory, indeed. *I*
can't recall any such incident with mine!"

Moorhead turned fiery-red, seeing at last the trap
she had set for him. Mr. Willoughby laid down his
knife and fork, and stared straight at him as if de-
manding an explanation.

Leonora bent her head a little and looked amused, casting furtive glances, now sidelong at her father, now under arched brows across the table at Moorhead, who could not help thinking, in spite of his misery, how pretty the glances were.

But the need of allaying the old gentleman's wrath was imminent, and it was written upon Leonora's face that she did not care, and meant him to get out of it as best he might.

Then a luminous, desperate idea flashed into his mind, and he looked up boldly and smiled. For the first time he felt that his legal training had not been wasted—he needed it all for this crisis.

"Pardon me, Mr. Willoughby," said he, pleasantly. "I don't wonder at your indignation, unless you happen to be aware of a rather new and distinctly absurd point of etiquette that was probably not the fashion before you withdrew yourself from the world—namely, that when a lady recalls a reminiscence a man must in courtesy seem to remember, and make an evasive answer rather than seem to doubt or forget. You doubtless see the point, which is rather a fine one even for social ethics? To set up one's own memory in opposition to a lady's is analogous to disputing her, and so may be considered a rudeness. Otherwise, of course, when the reminiscence is brought up for the sake of actual information, *then* one may venture to differ; but when it comes up in a merely conversational way—when the question is, as it were, only a form of narrative—you follow me, sir?—then the idea is that a direct difference of opinion is tantamount to a contradiction. I, of course, do not remember any such incident as that which Miss Willoughby has been pleased playfully to suggest, but how could I say so? Therefore I avoided contradiction by saying, 'Mr. Willoughby was very wet,' which was a truism, assuming (as one must) Miss Willoughby's reminiscence to have been real; and I said, 'The river was lower then,' which, you will remember, was the fact. I owe you an apology, sir, for the personal nature of the first remark. I was rather surprised at what had just been said, and it was the first thing that entered my head."

Mr. Willoughby burst out laughing. The absurdity of human fashions was a hobby of his, and Moorhead's explanation tickled him.

"The apology is due from *me*," he said. "Of course I had no idea, positively none, of this new point of decorum. No doubt there are ten thousand others of which we are ignorant here, just as in my day there were many quite as absurd. Yet I like them, with all their absurdity. They tend to make men careful in their conduct, I suppose, and, apart from their use, are a most amusing study. No more of your mischievous recollections, miss! I wonder what a figure you and I should cut to-day at a fashionable table?"

Tom was thinking that Leonora would "cut" the most glorious figure he had ever seen, and wishing he had a table of his own where she might preside. What Leonora was thinking of his excuse—whether she believed it or not—he could not tell, but he thought there was something almost congratulatory in the look she gave him.

Why had she dragged him into the dangerous land of memories? Did she suspect him? No, it was impossible, or she must surely have turned him out long ago. She would despise him if she knew, and she certainly did not despise him. What should he do? Why not let well alone for the present? But was it well? To be in an utterly false position towards the woman he loved was all wrong. Why not get out of it, then? Why not confess? But to confess would doubtless condemn him to go away in disgrace and never see her again. Would it not be better to be in disgrace with her than with his own conscience?

The misguided young man found the idea of the disapproval of conscience much the easier to bear. Yes; he could bear his own contempt better than hers. So he tried to dispose of the conscience, but it would not let him alone. A conscience may be reasoned *about,* but not *with.*

Leonora would, at least, let him alone after the first, *if* he confessed. The inward monitor would not, *unless* he confessed. But then she would let him too well alone. He decided to think it over. The more he thought, the more miserable he grew.

He wrote an angry letter to his brother, and kept it in his pocket, waiting an opportunity to send it.

Meanwhile Leonora put him to much torture. She brought up no more reminiscences in her father's presence, but when no third person was by she revelled in them.

" Let us forget that other time," said he. " It was unsatisfactory."

" Can *you* forget it?" said she; and he wondered, uneasily, what she meant by that.

Was it the very natural reproach of a girl whose lover speaks of forgetting the days of their first love (which is blasphemy in a lover), or did she mean that he ought not to be able to forget what he had never known ? He told himself that he was giving way to absurd fancies—that she could not suspect him.

Would she have teased his brother with those ridiculous reminiscences of hers ? Very likely—why, of course—if he had betrayed forgetfulness, it would have amused her to do so.

The rest of her conduct would have puzzled him less if he had not come out of his confinement in that office of his nearly or quite as ignorant of girls and their little ways as she could be of men. It never occurred to him to accuse that stately being of flirting ; and yet—

She would treat him for a day with great kindness and geniality ; would exchange little confidences with him, demand his sympathy, laugh at his jokes. The next morning she would hold him at a stranger's distance, with that extreme of courtesy that is little short of rudeness, and—which cut him deeply—would take any attempt at frivolous discourse in the most serious manner. Again, she would take entire possession of him, give no mark of favor in return, and order him about, with no thanks for his services. He took it all very meekly, glad of any chance to do her bidding.

Once she said : "I don't see why you waste your time out here. I should think a man ought to have some occupation that would keep him busy at home. His time ought to be valuable."

"Did you not write and say, ' Come at once ?' " he asked. He avoided any statement that she had written to *him*. "I came, and perhaps it was fortunate I did. I do not like to leave you while that —

creature — may still be somewhere about to trouble
you."

She gave a little exclamation of disgust. " Poor
creature !" said she ; " I think you treated him bru-
tally. I wouldn't boast of it."

" I was not boasting."

" I *wouldn't*," said she. " Is it so much for a man
who is evidently an experienced—'*bruiser,*' do they
call it ?—to beat one who is not ? I thought you
clever people of the world—you of the better class—
were proud of your excellence over the others in mind
and spirit, not in brute force or the skill of a prize-
fighter. Is it the part of a gentleman to *lay hands*
on a creature like that ? Perhaps it is one of your
new points of etiquette, such as you were telling about
the other evening at dinner ! I should have thought
you could have sent him away without that. It
would have been natural and no disgrace for you to
have been weaker than he in body and muscle—a man
may well be poorer than a brute in that; but surely
with your trained mind and soul you could have made
him do your bidding without scuffling with him.
To strike such a man is to come down to his level.
It's what *he* would have done to *you !*"

" Yes, he would, if I had given him the chance,"
said Tom. " There seemed no other way — at the
time."

" That," said she, severely, " is what I complain of.
There ought to have seemed a better way. I think
you have changed. You would never have done that
when you were here before. You would have gone
out and subdued him by dint of manner, caste, and
intellect."

Tom began to think she might be making fun of
him. But her voice and face were so grave and so
sweetly serious that it seemed impossible.

Yes; she still thought it was his brother. No wonder he seemed changed! He had not tried to imitate
Charles in any way since he had come to the valley,
and certainly his fight would have been but a poor
imitation of that careful and dignified personage.

He had been proud of his fight, and was deeply
hurt at her thanklessness. It was one of his fail-
ings to take the words of woman always in sober
earnest.

When he slept that night he dreamed that he was
in a dark place in the woods and a tall man stood before him. He could just see the outlines of the great
limbs and the flash of a knife. He seemed to fight des-
perately—not for himself, but for Leonora. Then he
heard a cry and saw the face of the maiden, pale and
white, peeping out from a bush, and he fought the
harder, till she cried, "Stop! You might have fought
for me if you had been Tom ; but you have chosen to
be Tom's brother, and you cannot fight !"

He knew in his dream that he had given up his own
individuality, and he felt ashamed and slunk away,
while laughter seemed to come from the trees all
about him.

He woke with the sense of a great shame upon him.
feeling that, in this great crisis of his life—his first
strong love—he was an impostor and a cheat; not
himself, but merely the counterfeit of another; that
as himself he had no right to be there, had no right
to Leonora's acquaintance. It was a morbid state of
mind perhaps — and perhaps not. At all events, it

was *becoming* morbid and gave him no peace. Should he tell her or should he not?

Sometimes a very small matter, alien to one's thoughts, ludicrous perhaps in itself, will serve to point a moral and help one to a decision when reason and conscience alike fail.

Moorhead saw Moloch over at the edge of the clearing sitting on a log. His face was preternaturally gloomy. He was holding a stout piece of twine, running it slowly through his hands. He looked up at the mountains and down at the grass and muttered to himself, but there was no hearing what he said. He seemed to be trying to make up his mind about something. He frowned terribly and put his hand to his head, and then set busily about making a knot in the cord. When this was done to his satisfaction he examined the undergrowth near by, and, after bending down several saplings as if to test their strength and spring, he selected a young cottonwood, and began to climb it till it bent with his weight. As it leaned he swung down and dangled by his hands, shifting his grip till he had grasped the top, which, bending lower, let him slowly to the ground. He tied the line to the top of the sapling, his countenance all the while becoming more lugubrious, till his expression was as black as the face that wore it.

"What is the matter with the man?" said Tom to himself. "Hullo, Moloch! what are you doing? Surely you don't mean to hang yourself with that fish-line!" he cried. "What's up? Can I help you?"

"Ah, Mr. Moorhead, sah," said Moloch, with a short-lived grin that changed suddenly to a look of unutterable misery, "I shall be mos' grateful for yoh 'sistance, sah! Would it be too much to ask yo' to hol' down the end of this slaplin' a minute? No, sah; I ain't goin' to hang maself. It's wuss 'n that physically, but bettah morally, Mr. Moorhead, sah!"

Therewith, while Tom held the end of the cottonwood, he fumbled at his face, and presently stood with his hands clasped, and the string dangling from his mouth, as from that of a hooked fish.

"Now, if you *please*, sah, *doan'* let it slip!" he said, in a beseeching tone, rolling his eyes apprehensively towards the bent cottonwood, and lying down under it with his arms folded across his big chest.

"Now, Mr. Moorhead, sah, would you kindly sit down on me, sah, an' hold my haid back?"

"Poor old chap!" said Tom. "Is it a *very* bad tooth? Will this work, do you think?"

"Yes, sah; I *hope* it will," said Moloch, fervently. "Now bend the slaplin' down close to ma haid, sah. N-o-ow—when I say 'Free!'—One! Two! Free!" Away went the sapling, and Moloch sprang up and sent Tom sprawling on the grass. A little something dangled from the top of the young cottonwood.

Years later, when that sapling shall have grown a great tree and been cut down, that something will be found, and a learned gentleman with theories and a taste for research will write a paper on the early Indian method of pulling teeth.

"How are you now?" Tom asked, with sympathy.

"All right, sah. Hurts, but nothin' to what it was," said Moloch, cheerfully. "I beg pardon for gettin' up an' frowin' you off so unceremonious, but at such times a man ain't altogether self-controlled, sah."

"Don't mention it," said Tom.

"Tell you, sah," said Moloch, "there's no luxury on earth like havin' a big toothache an' gettin' rid of it.   Bettah hab it out than bear it day an' night."

"Better have it out than bear it day and night!" The words kept repeating themselves over and over in Tom's mind, till he said to himself, "He's right," and straightway he went in search of Leonora.

XXIX

LEONORA sat in the drooping loop of a hanging vine with the tips of her little moccasins just touching the ground. One lovely arm, bare to the elbow, lay upward along the vine and her head rested in its soft curve. The boughs arched above, the ferns grew rich and deep on either side, and behind her was the darkness of the forest.

So Tom found her. She heard his step on the dry twigs, and her wide eyes seemed to ask what he meant by disturbing her in her retreat.

"Miss Willoughby," said Tom, "there's something I ought to tell you."

The change in her face surprised him. It had been calm—a little disdainful—rather weary; but now a gleam of some strong feeling came over it—a blending of eagerness and anxiety, of hope and fear; but she said nothing for a while. He, not knowing how to go on, waited in deep embarrassment.

"I don't think you *ought* to tell me anything unless you wish, Mr. Moorhead," said she, rather coolly. "Why should you? What have I to do with your affairs?"

"I'm in for it now!" Tom thought, and came right to the point.

"It is—it's—it is that I am an impostor—a cheat—a scoundrel—not fit to be in your presence!"

"Then why do you stay in my presence?" said the girl. But her voice was kind, and her face had a kind of triumph on it that he could not understand, and a smile that gave him comfort to go on.

"I'll tell you all about it," said he, bringing out his words slowly, for each was an effort; and the impulse to turn round, pack his goods, and disappear was strong upon him.

"About what?" said she, looking happy and a little mischievous.

"About my—my unpardonable rascality," said he, with self-accusing ferocity.

"I don't know that I care to hear of unpardonable rascality," said she.

"Please hear what I have to say!" he said, brusquely, almost angrily; for it is very hard for a man who has determined to confess to be deprived of the right of confession, and he had made up his mind that she should listen.

"I can't see why you should tell *me*, when I say that I *hate* such subjects," she answered, crossly. "Why not go and tell my father?—he's a great believer in unpardonable rascality—or Moloch?"

"It doesn't concern Moloch," said Tom.

"I do not understand how it can concern *me*," said she, "or, if it does, it surely concerns my father."

"No—well, yes—in a way it does, for I've been his guest under false pretences," said Tom, blurting out his words fast and tingling with hot shame. "I'll tell him instead of you, or do anything else you tell me. But if you'll let me, I'd much rather speak of it to you."

"You'll do anything I tell you?" said she.

" Yes."

" Good," said she. "That's like *you*. Norman—
Charles Norman, I mean—would have thought a minute, and said, 'Anything in reason.' *You* are rash,
are you not ? Think what things I might bid you do.
And then you must do them or break your word.
Well, then, if you'll really mind me, I tell you to say
no more about it, Mr. *Thomas* Norman Moorhead."

She rose, dropped him a grand, low courtesy, and
swept away to the house, leaving him too much astonished to speak or follow her.

" So she knows," he thought. "How long has she
known ? She must have divined it, just as Nelly
Merivale got the fact of Charley's engagement out of
me and thought I told her, when I had never said a
word about it ! Are all women mind-readers ?" And
all the sunny morning he wandered about alone, till
Moloch waked the echoes with a bugle of his that
meant lunch.

Then he went reluctantly to the house, wondering
what was in store for him. He looked apprehensively
at Leonora, then at Mr. Willoughby. She was sweet
and grave and happy, as it seemed ; her father was as
usual.

Afterwards, when Mr. Willoughby was deep in some
book and Leonora had gone out, Moorhead tried to
find her ; but all that afternoon she was gone upon
the hills.

In the evening she treated him pleasantly and
without constraint, seeming to think nothing of that
morning's conversation.

" What *shall* I do ?" he thought. "It cannot be
that she means to be friends with me now. She

knows, and takes no notice. It must be that she is too thoroughbred to have a 'scene,' and takes it for granted that I know enough to go—go at once—without any further allusion to a painful subject. And yet it did not seem to distress her or even make her angry. She was too proud to show it, that's all. Of course I must go. But first I must tell her—tell her the whole story: how carelessly I undertook this thing, how bitterly I repented it!" So he waited, but she gave him no chance to speak.

He hung about the house when she was there; when she had gone out he wandered over the mountain trails, hoping to meet her. It was in the course of these lonely wanderings that he came to a place where the narrow elk-trail ran along a ridge that was rocky and precipitous on one side, and on the other sloping and covered with timber. A curious stone on the ground caught his attention. He stooped to look at it, and stooped just at the right time, for the next moment he was rolling in the brush below the trail with a bullet in his left shoulder.

" Whoever did that did it on purpose," he thought. " It was a good aim for my heart if I had stayed as I was."

He lay still, waiting further developments, mastering his pain as best he could, but making no sound. He never knew how long he lay. A raven came croaking and barking overhead, and watched him with a hungry interest.

At last he heard a cautious step upon the trail—a slow, stealthy footfall, and evidently human.

He did not move. His position was such that he could see the ridge through the bushes that partly hid him from any one who might pass along its top.

The step drew nearer, and he could see, on the ridge, against the sky, a man sneaking along. He could not see the face, but he knew the rags, the long limbs, and slouching shoulders for those of the man he had fought and beaten for Leonora. His grip tightened on his revolver.

"That seems to explain," he thought. "But I must wait and make no mistakes. Better anything than such an error!"

The man drew near, crouching and looking often over his shoulder, examining every object about, peering into the brush as one hunting and hunted at once. He stood just where Tom had fallen, and caught sight of the wounded man's legs sticking out of the brush.

He stood still, and watched them and listened. "It may have been an accident," Tom thought. "Perhaps he mistook me for game, though it's not likely. I can't stand this any longer—I'll try him."

Tom moved his foot and groaned. Instantly the other's rifle went to his shoulder; yet he waited a moment as if calculating, from what he could see of his victim, the position of some vital part. Tom was tired of waiting. The halls of the echoes rang with a revolver-shot, and the objectionable suitor staggered and fell backward.

Tom crawled up on the ridge, and looked down the other side. Only a steep of rock falling straight away into the blackness of forest shade; only the sound of roaring water from the depths, and the raven, croaking and hovering lower and lower, a little way down.

The raven had transferred his allegiance. Tom dropped a bullet through his black back, and watched him falling into the darkness below. Then, spent with pain and loss of blood and the reaction from intense excitement, he went slowly back to the cabin and sought aid of Moloch.

"I helped you in a surgical operation the other day," said he, "and now it's your turn to do something for me." And he told his story, lamenting what had happened, and charging him to say nothing of the matter to his mistress.

" You done just right, Mr. Moorhead, sah," said Moloch, "an' thank God you ain't no worse. You owed it to Miss 'Nora to protect yourself, sah. Please to think of *that* if it troubles you, sah."

The bullet was not hard to extract, and the old butler tenderly ministered to the wound, and fed him, and left him to sleep. He slept well. It is a dreadful thing to have slain a man in his sins; but he knew he had done right, and Moloch's words, though the oracle was humble and the statement unlikely, comforted him.

"You owed it to Miss 'Nora to protect yourself!" If only that might be so!

XXX

In the morning Moloch helped him to dress, put him in a cool, shady corner of the veranda, where the sweet breeze came through the vines, and set beside him a table with books and a change of pipes, a jar of fragrant tobacco, and a cold jug of lemonade, tempered with good old Jamaica (*not* the ginger), to gladden his heart.

Mr. Willoughby came and regarded Tom with new interest.

"Are you quite comfortable?" said he.

"Thanks, yes," said Tom.

"If you will pardon me a personal remark," said Mr. Willoughby, "I am most happily disappointed in you, Moorhead. It took a cool head and strong nerve to wait for that fellow, as you did, without a sign, with a painful wound galling you. I did not think you had it in you. When you were here before, you seemed a totally different being. Well, I never shot any one myself, but I have often wished to, and I rather envy you the privilege of doing it lawfully. I congratulate you."

The old man held out his hand, to the great disgust of Tom, whose soul revolted against treating such a matter lightly.

"Sir," said he, "I am glad, indeed, to shake hands with you as a friend; but pray understand that I consider what I have had to do a matter of pity, not congratulation."

"Quite right," said Mr. Willoughby, with a slight sneer. "A very proper spirit. All the more credit to you for doing it so well. But when you know men as *I* do, you'll understand my point of view. Gentle or simple, rich or poor, priest and layman, they are much alike; much like that poor wretch who has got his deserts at your hand, except that they have more tact to disguise their feelings and control their actions, in fear of the law.

"So they use sneers for blows, lies instead of ambush; they give heartaches and agony of mind instead of rifle-shots and festering wounds; they are much the same — fraud or force; and that is why, when one catches them jumping the limits of their sheltering pen, the law, he is to be thanked for killing them for what they are—the most dangerous and treacherous of animals; the only ones to which the devil can teach his tricks; the only ones he can break to his yoke!"

Tom understood fully now the old man's reasons for living apart from his fellows.

His hatred of man amounted to a monomania, which showed itself less in his words, which savored too sadly much of reason, than in his flashing, eager eyes and frowning brows, his clinched fist and heaving chest. "I tell you," he began again—but Leonora came out and laid her hand on his arm and looked into his eyes, which grew mild at the sight of her sweet face, and caught a tender light from hers. His brow lost its deep lines; he smiled and kissed her before the young man's envying face; and, turning to him, said,

18

gently: "Yet there may be—*there are* human beings that are God's own creation, and have never lost the glory that He breathed into the nostrils of the first man. You—you never knew my wife, sir."

And Mr. Willoughby pulled his broad hat down over his eyes and went away to his fishing.

"My father doesn't mean half what he says about people," said Leonora. "He was angry and bitter when he came away. He has hardly seen any since in all these years; so he has had no chance to change his opinions, but has brooded over them till he thinks he really believes in them."

"I'm afraid too much of them are true," said Tom.

"That is not the point," said Leonora. "What if they are? I did not say believes them, but believes *in* them—thinks they are *right* to act upon and live by. If only I could get him to see that, bad as humanity may be, we are a part of it and not *apart from* it! Well, sometime, perhaps, I can. But you — you have had a narrow escape and a hard experience: Moloch told me, in spite of your injunctions. I can think how you must feel; but it had to be, did it not?"

"I suppose it had; and yet why should it? I'd as lief, if I had thought of everything, have lain still and let him finish his work."

"Stop — don't speak so! Come — you are down-hearted and suffering."

"You are right," he said. "One must not whine."

Now, Leonora knew that it was not only his adventure on the ridge that troubled him, and he seemed so unhappy that she relented and took pity.

"Can I not help you to be—happier?" she asked.

"Yes," said he. "I *am* downhearted—I *am* suffering. But it's not this—it's something else. You *can* help me—no one else can."

"I will — perhaps," said Leonora, smiling beautifully.

"It's what I was telling you the other day," he continued. "You knew that before, though I did not think so when I confessed."

"I am glad you told me when you thought I did not know," she said. "It made a difference."

"I wonder how much more you know of what I was going to say? At all events, that is what I need— to tell you all about it—everything, from the beginning."

Her face grew grave with something of that anxious expression he had seen before.

"Go on," said she. "You may tell me."

"It was a shameful, a wicked fraud—"

"What was?" said she. "Tell me what happened, and let me decide about that."

"I came here intending to pass myself off for my brother," said he.

"Why?" said she.

He sat silent before her, thinking: "Suppose she does not know the whole? Suppose she thinks my brother still loves her? How can I tell her he does not? How can I tell her that *I* love her, if she does not know about his faithlessness—if by any chance she still cares for him? It's a hard thing that a fellow must either tell the girl he loves that his brother is a rascal, or seem to be making love on his own account to his brother's *fiancée*, or say nothing."

"Why?" Leonora asked again.

"I—I find I *can't* tell you that."

"You *must* tell me that.   I have a right to ask."

"Then you don't know ?" he said.

"How should I ?"

"One thing I must tell you," said he.   "I meant to take his place and marry you ; and I consented to try to do so for a *price*, before I ever saw you."

He looked so miserable that a shade of compassion came over her face, and she said, quickly, "Forgive me.   You deserve it; but I forgot that you were hurt; and now—just because you are ill, and for no other reason—I'll let you off and not tease you any more. I'm coming right back."

She went into the house, and brought back an open letter which she gave him.

"There," said she, "you've made your confession like a man, and tried to shield your brother.   Now read that !"

"MY DEAR MISS WILLOUGHBY,—

"As a dear friend of Mr. Moorhead, I write to tell you, for his sake and your own, some bad news.

"It is best you should know at once that marriage between you is an impossibility.   I will not try to give all the reasons, of which there are many, why it would not do—most of them you could hardly be expected to understand.   You are said to be a great reader.   Your books will tell you of the evils of ill-assorted marriages.   I say this to prepare you for what is to come.   *He* has seen his mistake, and wishes (forgive me if I hurt you, but it's better you should know, as you'll see when I have done) to be free from his engagement, for your sake as well as his.   But he will not—cannot, as a man—break it off.   It is your place to do this.

"Being unable to bear the idea of this engagement to you, and equally unable to write and tell you so, he has taken this singular and unheard-of way of getting out of the difficulty.   His younger brother, Thomas Norman Moorhead, who, in appearance, is much like him, is going to visit you, and, if you mistake him for your *fiancé*, Charles Norman Moorhead, will carry out the deception and marry you in his brother's stead, *if* he finds it his pleasure to do so. It is a wretched and foolish plan, and I think it my duty to warn you against it, both to show you how impossible and wrong a marriage between you and Charles Moorhead would be, and to keep you from marrying Thomas Moorhead, who is a disgrace to his family, and an adventurer, of no character or means.

"Very sincerely,

"SARAH J. BRADLEE.

"P. S.—Thomas Moorhead is to be paid a large sum by his brother for marrying you."

"Well?" said Leonora. "Is it true?"

"Yes."

"That you are to be paid?"

"Not now. It *was* true. Will you let me tell you about it, or are you too utterly disgusted with me?"

Leonora laughed. "Curiosity is stronger than disgust—in a woman," said she.

Tom told her of his brother's new infatuation for his old love, of all the pressure so ingeniously brought to bear on him, of his obligations to Charles, of the marvellous way in which Mrs. Merivale had extracted information from him, of his brother's anger and grief, of her encouragement, of how he had said he could not support a wife, and of his brother's offer to make him able to marry.

"I thought you were not exactly a dramatic villain," said Leonora. "You seemed more like a schoolboy, all the time. But I didn't think you were exactly. stupid—not *so* stupid. Why can't you see—*can't* you see?—that those people—your brother and Mrs. What's-her-name—had it all arranged between them for some reason ? You didn't tell her anything; she knew all about it beforehand. Well—about the money. Are you to have it ?"

"No !" said he.

"Why ?"

"Why ? Why, Miss Willoughby, what do you take me for ? Don't you see how different it all is ? I didn't *know* you then. Since I have known you I would no more think of doing such a thing— Oh, Leonora, you have changed me ! I'm a different fellow now ! If you would only believe me—here— wait a minute—I have something to show you !"

"Don't get up," she said.

"Oh yes !" said he; "I'm well enough to walk about." He went to his room and came back with a blank face. "I had a letter too," said he, "and now I can't find—oh ! here it is. It was in my pocket all the time. Read it. I wrote it some time ago, but there has been no chance yet to post it."

He tore off the envelope and handed it to her. She read, as follows :

"CHARLES N. MOORHEAD, ESQ.,—

"I have come to my senses.

"I'll have nothing more to do with the dishonorable plan by which you have sought to rid yourself of as lovely a woman as the Lord has made.

"Keep your money, and, if you are not quite devoid of sense and feeling, give up your silly infatuation and ask her to receive you again.

"Rest assured of one thing, however: you shall not have her if it be in my power fairly to win her from you !

"I love her too well.

            "THOS. N. MOORHEAD."

"I never meant you to read that last part," said

Tom, very red, and looking away. "I had forgotten that."

"Forgotten—so soon?" said Leonora, looking away also. You *are* alike in some things, then—you brothers."

They both sat without a word for a while. Then Tom said, very gloomily:

"It's a pity my shoulder's in this fix. I ought to go at once. But I can't carry a pack. I didn't know *you* when I let myself be hired. Since I have known you I have been bitterly ashamed. I wish I had met you in some other way—not that I'd have had a chance. I—but never mind. It's all over—now, and there's no use talking about it.

"I'll alter that letter before I write to my brother, and leave out those words I ought not to have written."

"What words?" Leonora asked, glancing at him and turning away again while she listened to the answer.

"I had no right to tell him I—I loved you."

"Let that stand," said she. "Send the letter as it is."

"Thank you," said Tom, gratefully. "I'd rather, if I may; and, as soon as I can, I'll relieve you of my presence."

"Oh! I wouldn't do *that*," said Leonora. "I think" (shyly) "if *I* had done anything I was ashamed of, and people didn't seem inclined to forgive me for it, I'd stay, and take the consequences, and—live it down!"

XXXI

TOM was soon free from all bad effects of his slight wound. To have one's mind diverted from any ailment greatly helps recovery (if it does not lead to carelessness), and Leonora diverted his mind effectually. Being a maiden of her word, she did not seem inclined to forgive him too easily, and took great care that he should not be allowed to forget his offence in a hurry.

A girl is armed by Nature with as many subtle and ingenious instruments of torture as any mediæval tyrant ever dreamed of in his happiest visions, and lack of former practice seemed to detract in no way from her skill in using them.

As a keen reader whose library is limited by adverse circumstances to three or four books knows them word for word and thought for thought, so she, with her few volumes of human nature to study, was quickly aware of every phase of character. She took pleasure in finding out Tom's tender points and using them to his grief. He was teased, snubbed, puzzled, hurt, disappointed, and made foolish in his own eyes, by turns, every day and all. But he liked it, and was happy, because he was out of his false position, himself again, clear of obligation, free, in the eyes of Leonora. One thing only troubled him, and that not nearly as much as it ought.

He was penniless and without prospects. Most young men in love and good health think but lightly of such small and sordid matters, and go right on making love, sure of their happy destiny and the prosperity that doubtless lies in store for them. "Why not," they say, "when I have *you* to work for? How can I fail?" But Tom had had too much trial of what it is to be penniless in the world to ask the girl he loved to share a life free from all such mean and mercenary considerations as dollars and cents.

Then of course there was also the question, "Would Leonora ever have him at any price?" He would not ask her till he could give her a home. This plan, at all events, he felt, with reasonable certainty, would give her plenty of time to get over her disappointment, if any, in regard to Charles. Had she any regrets about Charles? When she had thought that he was C. Norman, during the first few days of his stay, before Mrs. Bradlee's letter came, she had shown no great enthusiasm for him; but then girls were queer.

He would not ask her any questions yet. He would plan his campaign there in the valley; then he would go out and do battle with the world, win or lose, and Love must bide the issue.

The more he thought, the less practicable it all seemed. He could not afford to practise his profession, but for what else was he fit? He was no accountant—no clerk—no salesman. He had tried to find work before, and had found only this—that every honest and regular means of subsistence known to man demands one or both these things—capital and experience.

For an independent position one must have capital;

for a subordinate one, experience and, generally, references. Tom had nothing. He broached the subject once, indirectly, to Leonora.

"You have your profession," said she.

He laughed. "You might almost as well say, in these days, 'You have your sword.' One is as marketable as the other. The profession would be good if I could wait ten years or so while the public was becoming aware of my great value. The sword would be good if I could go through West Point first."

The sword, in fact, would be better, because one could pawn it in case of great need; but one can't even do *that* with a profession.

"A great many people have risen from nothing," she said. "One's always reading of some one."

"One in thousands; but of the *thousands* you *don't* read; so the one impresses you, and you judge by him. To be reasonably sure of success on nothing, one must be either a genius or a fraud."

"I can't say that I have seen any sign of your being a *genius*," said she, "and you do not enjoy—"

"Being a fraud? No, I've had enough of that," said he, with becoming meekness.

"Enough to satisfy an ordinary person," she added, "and I think you seem to be an ordinary person, as well as I can judge. So I really do not see how you are to become a success."

Tom stayed on in the woods, putting off his departure from day to day. The cordiality of Mr. Willoughby's manner began to fade as he observed a growing understanding between his daughter and Moorhead.

"What is your profession, sir?" said he, one day.

"Law, Mr. Willoughby," said Tom.

"Doubtless your clients can ill afford to spare you so long, sir," the old gentleman suggested.

Both men were watching Leonora's face to see how she would take it. That lovely luminary clouded with a slight shade of dismay. Tom was delighted at this, and the old gentleman's eyes twinkled with a kind of malice.

"You agree with me, Leonora, that Mr. Moorhead's clients must be at a loss?"

"It may be they can find other counsel," said Leonora, "but that is Mr. Moorhead's affair."

"I'm afraid *all* Mr. Moorhead's affairs are suffering for lack of attention, are they not, Mr. Moorhead?" said the father. "It is within the bounds of possibility that the clients may be able to find other counsel, for where violence and treachery, failure and death and evil are rife there is never lack of lawyers; but will it be so easy for Mr. Moorhead to find other clients?"

Leonora was on Tom's side in this discussion. "Don't misunderstand my father's speech, Mr. Moorhead," she said, graciously. "He means, of course, that where the enemies of Law are many there are her knights in the press of battle to guard her and aid her subjects."

"I mean nothing of the kind, my dear daughter," said Mr. Willoughby, coolly. "But, as you have so gracefully put it, Mr. Moorhead's post is where the Law needs him, and her subjects—his clients—need him; and his post has long been deserted."

"I think my clients—if I had any—would forgive the desertion," said Tom. "But I have none."

The old gentleman smiled, and spoke more kindly :

"I do not mean to be rude, my dear sir ; forgive me if I speak frankly : you have been a friend, and nearly lost your life by it. You have adapted yourself to our ways, and, little as I care to see of men, I have had pleasure in your company ; but our life is not for you, nor yours for us. Your place is in the world— you have duties there. Doubtless the world can well dispense with your performance of them —but *you* cannot. If you intend to cast off, as I have done, all intercourse with men and civilization—well and good —do so. But if you mean to hold a place among men, you have assumed responsibilities that you cannot discharge here. A young man must choose his way, and, having chosen, must stick to it. You are wasting your time, and it is not well that you should do so."

"All right, sir," said Tom. "I'm off to-morrow."

He had not meant to make love to Leonora yet. But they happened to be together, and somehow the subject seemed to occur to them both at once, So, as a ship that has drifted near a lovely island and most desirable refuge—the crew eager to land, but afraid of reefs and shoals and unknown dangers round about— stands off and on and tries how near it can come to land without running aground, each shyly approached and avoided the topic, and kept drawing a little nearer.

"Will you forgive me ?" said Tom, at last, "if I ask you—I have a *reason* for asking—if it was very painful to you to get that letter telling about Charles's faithlessness and folly ?"

Leonora picked a spray of willow, and put it in her

hair, looking demurely dismal and woe-begone. Then she burst out laughing.

"Oh, so painful!" she cried. "You notice how I've pined, how faded I am getting, how I mope and mourn? Why, Tom, nothing in the world ever gave me such pleasure as that letter! When your brother came here I liked him. Then he began to make love to me, and I liked that. I'm afraid I was worldly—he taught me to be worldly—and I began to feel discontented with my dear valley and wish to belong to the world, and go in flocks and herds and droves, like other folk; and it seemed to me it would be pleasant to be his wife and have the luxuries he offered me. So I *persuaded* myself—deliberately, if unconsciously, persuaded myself—I cared for him. But happily I could not leave my father. I stayed by my duty, and that was my safeguard. For after your brother was gone I found I did not care for *him;* that I had made a horrible mistake; that it was too late to withdraw, for he had set his heart on me, I thought, and I would not disappoint him. Then I was miserable. But I made up my mind to keep my word to him. Then you came—after a long, long, miserable time, and at first I thought you were he. But still you seemed so different. I thought, 'I believe I can love him, after all.' Oh, what have I said!" she cried. "Of course I don't mean *that*, Mr. Moorhead," and she reddened with shame at her self-betrayal, and rose to go away.

"Stay, stop one moment, *please!* Don't go away. Think—I may never see you again, after to-morrow."

"Well," said she, crossly, looking at him with deep disapproval; "what is it?"

"Leonora," he said, standing by her and taking her hand, "my brother told me you would never let him kiss you."

"I should think not," said Leonora, drawing aloof and eying him coldly. "I could never have done such a thing."

"Of course not. Leonora?"

"Yes?"

"Couldn't you—do you think—won't you let *me* kiss you?"

"Oh! You? You are different," said Leonora.

Next morning Tom was off with Moloch and the ponies for the sound.

"Now, my dear," said the old gentleman to Leonora, looking hard at her to see how she took it, "you and I can be at peace awhile."

But Leonora did not answer. She was supremely happy—doubtless with the sense of having conferred a benefit—for, just to show that she bore no ill-will, she had let Tom kiss her again before he went away, and she thought he had seemed to like it.

XXXII

Tom posted his letter to his brother and wrote another, saying :

"Mrs. Bradlee was kind enough to write and tell Miss Willoughby the circumstances of my coming here. You owe me nothing for my services, but I owe you something for the temporary loss of my self-respect. I think I shall be able to pay.

"Marry Mrs. Merivale, and one of these days you shall see Miss Willoughby and your wife side by side; shall compare what you have won with what you have lost; and I think that will be enough."

"And he *shall* see them together," Tom vowed to himself, as he posted the letter—" my wife and his. And I *will* win her ; and, what's more, I'll make that old misanthropical patriarch my very good friend and father-in-law elect, the worthy Mr. Willoughby, come out of that valley, so that she can come, too, and marry me, and live like a Christian."

All of which, being a man of his word, he now set out to accomplish, with a strong constitution, a heart full of hope, and a staff in his hand of the good yellow cedar that grows far up on the heights.

Now, to a man who seeks work a strong constitution means a vast appetite, a heart full of hope, a tendency to be unpractical and chase delusions, neither of which is well for him.

But a staff of good yellow cedar is a right good thing and may work wonders, as we shall see.

Tom had but a poor hunt after work.

Leonora had told him to see, first of all, if he could not manage to find something to do at his own profession, saying that she liked lawyers, so far as she had been able to observe them (for she had given him, before he went away, much good, practical advice, such as one's nearest and dearest, of least experience and greatest faith, pour freely into one's ears at the hour of one's setting out for scenes particularly unknown to them).

So, out of respect to his profession, he went about among the lawyers' offices.

Seattle had risen vainglorious from its ashes, and many more thousands had been found to share its comforts.

He went to many an office and was urbanely received, but found no likelihood of an opening.

At last he bethought him of Solomon Druby.

"You couldn't have done better," said that gentleman, heartily, "than to strike Seattle just at this time."

"If I may take up your time, I'd like to ask a few questions," said Tom.

Druby looked at his watch. "Time," said he, "is precious. Brother — beg pardon, I didn't quite get your name—Brother Moorhead—but always, as you and I know, at the service of fellow-members of the Bar."

"Thanks! At what rent could I get an office here?"

The legal gentleman brightened, scenting business.

" Office-rent, like everything else, is booming here
—'way up; *we* could let you have a set of offices in
this very building at—well, you want the best, no
doubt—a hundred and fifty a month."

" My limit is very low," said Tom.   "I am just
beginning."

" I see—I see—"

" And what I want to know is not the *highest* but
the *lowest* rent at which I could get a small office—
single room."

" I don't know of any at less than fifty dollars a
month—in advance."

" That's 'way beyond me," said Tom.

" I understand," said Druby, with sympathy.   "Bless
you, when I came here to practise I piled slabs and did
odd jobs about the wharves for a living.   Well, why
not get desk-room in some office ?"

" Do you think I could pay for it with my services ?"

" Possibly—possibly."

" Can you—on those terms ?"

" Well—no, we can't.   I should like to oblige you,
Brother Moorhead, but you see there are several young
men here already, and we've not overmuch for them
to do.   They merely take up room."

There *were* several young men there, and they certainly *were* doing nothing, and *did* take up room.
They came out of their fits of abstraction and laughed.

" Clients !" said one.   "Haven't seen such a thing
since—"   The others turned upon him and frowned
him into silence.

" Practice is not as brisk, then, as it might be ?"
said Tom.

" Practice," said Druby, confidently, "is booming.
19

To be sure, since the fire people have been too busy to go to law much, but they'll have to soon. You've come to the right place, sir. Sorry we are not in a position to do anything for you. Good-day. But wait. I'm still, incidentally, in the undertaking business, though Law and Real Estate have the precedence, outwardly, just now. Can you drive a hearse? If so—"

Tom declined.

"I think you're silly," said Druby, "downright foolish. A man's got to begin at the bottom, you know, and work up. Take my advice, an' 'witch th' world with noble *hearse*manship' till you git well known in town and see an openin'. *Then* 'hang up your shingle on the outer wall.'"

Tom found that the town was flooded with lawyers, all trustfully waiting for the coming prosperity. He was inclined to believe that Solomon Druby had been right, and that the way to begin was by piling slabs and doing odd jobs. But, alas! the slab-piling industry and the odd-job business alike were crowded. He could not even get employment digging on the streets. He drew the line at driving a hearse.

Everybody assured him that it was a "great country, that was what it was," and he had "come to the right place, that was what!" But nobody wanted him.

Day after day he walked the streets with weary feet, up and down, and his little stock of money dwindled, and nothing was accomplished, and he found nothing to do till at last he had but two dollars in his pocket—enough to take him back to the woods, where he could support himself by hunting and fishing. He was discouraged, and did not seem much in the way of making his fortune and doing those several things he had promised himself — to get old Mr. Willoughby out of the valley, marry Leonora, and shame his brother.

There sat in the street an old Siwash squaw, begging. She was a very old woman indeed; her face was seamed by countless wrinkles, and she was bent and infirm, tottering even as she sat. She crooned to herself, swaying tremulously back and forth, and now and then greeting a passer-by in shrill Chinook.

A teamster backed his cart up to the sidewalk to deliver a load of furniture. The old woman was in the teamster's way, and he called to her to get up and be off. But she either could not or would not hear, and the man—a hulking brute of a fellow—gave her a savage cut with his whip, and would have followed it up with another, but Tom, furious at the sight, ran towards him with a shout. The teamster, turning, gave him the blow, and, being a much larger man than he, asked him what he meant to do about it?

Tom ran at him. The teamster struck a downright blow with the heavy-wadded butt of his mule whip. Tom raised his good stick of yellow cedar above his head, slanting downward to the left, so that the blow slipped along its smooth length beyond his left shoulder and struck the air, throwing the enemy off his balance; then, with a quick turn of the wrist, he brought the heavy staff round in a wide swing of three quarters of a circle, straightening his arm just as the circle was complete, and catching the teamster with the full force of the blow on the side of the head. It staggered him, but his head was not his sensitive point, and it would have been a sad day for Tom if a tall man had not run across the street to his assistance. The teamster jumped into his cart.

"Well done," said the stranger. "Hurt any?"

"No," said Tom. But he *was* hurt, and not very well; he had been economizing too much; he was discouraged, and the excitement had made him almost hysterical.

The old Siwash was raising her hands towards the sun and calling down blessings on his head in her strange tongue.

The stranger looked hard at him, and kindly said:

"Anything I can do for you? I love sand and grit, and you look, if I may say so, as if you wanted something."

"I want a job," said Tom.

"That's not such an easy matter. What kind?"

"Anything."

"Had any experience logging? That is *my* business."

"No," said Tom.

"Then I don't see how I can use you. That's what I don't," said the other; "but maybe—hello! That's a right good club you hit him with."

"That's a cedar stick I cut in the mountains," said Tom.

"Lemme look. Cedar, eh? So it is. But, boys! O *boys, what* cedar! Heavy an' close-grained, and what a polish! Never saw any like it before. Any more of it up there?"

"Yes, hundreds of acres. This yellow cedar grows high up on the Olympics. So far, out of reach for all practical purposes."

"Grow large?"

"Immense.   As big as any trees I've seen."

"'Way up where no one can get it except the devil, I reckon?"

"I think it might be got at."

"Might? Well, sir, if you'll find the way back and take one of my timber-cruisers along I'll make it worth your while."

"I can't take a man out there at present," said Tom. "But I'll tell you what I'll do. I'll go out and do your cruising myself. I'll look it over and see just what can be done, and let you know."

"Well, sir, it'll pay you to do it," said the lumberman, earnestly. "That's what! And here's where to find me." He scribbled an address on an old envelope. "Burns, of Shelton—that's me. There's no such wood as that on the market; and if it's as plenty as you say, the man that brings it down to the sound makes his pile right so!"

The next week found Tom encamped on the ridge over the valley.

XXXIII

THE autumn came and brought heavy showers, and also a few clear, sharp days, when the forests gleamed with hoar-frost: then the long, continuous storm, which is snow among the mountains and rain on the low woodlands along the salt-water, set in. The snow lay deep in the valley, and, resting in masses on the broad boughs, shut the light out of the forest.

The river muttered under its ice, and wild beasts came down from the heights and were seen among the haunts of men.

Sometimes a Chinook wind, with its warm, sweet breath, came like a touch of spring. The heavy drops dripped tinkling and pattering from the trees; the forest was splendid with icicles; the mountains thundered one to another with the sound of new-born torrents, and the river roared and rose high over its banks, flooding the lowlands, and making an island of the knoll where Leonora lived and waited for the spring. It was a glad winter for her, full of relief from past trouble, and of promise for the days to come.

Tom had come to the valley late in the summer, and had built himself a hut on a shelf of the ridge. He had had a long talk with Moloch, and Moloch had grinned and promised aid. Between them they had accomplished great ends ere the winter's long storm began, and Leonora had helped them, doing a good man's work with axe and chain upon the slopes.

Mr. Willoughby had known nothing of all this. He had been revelling in Voltaire all winter.

So when the rain had grown less chill day by day, and the river had risen nearly to the clearing in its last great spring flood, and had gone down, leaving green grasses and budding shrubs along its banks—when the snow was all gone except on the heights and northern slopes, and the forest rang with the song and twitter of mating birds—the old gentleman, having gone far down the river to the end of the valley to renew his acquaintance with his speckled friends, and sitting by a favorite pool in immense enjoyment of his solitude, was surprised and infinitely disgusted to see a party of men, with packs and rifles, coming up the trail in single file and examining the country as they came.

He drew back into the brush to watch them unobserved.

They were led by a lean, wiry, sharp-eyed fellow, with the long, light step and spring of the knee that mark the practised mountaineer. One of the others was a great burly man, whom they called Burns. The rest carried axes and surveyors' tools.

"Here's the place, Mr. Burns," said the leader, stopping and turning to the portly soul, who puffed and blew, and looked at the river and then up to the ridge.

His eye brightened. "That's the stuff up there," said he; "hundreds and hundreds of acres, just as he said. Now, how does he think to get it down, Sam?"

"You see that rock," said the timber-cruiser, pointing where the river swerved, foaming and eddying round a gray mass of stone that had fallen long ago from the ridge, "and you see the gulch below it —the old river-bed. You've seen that old channel all the way up from where it runs into the present course, and how straight an' deep an' clear it is?"

"That's what," said Burns.

"He was dead right when he said it wa'n't goin' to take much blastin' to coax the stream back where it used to be when that rock come in an' slewed it off, wa'n't he, Somers?"

"*Dead* right," said a man carrying a note-book. "A gang of hands to clear that loose stuff, a blast here and there, a few trees felled across the stream where she runs now, and away she goes in the old course, fit to carry your logs ten abreast clear to the sound."

"That's what!" said the chorus.

"Well, you may make your specifications, and we'll go up and look at the timber."

"All right! Here's the blazed tract he spoke on," said the timber-cruiser; and the party filed up the ridge above the bend of the river.

Leonora had never seen her father so disturbed as when he came home that night.

"They've come at last," said he. "There is a party of men down at the foot of the valley making arrangements to cut the timber off the ridge and float it down the river." His voice was that of a heart-broken man.

She said nothing, but came and stroked her father's hand, and felt guilty and ashamed. For was she not a party to this outrage? Moorhead had persuaded her;

she had allowed herself to listen to his plans, and had helped him, knowing, but not realizing, how it would ruin her father's peace.

Now the old man sat with head bent down and trembling lip. "In a little while, dear," he said, in a querulous voice, "the valley will be laid waste. Throngs of rough boors will come and camp at our very door—we cannot prevent it; the peace we love will be driven away with the sound of axes and saws and shouting men by day, of drunken blasphemy by night. Our lovely home will be but a barren, treeless waste, strewn with wreckage and the mutilated limbs of the old giants that have watched over us so long. The place of your mother's grave will be no longer sacred; these barbarians will overrun everything, and bring ruin and destruction with them. I cannot stay to see it; and I am too old to seek a new home in the mountains. What is there left but to go back to men and cities, to dusty streets and ugly structures, to lies and meanness, jealousy and selfishness, bickering, malice, everything foul, everything I hate?"

Leonora could not give him a kiss of comfort, could not even speak; it would have been hypocrisy.

By-and-by he said, more quietly: "It may be better so. Perhaps I ought to have gone before: I promised your mother, and year by year I have put it off. It may be I should never have kept my word to her but for this. Yes, she would rather have it so than that I should stay on and let you waste your beauty in the forest, my daughter. I owed it to her, and ought to have kept my promise to her, and now it is well that I *must* do so."

Then Leonora was comforted, and kissed him, and

told him how they would find a home in some quiet place where he could pass a peaceful life.

"Moloch cannot keep on working for us always, father," said she. "There will come a time when his strength will leave him, and he must rest; and then what would become of us if we were here? We could bear the summers, but if winter found us here alone? He and you have earned your rest; and could you rest here, with only a girl to hunt for you and get in wood and strengthen the house against the winter storms? Yes, it must be sometime. Why not now?"

She left him in a happier state of mind, and went out and met Moorhead, who was waiting for her on the mountain trail, by a tree which was their place of meeting, and in whose friendly hollow they put letters for each other.

"They have come," said Tom, "and everything is in trim."

"He knows it," she answered. "He saw them and heard them talking."

"How does he take it?"

"He was miserable at first; he seemed ready to break down. I was afraid for him. But he suddenly remembered that he had promised to go, and ought to have gone before. I almost fancy that he likes the idea, now he's made up his mind to it."

"Then there's one thing accomplished. Now, 'Nora, it's all done. This yellow cedar is valuable, you know, and this is the only place that has been found where it is accessible. I have every strip of it under control. Moloch and I filed claims on part of it, you know. There was a lot left, and I got six men

to come out here and file on the rest of it, on condition
that I would agree to buy of them at a certain price
and time.   Burns, as soon as I convinced him what
we had here, formed a company to come out and work
the cedar; and the whole thing has only been waiting
till the State should accept the survey—the survey
that you and Moloch and I made—so that the claims
would hold.   The survey was accepted last week.
Yesterday I transferred Moloch's claim and mine
and my rights in the other six claims to the company
—part payment cash and part in shares.   Why, even
Moloch's a capitalist to-day.   It's the only yellow
cedar in the market.   The quality is perfect, the
supply enormous.   So, as I said, I'm rich.   But that
isn't the point, Leonora."

"Oh! what is the point?"

"That I shall have you, and you me.   So what does
it matter about anything else?"

Soon a great force of loggers were encamped in the
valley.   All day the hills echoed with harsh sounds; the
frightened deer fled far into the mountains; hawk and
eagle, scared from their ancient strongholds, hung
poised against the blue, watching the strange things
that came to pass; by night the camp-fires lighted the
ridges on either side; and rude songs and hoarse
laughter frightened away the silence of the doomed
forest.

Mr. Willoughby was furious, and, after a short
time, talked of nothing but getting out of this camp
of savages into civilization.

"Mr. Moorhead, I don't know how far you are
responsible for this change in our lives, and will not
inquire.   It had to be made, and for my daughter's

sake, and for no other reason, I am not altogether sorry. One favor I ask of you, and if you have caused our exodus it is the more your duty. I am leaving behind the spot I hold most sacred on earth — the grave of my wife. I cannot bear to think that when I am gone, and there is none to guard that spot, it shall be held sacred no longer—trampled and desecrated and forgotten. If you—"

"I will prevent it, sir," said Moorhead.

That afternoon he explained the situation to Burns, who put men, cattle, tackle, and derricks at his disposal. By afternoon the cross and cairn having been tenderly removed by Leonora's and Tom's and Moloch's own hands, a great fragment of rock came swinging and rolling by lever and derrick down the ridge, and was gently lowered on the grave, so covering it that the foot of man might never disturb the sacred earth.

XXXIV

THE west wind brought home the news of Leonora's marriage and heralded her coming, and the people wondered. They wondered who was this person, and why had one of the Moorheads married her?

Then Mrs. Norman Moorhead, *late* Merivale, *née* Trask, was sore at heart with a trouble she had not foreseen. She was far more fond of her husband than she had ever meant to be of any one, and, being of a jealous disposition, began to fear the effect upon him of Leonora's arrival. How much of his defection from that former allegiance was due to her own superior charm? How much to his forgetfulness of Leonora? These questions troubled her night and day; she began to hate the woman whose happiness she had not scrupled to destroy, and who might well ruin hers in turn. She did a silly thing. She went about (to make Leonora's *début* easy for her) hinting what manner of person was likely to come out of the backwoods, and suggesting that folk ought not to expect too much of her in the way of manners, dress, or conversation, and that it would be well to be lenient towards any little *gaucheries* that such a woman might be apt to display. Her efforts in behalf of her sister-in-law were so successful that Mrs. Thomas Moorhead became famous.

It was said that her husband had married her, partly for money, somehow suddenly amassed by her pioneer father in a sober interval, and partly for a kind of coarse beauty bred of an outdoor life.

That he had married her (for Charles Moorhead's household had caught a significant word or two, and there are people who will listen to the gossip of their friends' servants) at the instance of his brother, who had been wise enough to wish to break his own engagement to her, and had paid a good round sum for the privilege.

That she would give a rare exhibition of the ways of the wild wood and express her feelings in choice bits of Western slang.

That she was not altogether a Caucasian, and spoke Chinook when excited.

It was agreed that Tom didn't care, so long as the pecuniary consideration, whether from his brother or father-in-law, was forthcoming.

It was felt to be a sad pity that this should have happened to Tom just when his rehabilitation had begun to seem so real and thorough.

Mrs. Bradlee was sadly put out. " I have been a mother to those boys!" she complained. " I saved Norman from that *dreadful* entanglement—and I did my best for poor Tom when I heard of his infatuation; I actually *wrote* to the girl herself, and explained in the *kindest* way how utterly *impossible* it was that she should marry *either* of them. But it was not to be supposed, of course, that any sense of the fitness of things could be brought home to such a person. Well, he has taken his own course, and he must ' dree his weird ' !"

" Then you knew of it beforehand ?" said an inquisitive friend.

"And the elder brother *was* engaged to her, too?" said another.

"Oh, do tell us, Mrs. Bradlee!"

The good lady was not quite prepared to answer all these questions, and there was a moment of silence.

Mr. Timmons, who had come to call, had fallen unawares into a large feminine assemblage, and had waited long, careless of his tea, upon the edge of his chair, biding his chance to speak, seized the opportunity.

"It seems to me," said he, "that Tom Moorhead's 'weird' is none so hard to 'dree.'"

The ladies looked at him with cold disapproval.

"Why?" said one.

"Pray let us have the grounds of your opinion," said another.

"Mr. Timmons's ideas are always *so* original," said a third.

"I've seen her," said he.

Never was man raised more suddenly from utter insignificance to the pedestal of popular favor and importance.

Metaphorically, the ladies threw themselves at his feet.

"Oh, Mr. Timmons!"

"When?"

"Where?"

"*What* is she like?"

"Oh, how *nice* of you to come and tell us!"

"*Why* didn't you tell us before?"

"I couldn't, without interrupting," said he.

"Well, we are waiting!" said they.

Timmons smiled, close-lipped. He would be revenged for their late indifference.

"I met them in Montreal," he said. "They will be here in a few days—or a week or so."

Again the chorus:

"What *is* she like? Oh, *tell* us all about her!"

"I fear my descriptive powers are hardly up to it," said Timmons, modestly. "Then, my judgment may be at fault. I hardly dare try to describe, much less express an opinion on, a subject of such intense interest."

"Oh, Mr. *Timmons!*"

"I'll tell you what to do: Call upon her, and invite her—when she comes. Then you can see for yourselves." And Timmons, smiling blandly, made his adieux.

"Invite her, indeed!" said the ladies. And yet, when Leonora came, she found herself both called upon and invited.

"How many friends you have, Tom, and how kind they are!" said she.

"Very!" Tom grinned cheerfully. He knew that all these cards and courtesies were the result of curiosity, for Timmons had given him some hints as to the trend of common talk. He looked forward with keen pleasure to the dawning of his bride's loveliness on an unenlightened community, and was not disappointed. They went where they were bidden, and, as the snows in her own valley at the coming of spring, the chill of reserve and prejudice melted away before her presence; as the flowers open in the new warmth, kindly thoughts and good feelings answered her sweet and genial nature everywhere.

People turned upon Mrs. C. Norman Moorhead and demanded explanations. The latter saw Leonora once, went home early with a sinking heart, and from that time did all she could to keep the susceptible Charles out of her way. She might have succeeded —for he shrank from meeting either his brother or his brother's wife—but for the fondness of Mrs. Bradlee for usurping the functions of Destiny. That lady, beholding Leonora, and forgetful of her own recent remarks, had easily persuaded herself that her letter had been intended to warn the maiden against any lingering regard she might have had for the faithless Charles, and to make the way clear for the deserving Thomas. She went here and there, exulting, to claim the whole credit of having conferred Leonora upon the civilized world.

Meanwhile the Moorheads never met. Each of the brothers had something to say to the other; but Charles, for whom the task was likely to be anything but pleasant, put off the meeting by every means in his power; and Tom, eager as he was, could never find him.

The elder brother was very unhappy at this time because of his wife, whose conduct towards him had utterly changed. She watched him as if she would not let him out of her sight, yet had hardly a kind word or look for him. Her brightness and charm of manner were gone; she was sad and dull and cross. He could not understand, nor would she give any explanation of the change.

Now people began to talk freely of these things, and Mrs. Bradlee, grieved that any combination of circumstances should exist without her intervention,

20

undertook the formidable task of peace-making. To
this end she determined to assemble the hostile Moorheads about her own hospitable board, and, seeing
no other means, asked them all to dinner, saying to
Charles and his wife, "There will be no one but ourselves." She appeased her conscience by explaining
to it that "ourselves" (whatever her guests might
understand by the word) meant "the family."

When escape was no longer possible Charles found
himself taking Leonora in to dinner, while Nelly laid
two cold fingers on the arm of Thomas and walked
in bitter wrath beside him into the gloom of Mrs.
Bradlee's dining-room.

Regarded strictly as a dinner-party, the feast was
not a success. Mrs. Bradlee beamed upon her guests,
but beamed in vain, and began to wish, for once in
her life, that she had not meddled. Charles sat down-
cast at her right, afraid to meet the eye of Tom, opposite, or speak to Leonora by his side, and cast now
and then a furtive and deploring glance at his wife,
who gave him no sympathy. She, at the farther corner, saw his miserable face and thought, "He repents
his choice already." So her self-possession and easy
flow of words deserted her, and she sat with burning
eyes and a voice like a low winter wind, and bore
it all as best she might. Tom watched his brother
sharply with a kind of savage amusement, thinking
the same that Nelly thought, and adding, "And
before I've done with him he'll be sorrier still."

Mrs. Bradlee had intended to put them all in good-
humor with a conciliatory speech, and even, if necessary, to bring up the subject of their differences,
smooth it over with a jest, and laugh it off; but those

three gloomy faces frightened her; she saw that the trouble was beyond her depth, and her tact was not equal to the task in hand.

Only Leonora was completely at her ease. She had nothing whereof to be ashamed. She bore no one ill-will, and she had the absolute fearlessness of inexperience and the joy of youth in a new state of things. She talked pleasantly to all the rest. Her sister-in-law tried to snub her and did not succeed; Charles answered her with faint civility and wished she would let him alone; Tom was silent and abstracted. Mrs. Bradlee was heartily grateful to her, and showed it in voice and manner.

At last the awful function was over, the ladies went up-stairs, and the two brothers were left together in the gloom of Mrs. Bradlee's dining-room.

No one could have mistaken one for the other now.

The one had a stalwart, upright frame, a well-browned face, fresh as a boy's, but full of energy and strength of purpose; trouble, hardship, love, labor, success, and triumph had made a man of him.

Charles looked much older, pale and thin; his shoulders drooped; his face was full of care, ill borne, and something he had on his mind at the time gave him a hang-dog look.

"Tom," said he, in a pleading tone that irritated his brother.

"Well?"

"My dear brother," he said, fretfully, "I *wish* you would take the money and other property I offered you. It's only right you should; it is your share of the estate, you know, and—"

"That will do," said Tom. "I don't care to hear of it."

"Have patience a minute. You don't know why I made you that offer, or how much your taking it would mean to me!" And, stammering much, Charles made a clean breast of the part he had played in disinheriting his brother, and of his project for repaying him without the bitterness of confession. "You'll take it now, won't you?" he asked, piteously.

Tom was deeply touched at his brother's shame, but would not show it. He had something else to say first—a taunt he had treasured up against him, and had waited for too patiently to forego.

"Give it to some charity, if you like," said he. "From what you say, you would seem to have *earned* it, after a fashion of your own. I'm not surprised. You are very welcome to the whole."

"But you'll need it!" said Charles, more unhappy than ever in being denied his atonement.

"I? Man, I could buy you out—you and your offer three times over!" said Tom, brutal in his independence. "No, let that pass. I could easily forgive all that, but you did me a worse wrong when you put me under obligations to you and deprived me of my self-respect, so far as to make me enter into your place to cheat the woman you thought hopelessly in love with you. She never was. I have promised myself my revenge—to bring her and your wife together, and let you see them—what you have won and what you have lost. What do you think now? How could you throw away your chance of *her*—for your wife? What do you think? Were you not a fool to make the exchange? Are you not sorry for it now?"

He hated himself for the words as soon as they were spoken. It was a mean revenge, he felt, a dastardly thing to do—to show a man his wife's inferiority to another woman.

But, to his surprise and immense relief, his brother smiled and said, looking him straight in the eyes for the first time, so that he knew he spoke the truth :

"Tom, you don't understand. Leonora is a lovely woman, and I believe that you are worthy of her and that I am not. But so is Nelly, my wife.. I love her, Tom, and you could not disparage her in my eyes if you put her beside a woman ten times lovelier than even your wife. She and I were made for each other."

"Charley," said Tom, "you're a better fellow than I ever knew you were. I beg your pardon. I was angry ; and thank God my words have not touched you. Come, let us go to our wives."

Later Tom told Nelly what he had said to Charles. It was hard to tell, but he prefaced it so kindly and spoke so gently that she listened in spite of herself, and when he had repeated what *Charles* had said to *him* she went to her husband with a happy face, and he, relieved of his trouble and the burden of his conscience, was content.

Nelly had suffered terribly for fear of Leonora ; but when that was over, Tom's wife soon won her, and found her a stronger friend than she had been an enemy.

There is a tall, stately old gentleman who frequents the clubs and places of amusement—an exceedingly well-read man—prosperous, genial, and at peace with the world.

Everybody likes him, and he, on experiment, finds that he likes everybody, although he is known to have fled for years to the wilderness to shun his kind. He is attended by the blackest and most courteous of beings, who answers cheerfully to the name of Moloch. His only sorrow is that his daughter has so many friends that he sees less of her than he would. But he finds a fund of consolation in teaching his grandchildren to fish.

THE END

www.ingramcontent.com/pod-product-compliance
Lightning Source LLC
Chambersburg PA
CBHW060526030726
47498CB00004B/1096